HME at *Last*

Award Winning Author

JAN SIKES

RiJan Publishing

This story is dedicated to our girls, Lily and Nicole, who worked alongside us, endured many hardships and deprivations and never complained. Luke loved them with all of his heart and soul and would have killed to protect them.

This is a true account of happenings, with (of course) lots left out. The main focus of this story was to get Luke back to what he was meant to do in life and that was to make music!

REVIEWER QUOTES

"Jan Sikes writes with heart, with compassion, and with great psychological insight. Her writing flows with ease, helping the reader race through the pages…"~B. O'Hare

"I love the way the author told her story it was quite captivating and interesting…"~ E. Lindsey

"Jan Sikes is a magician, a wordsmith extraordinaire…" ~ C. Herron

Chapter 1

Texas 1985

Into the unknown they traveled
Like a band of Gypsies
Their life came unraveled
Not knowing exactly what lay ahead
Holding onto dreams like a golden thread…

A hot July sun bore down on the maroon Chevy Malibu as it headed west. The lush green East Texas pines had long turned into mesquite and scrub oaks. Darlina Flowers brushed a strand of auburn hair from her face. The air conditioner had gone out back around Waco. With the windows open, the Central Texas air felt much like a furnace. The faces of the two little girls in the back seat were flushed and red.

"Luke Stone broke your heart once. He'll do it again." The words echoed in Darlina's head as the tires hummed on the scorched asphalt.

"No, Mama. This time it's gonna be different. I swear he's a changed man and I love him," she'd argued.

"You sure better think about what you're dragging these precious girls into. A man that's been locked up for as long as he has..." Darlina's mother hadn't attempted to hide her anxiety the last time they'd spoken.

"Are we there yet?" A small voice complained from the back seat, interrupting her thoughts.

"Not yet, sweetie, but we're getting close."

A road sign told her their destination was only a few more miles ahead. She spotted a deserted roadside rest area and pulled in. The girls clamored from the back seat in a hurry to escape the confines of the car.

"You can get out but I want you to stay close. There are rattlesnakes out here." Weary, Darlina rubbed the back of her neck and shoulders.

Darlina watched as the two children chased each other. After a few minutes of letting them play, she called, "Lily, Nicole, you girls come here. I need to make you presentable before we get to Coleman."

Lily ran to her mother. She was nine years old and took her job as the older sister very seriously. She stood patiently while Darlina brushed her strawberry blonde hair, pulling it back into a pony tail. The mother then cooled her child's flushed face with water from the cooler.

More than anything, she wanted her girls to be accepted and loved by the new family they were joining.

Placing a kiss on her cheek, Darlina hugged her. "Thank you, Lily. I'd like for you to get back in the car while I freshen up your sister."

"Okay, Mama." Lily opened the car door and sat on the edge of the seat swinging her legs as she waited for her younger sister.

Darlina turned her attention to Nicole, barely six years old. She brushed back her daughter's blondish-brown hair and kissed the row of freckles that marched across her nose like proper little soldiers.

The two girls were as different as night and day. Lily preferred reading books and keeping to herself, whereas Nicole treated every stranger as a friend and would rather color in the books than read them. Darlina loved the sweet spirit in both her girls and hoped against hope that she'd made the right decision.

Leaving behind everything secure and comfortable for the second time in her life, to join Luke Stone, was a gamble she was willing to take.

She quickly ran a brush through her own hair and gave the girls one last inspection before closing the doors and restarting the engine.

Fifteen miles down the road, she got her first glimpse of Coleman and her heart sank. The dusty, dirty, small Texas town didn't provide much of a welcome. Darlina drove slowly, following the directions Luke had provided.

"Mama, where are we going to live?" Lily's voice quivered.

"I'm not sure, honey. We'll find a nice place."

"I miss Granny." The rearview mirror reflected big tears welling up in Nicole's blue eyes.

"I know, sweetie, but everything's going to be all right."

How could she sound so reassuring when she had the same doubts and fears? As she drove under a railroad bridge, a sudden wind whipped down the unpaved dirt streets, pelting the car with sand.

"Close your eyes and cover your mouths, girls." She tried to ignore the apprehension that knotted her stomach like a tightening noose while she rolled up the windows.

She'd spoken with Luke's mother by phone several times and knew they would be welcome in her home. However, many questions remained unanswered.

Fifteen long years had passed since that fateful day the judge had sentenced Luke to seventy-five years in prison. Would he be the same man she'd fallen in love with so long ago, or would the many years behind bars have turned him bitter and cold?

The fact that he'd been granted parole was a miracle far beyond anything they'd dared to hope for. With family and a promise of work in Coleman, Texas, he'd chosen the small town as his parole destination.

Surveying it up close, Darlina now wished she'd advocated a little harder for a parole to Shreveport, where she'd had a good job and nice home.

She brushed that thought aside. It was too late to go back.

It'd been a lucky break when her neighbors bought her house in Shreveport. Things for this move had come together easily, and to her, that was a good sign. It had to be. Everything was hinging on it.

At Luke's insistence, his oldest son, Joseph, and nephew, Gary, drove to Shreveport, loaded a rented U-Haul truck and moved Darlina's belongings. She would breathe easier when she saw her things again.

"We're here," she announced, pulling onto a caliche driveway.

The girls peered out, eyes wide with curiosity.

"Is this our new house, Mama?" Nicole scooted close to her big sister. She couldn't clearly pronounce her R's so they sounded like W's.

"No, honey. We're just gonna stay here 'til we find a nice place for us to live with Daddy. Let's go in and say hello."

Before they could get out of the car, the screen door flew open and a short, rotund, gray-haired lady stepped out onto the porch. "Well, my lord! I thought you kids were never gonna get here. I've been on pins and needles all day. Come in out of this God-awful heat."

Darlina and the two girls hurried out of the car and up to the front porch. "You're sure right about the heat, Mrs. Stone. Our air conditioner went out back down the road and it's been pretty miserable."

Mrs. Stone leaned down, hugged each of the girls and ushered them inside the cool house. "Well, I'm sure glad you made it and please don't call me Mrs. Stone. After all, you're going to be my daughter-in-law in a few short weeks. I'd like it if you'd call me Mom and you girls call me Nanny."

"Okay, Mom." Darlina placed a hand on the shoulder of each child. "This is Lily and Nicole."

"I'm very happy to meet you, Lily and Nicole. What pretty little blue-eyed girls. I baked a pie. Would you girls like a piece?"

Inside, Darlina looked around the modest house. She remembered another time that she'd been in Luke's parents' home many years ago in Brownwood, when the welcome hadn't been quite as warm. In fact, the atmosphere had been downright chilly since Luke was still a married man back then.

"Girls, do you want a piece of pie?" Darlina repeated.

Nicole's eyes sparkled. The child dearly loved desserts. "Is it a strawberry pie?"

"No, sweetie." Mrs. Stone chuckled. "Do you like chocolate?"

"Oh yes!" Nicole replied. "I like chocolate but not as much as strawberry."

Lily stood slightly behind Darlina as though trying to make up her mind about this move and strange new woman welcoming them into her life. Her voice was quiet and matter-of-fact. "I like chocolate the best."

"Here, let me help you, Mom." Darlina opened a kitchen cabinet, only to jump back in horror. Cockroaches fell out of the cabinet onto her arm and scattered in all directions.

"Oh, don't pay them no mind. I've been meanin' to get an exterminator out here. I haven't cared about much of anything since Al died. It's hard to believe he's been gone twelve years already." Her words trailed off into a mumble.

Darlina placed her arm around Mrs. Stone's shoulders. "I know you miss him, Mom, and that you can't wait for Luke to get home. How about I go tomorrow and get some bug spray? We'll see if we can run them out of the house."

Mrs. Stone gave her a bright smile. "Yes, having my son home will make everything better. You can go get bug spray if you want." She set plates with pie slices on the table. "You girls eat up."

The girls sat at the small round table in the kitchen, eating their pie, when suddenly Darlina jumped up. "Oh dear! I forgot that Amanda is still in the car. You remember we have a cat, don't you, Mom?"

"Of course. Go bring her in. I don't mind at all. I love animals. After the girls finish their pie, I'll take them out back and introduce them to my pet sheep, Baby."

"A sheep?" Nicole's eyes widened.

"Yep, a sheep. I've had her since she was tiny. She was the runt of a litter. I brought her in the house and bottle fed her until she was big enough to make it on her own."

"I've never seen a real sheep." Lily popped a bite of pie into her mouth.

Darlina returned with a crate the cat had been confined in since they'd left Shreveport. Amanda, the cat, shot out the open door and quickly darted behind the refrigerator. She mewed forlornly, refusing all Darlina's coaxing to come out.

"Oh she'll come out and explore once she settles down." Mrs. Stone began clearing dishes from the table.

Finally, Darlina gave up and stood. "Where do you want me to put our things?"

"I'll show you. You three are gonna be right here in this bedroom. It used to be Luke's and Bobby's." She pointed down a short hallway.

The room held two beds amidst piles of material bolts, boxes and chests. "I probably need to get rid of all this material. Doubt I'll ever do much sewing again with this broken arm that won't ever heal. Just move stuff over to make room for whatever you need."

"Thanks, Mom. We'll be just fine in here."

"Come with me girls," Nanny Stone called. "We'll go see Baby while your mama brings in your things."

"Oh, Mom, I forgot to ask. Did the boys make it okay with the truck?"

"They sure did. It's parked down at Bobby's."

Both girls eagerly followed her out the back door while Darlina stood in the middle of the room looking around. Well, it could be worse. This place could sure stand a good cleaning though. She'd do what she could without hurting Mrs. Stone's feelings.

In no time, she had what they needed from the car and went to find the girls. They were standing in the middle of the yard with Mrs. Stone, hand-feeding and petting a full grown sheep.

Darlina's breath caught in her throat. In the far back corner of the yard sat the familiar Rebel Rouser's band trailer. The rebel flags on each side were faded and peeling and weeds grew around the flat tires.

A rush of memories came flooding. The many nights she'd sat beside Luke in the Lincoln Towncar as he and his country band drove the roads of Texas to play music. The countless hours she'd lain in his arms warm and secure, making sweet love convinced that nothing on heaven or earth could separate them.

Tears stung the backs of her eyelids. Luke was coming home. In a few short weeks they'd be married. After what seemed like a lifetime of waiting, she would finally become Mrs. Luke Stone.

Just being with Luke would make everything right again. He'd vowed to love her girls as his own. The hundreds of letters they'd written to each other over the long fifteen years, filled with their hopes and dreams, would have a chance at last.

She could put up with the cockroaches, the dirty desolate little town and the heat as long as they had each other. Their love could overcome any obstacles they faced. That's just the way it would be. She had no doubts about that.

Darlina, Lily and Nicole 1985

Chapter 2

August 17, 1985 dawned a typical blazing hot west Texas day. Darlina's cotton blouse and skirt stuck to her damp skin and she wished the air conditioner in the car would magically start working.

She gripped the steering wheel with sweaty palms. Her heart raced, keeping time with her thoughts. The twenty-eight miles between Coleman and Brownwood seemed to stretch forever. In a few short minutes, Luke would step off the Greyhound bus and into a new life as a free man, as her husband and father to her girls.

The anticipation, almost unbearable, weighed like a heavy cloak around her.

There was a certain exhilarating fright about dreams coming true. Like dreaming a dream that you were scared you'd wake from and find it was only a dream.

Her breath came faster as she rounded the corner and the big gray dog on the sign above the bus station came into view. There was no activity, so she knew she was early. She went inside the cool building to freshen up and wait for the coach from Kansas that would bring Luke Stone back to freedom and into her arms.

***

What if it had all been a mistake? Luke's heart leapt into his throat each time he spotted a highway patrol car. What if they stopped the bus, dragged him off and back into the cage that had imprisoned him for so long? He fought to push those paranoid thoughts aside.

His eyes had been glued to the outside world since he'd left Kansas. Each breath of freedom thrilled him all the way to his toes. Fifteen long years behind bars for a crime he hadn't committed was now over. He'd been given a second chance at life and he damned well intended to make the best of it.

He held the lovely vision of Darlina's face firmly in his mind. But more important than just seeing her again, he'd have the pleasure of holding her in his arms and feeling her warmth pressed against him. He almost groaned out loud. This time he'd never let her go.

It had been over a year since she and Lily had visited him in Leavenworth Penitentiary. She'd agreed to marry him then, with no idea of when freedom from prison would come. He couldn't deny that it was her determination, persistence and money that had obtained his parole. Now it was time to make the kind of life they both longed for and dreamed of and he was more than ready to get started.

The air brakes brought the lumbering bus to a stop and the door flew open. Luke stood and gathered his meager belong-ings, consisting of a cheap cardboard case with a change of underwear, one change of clothes, a comb, toothbrush and shaving razor he'd been issued when he left prison. In his pocket, he carried his parole papers, which he'd glanced at often since leaving Kansas.

When he spotted Darlina at the entrance of bus station, he swallowed hard.

He maneuvered his lanky frame to the front of the bus and stepped off. He dropped his case and wrapped his arms tightly around her when she ran forward. They stood quietly, barely breathing.

His chest tightened when he saw big tears welling up in her blue eyes. He hated to see her cry, even if they were tears of joy.

"Oh Luke. You're finally home," her voice quivered.

He cleared his throat. "It's damned time too. Let's get out of here. All of these people make me a little more than nervous." Luke picked up his small case.

"Sorry, the air conditioner in the car doesn't work. It's damned hot," she chattered nervously.

Luke nestled his free hand in hers and let her guide him to the maroon Chevy.

"Honey, it wouldn't matter to me if you had to pick me up with a wagon and team of mules. God, it's good to be back in Texas. All the way here, I kept thinking to myself, 'Toto, we're not in Kansas anymore'."

Standing beside the car, Luke threw his case into the backseat and pulled Darlina into his arms. He kissed her waiting lips and slid his hands slowly down her back, savoring the feel of her beneath his trembling hands.

Darlina let out a long sigh. "I've waited so long for you to hold me, baby. I thought today would never get here."

Luke struggled to steady his voice. "Not nearly as long I have, sweetheart. Let's go home. But, first I want to stop at a five and dime store and get some little presents for the girls. They gave me fifty dollars when they let me out of prison and I get another fifty when I check in with my parole officer, which I have to do within twenty-four hours."

"They'll love that. They're so excited and you're all they've talked about for days. They're staying with Bobby and Cindy tonight so you won't see them until tomorrow."

Luke chuckled. "Why is that? Do you have something special planned for tonight?"

Darlina ran her index finger lightly along his jaw line then traced his lips. Oh how her touch made his heart pound. And, the twinkle in her bluebonnet eyes said it all.

"I might have a thing or two up my sleeve. Your mom can't wait to see you, but I explained it would be tomorrow before you'd see any of them. I want you all to myself for twenty-four hours," she whispered.

"Sweetheart, I can't think of anything I need or want more." He opened the car door and Darlina slid across the seat to the driver's side.

With his hand wrapped in hers, she steered the car out onto the street and turned in the direction of Coleman. He was sure he could hear her heart pounding in rhythm with his own. God, how he wanted to wrap himself up in this woman.

"Baby, you look so different from the last time I saw you. What made you decide to cut the long ponytail and shave the beard?" Darlina asked.

He chuckled. "I figured it'd be hard enough to fit in just being an ex-con, without the long hair and beard." He squeezed her hand.

"You don't look anything like a convict. Maybe the Godfather, but not a convict. And you're so tanned and thin. Me and your mom will have to fatten you up." She tightened her fingers around his in response.

In the variety store, he relied on Darlina to help him choose gifts for the girls. She picked out a red silk rose for his mother, a book for Lily and stuffed animal for Nicole. He kept his arm protectively around her waist and the nearness caused him to quiver inside. Each moment he spent not wrapped in her arms was too long to suit him.

Even though he fought to stay calm, being in a store of any kind for the first time in fifteen years made him a little more than nervous. When a customer dropped a vase on the next aisle, shattering it, Luke jumped as though he was shot.

"Let's get the hell out of here," he growled. "It's gonna take me a while to get used to being out in the world again."

They headed to the checkout stand, where he quickly paid for the purchases and exited the store.

During the ride back to Coleman, Luke never let go of Darlina's hand. He savored the countryside that he'd known as home for all but the last fifteen years of his life. The prickly pear cactus grew wild in the pastures and along the roadway amongst the cedar and mesquite trees. A lot had changed in fifteen years, and yet so much remained the same.

The moment they stepped through the door of the small apartment Darlina had rented for them, Luke drew her into the circle of his arms and kissed her, savoring the uninhibited way she returned the kiss.

He ached for her in ways that only a man who'd been deprived for years could ache. The need and raw hunger overtook everything else.

In minutes, the two lovers lay on the living room floor with remnants of clothing scattered about. It didn't matter that they hadn't made it to the bed. Nothing mattered except losing themselves in the moment.

Luke's insatiable appetite grew more with each release. They devoured each other lost in a span of time and space where the entire Universe stopped spinning just for them.

Finally, out of breath and spent, Luke sat up with his back against the sofa and gathered Darlina close beside him. "You have no idea how many nights I dreamed of this and how those dreams kept me going when there didn't seem to be any other reason."

She snuggled into the crook of his arm. "I've died and gone to heaven. I looked for some way to replace you after you left, but I never found it."

"You scared the hell out of me with all the shit you did. Now, I'm here and I'll make damned sure nothing ever hurts you or the girls."

"I have a gift for you." Darlina stood and pulled him to his feet.

"Sweetheart, you've already given me more than any man could ask for."

Fetching a brightly wrapped package from the top shelf of a bookcase, she put it into his hands.

Within seconds, he ripped the paper off then looked down at her, tears shining in his blue eyes. "You didn't have to do this."

"I wanted to. I know it's your brand."

Luke popped the lid open on the box of King Edward Cigars and unwrapped one.

"Welcome home, baby. Would you like something to eat or drink? I have some Crown Royal Whiskey that a salesman gave me at the refinery in Shreveport." Darlina handed him a lighter.

Smoke curled from the King Edward as Luke drew hard on it. He draped his arm around Darlina's shoulders. "I don't need anything but you, darlin'. Whiskey is the last thing on my mind right now. Show me the rest of the house."

Darlina laughed. "There isn't much to show. The girls' bedroom is upstairs in the loft and ours is in here."

She opened a door revealing a bed with a beautifully hand-knitted rainbow colored spread across it.

"Well now, that's damned inviting." Luke put out his cigar, gently laid Darlina on the bed and then joined her. She allowed herself to remember the many nights she'd dreamed of Luke while lying on this bed. Never again. Those dreams would now be reality.

This time Luke leisurely explored every inch of her warm and waiting body. "My princess. I'm gonna make sure you never regret one second of loving me. You are my everything and I intend to show you in all of the ways that a man can possibly show a woman." Luke's breath ruffled Darlina's hair as he moved over her. He felt as if he needed to pinch himself to make sure he was awake and not still locked in a cage, dreaming again.

Tears clogged her throat as she gazed at the man she loved with her entire body and soul. "I know, Luke. I know." She caressed his back, outlined the frame of his face and placed feather touches on his lips. "We've got the rest of eternity to love each other and as you told me so often in your letters, even death won't separate us."

"That's a promise you can bet the farm on, sweetheart. I won't ever get enough of loving you."

"Life is finally beginning for us, Luke. Finally. And I'll never close my eyes when we make love because I don't want to miss a single expression on your face." She touched his face and sighed contentedly.

Their long journey had finally brought Luke home. Home to her, home to a family and home to stay.

Darlina and Luke Homecoming

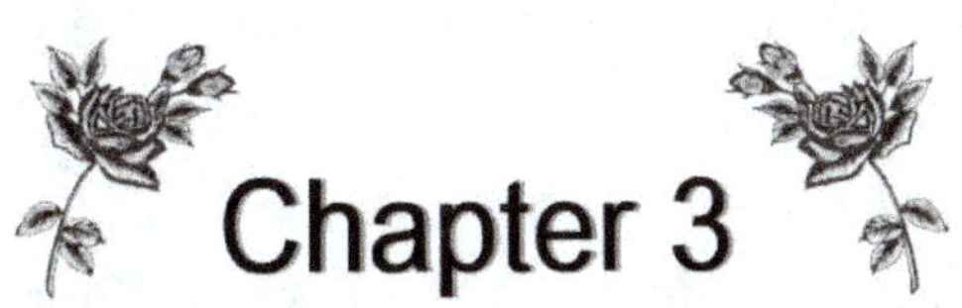

Chapter 3

Long after Darlina had fallen into a deep slumber, Luke lay awake listening to the outside noises. It had been many years since he'd heard cars going down the street or crickets chirping. This would take some getting used to. In prison, his very life depended on sleeping with one eye open attuned to the sounds around him.

Overwhelmed by the gift of freedom he'd been given, his gaze caressed Darlina, who lay sleeping as peaceful as an angel beside him. Her soft curves molded against him perfectly. Never again would he hurt her or allow anyone else to. And only a fool would mistreat the little girls or they would have him to deal with. This was his family now and in just a few days, they'd be husband and wife.

The wedding ceremony was a mere formality for family's sake because he'd never be more married to this woman than he was right this moment.

As though feeling him watch her, she stirred. He pulled her close, brushing her auburn hair from her face. He watched her until he finally fell asleep, knowing that her face would be the last thing he would see every night for the rest of his life.

When his eyelids fluttered open, the bright Texas sun filtered through the curtains, embellishing the vision of Darlina, still deeply asleep. Her soft arm draped across his chest filled Luke with renewed desire.

She came awake by degrees as he kissed her face, her parted lips and eyelids. She moaned softly under his caress. Luke's heart raced. He'd never seen a more amazing woman, and she belonged to him.

After more lovemaking, Darlina finally pushed herself away, much to Luke's disappointment. "Baby, if we keep this up, we're gonna kill each other. I'm starving. Do you realize we never ate yesterday?"

Luke chuckled. "Food was the last thing on my mind, angel. I kept thinking I was dreaming and I'd wake up back in my cage. I never want to spend a night away from you for any reason."

"And you won't have to. But, right now, if I don't get us some food, our life might not be very long." Darlina giggled like a young school girl.

Just as she moved to get off the bed, Luke pulled her back for one more kiss. "You've got a point. I'm gonna take a shower, then I'll meet you in the kitchen. I have to report in to my parole officer today."

When her feet hit the floor, Darlina groaned. "Luke, I think every muscle in my entire body is sore. You gave me quite a workout."

"Yeah? Well, at least you don't have carpet burns on your knees." Luke grinned.

She stopped just short of opening the door. "I've missed that crooked smile of yours for an eternity, baby."

"Well, no more. Everything I have, every part of me, belongs to you." He embraced her, then turned in the direction of the bathroom.

A short time later, Luke padded into the kitchen with a towel wrapped around his waist. To hear Darlina humming to herself while she made coffee, eggs and toast, sent joy coursing through him.

He walked up behind her and wrapped his arms around her waist. She turned into the embrace and smiled up at him.

"Nothing can wipe the smile off my face today, Luke Stone. My heart is finally whole and we'll never be separated again."

"You can count on it, sweetheart."

***

Darlina knew she'd been selfish keeping Luke all to herself, but part of the day had been taken up with reporting in to the parole officer. She'd been acutely aware of how Luke fidgeted as they drove to the State of Texas Parole office in Brownwood. He didn't say the words, but she sensed his gnawing fear of being sent back to prison. Thankfully, all went well and the routine meeting ended quickly with instructions on reporting in, and another fifty dollars being put in Luke's hands.

The State parole officer made arrangements for the federal officer to meet with Luke at the apartment the next week.

With Luke by her side, Darlina pulled the Chevy into Florence Stone's drive.

Lily and Nicole bounded out of the front door before the car came to a complete stop.

The minute Luke opened the car door, they both flew at him. "Daddy, Daddy!" Nicole yelled.

"Let me get out of the car, girls, then I can give you both a big hug."

Darlina watched, misty eyed, as the girls grabbed Luke's hands and pulled him toward the door of the house. Luke glanced back over his shoulder at her. "Come on, Mama. Let's join the party."

She smiled and caught up with them.

The entire family had gathered to welcome Luke home and Mom Stone had prepared a feast including homemade chocolate pie.

Tears and laughter filled the air with joyous celebration.

When Mom Stone hugged her son, she sobbed into his shoulder. "Bubba, I didn't think you'd ever get home."

"Don't cry, Mom. I'm here now and I'm not going anywhere else." He reached for Darlina who wrapped her arms around them both.

Luke's eyes misted when he hugged his only brother, which in turn brought a lump to Darlina's throat. Because of cancer, Bobby no longer had any vocal chords and after suffering a stroke, he walked with a cane, and dragged his left leg.

Voice hoarse with emotion, Luke hugged Bobby a second time. "It's damn sure good to be home, stud."

Bobby wiped his own eyes with the back of his hand and held a small device that looked like a narrow plastic straw in the corner of his mouth to produce an electronic voice sound. "I know, brother."

The homecoming went on into the evening hours with cousins, aunts, uncles and friends stopping by to welcome Luke home.

Darlina watched as Luke began to come alive. Her heart ached for the deprivation he'd endured, but that was over now. It was time to move forward and build the life they'd dreamed of for an eternity.

By the time they left, Luke had made a list of repairs for his mom and brother. He would not be idle.

In the car, with two tired girls in the backseat, Luke held Darlina's hand as she drove the short distance to their apartment.

"One of the first things I want to do is get our own place to live. The apartment is fine for now, but we need a real home."

"I couldn't agree more. We need a place the girls can grow up in and call home." Darlina squeezed his hand. "I love you, Luke."

"And I love you sweetheart, more than I can ever tell or show you."

***

The next week was a flurry of getting settled in addition to make wedding preparations. It seemed that one day barely ended before the next one began. But, the nights were the best of all, when Luke and Darlina could love the world away and meld into each other.

Darlina moved as if in a dream. She was hardly aware of anything around her but Luke. She went through the motions of cooking and taking care of the girls, but her attention was always on Luke.

She understood the struggle he faced coming back into the land of the living. Everything was new from the daily noises to re-learning how to drive. When Luke had been taken away, there were no center turn lanes, freeways or microwaves.

Oft times, Darlina would find Luke standing outside, looking up at the stars. She wondered at the pipe ritual he performed daily blowing smoke into the four directions, but didn't question.

She held his hand as they walked around the old band trailer. Luke bent down to pull some of the weeds from around the tires, then with a hammer, broke the lock and pulled the rusty doors open.

Nothing much had been salvaged. A few microphone stands, cables and empty boxes were all that was left of the honky-tonk lifestyle he'd lived.

When a car backfired on the street one night, Luke sprang from the bed, taking a fighting stance. With her heart pounding, she soothed his frayed nerves.

She had one focus, and that was to help make this transition as easy as possible for Luke, and loving him through everything he faced.

When he went to the local market with her, his shock over prices caused him to burst out, "They may as well use a gun and rob us, for the price of a loaf of bread."

"Maybe so, honey. But, we've gotta eat."

She shared every detail of the wedding plans with Luke. Norma, her older sister, had volunteered to make the cake and for a wedding present, hired a local photographer to capture the event. Darlina's entire family was coming, including her reluctant mother.

Purple satin brocade dresses, which Darlina had purchased for the girls while still living in Shreveport, were pressed and ready.

An ivory chiffon dress with a sweetheart neckline, cap sleeves and off the shoulder style had been Darlina's choice for the big day. It cinched tight at the waist, then flowed in soft layers to the floor.

Luke didn't have a suit to wear, so his cousin, Johnny, graciously offered to loan him one. Now, she crossed her fingers that it would fit. A single red rose would be pinned to the lapel.

Luke's brother, Bobby, was in charge of the music. The song Darlina had chosen for the ceremony was Lionel Richie singing *Truly*.

***

The minute her eyelids fluttered open, on Saturday, August 24, 1985, Darlina's blood raced with excitement. Their wedding day had dawned with a stifling heat that can only be found in a West Texas full-blown summer.

She turned to Luke, surprised to see him awake and watching her.

"It's here, baby. Our wedding day!"

Luke pulled her toward him and kissed her. "This is only a formality. You know as well as I do that we're already married in every way possible."

"I know, but now our families get to be a part of our celebration. I can't believe that my best friend, Sally, found her way here from Shreveport at three o'clock this morning by herself. She was determined, in spite of her ass of a husband."

"She loves you. That's plain to see and because of that, I love her. I'll try to refrain from punching the asshole in the face if and when I ever meet him."

"That'd be real nice of you, sweetheart." Darlina bounded out of bed. "We've got a lot to do. Let's get moving."

"I have to tell you, I'm a little nervous about meeting your mom today. I know what she thinks of me and I don't blame her. But, if she'll give me half a chance, I'll prove to her that I'm gonna love and take care of you girls."

"Don't worry. Mama isn't the kind to cause a scene. She'll just keep her distance. And I have no doubt you'll eventually win her over. We've got a lot to do. Let's get movin'."

"Not so fast, little lady. Get back over here and give your husband a good morning kiss."

Giggling, she jumped back on the bed, pressed her lips to his, then jumped back off before he could grab her. "Johnny will be here any minute with your suit and you need to make sure it fits."

Groaning, Luke got off the bed. "I don't see why we have to get all dressed up."

"Because it's my wedding and it's what I want. I'll go make coffee while you shower." Darlina wrapped her arms around Luke and kissed him again before she left the room.

Luke patted her on the bottom as she walked away. "I love you, princess."

"I love you too, my husband. Let's go get married!" She threw back over her shoulder.

***

By the time they reached the church that afternoon with the wedding dresses, the girls and flowers, the temperature lingered close to the one hundred degree mark. Thank goodness the church had air conditioning.

Sally, along with Darlina's sisters, Norma and Leann, helped Lily and Nicole into their fancy dresses.

Once Norma and Leann had Lily and Nicole's hair curled and combed, they painted the girls' fingernails purple to match the dresses while Sally helped Darlina.

The door to the Sunday school room opened and Darlina looked up to see her mother. "Mama, come on in." She stood and leaned down to embrace the short, rotund woman, while Sally went to check in on the girls.

"I just wanted to see you before everything starts. Darlina, are you sure about this?"

"Mama, I've never been more certain about anything in my life. I know this is hard for you and you're worried for me and the girls, but I promise you that Luke is going to take real good care of us."

"I hope you're right." She opened her purse, took out a small lace handkerchief and dabbed at her eyes.

"Try to be happy for me, Mama, even if you don't feel it."

"I can only pretend." She sighed. "I just want what's best for my girls."

Darlina took her mother's wrinkled hands in her own. "I know, Mama. But, this is what's best for me and for the girls. They have a real daddy now. One that will do anything in the world for them."

"Time will tell. Guess I better go sit down."

After another embrace, Darlina's mother went to look for her granddaughters.

Leann peeked through the door. "You okay, sister?"

Darlina patted under her eyes. "Yes. I'm ready to get this over with. Are the girls ready?"

"Yep. They're cute as bugs. It's almost time. Do you need anything?"

"Can you help me get this necklace on? My hands are shaking so bad, I can't fasten it."

"Oh, this is the necklace Luke bought for you in 1970. His first gift to you."

"Yes. I wanted it to be the something old that I wear today for that tradition."

Just then Sally came through the door. "And I have something I want to loan you, so you'll have something borrowed." She opened a small box and took out a baby blue garter. "It also takes care of the something blue."

"Oh Sally, you thought of everything."

"Okay. I'm going to go out and join the family." Leann gave her sister a quick hug. "See you in a little bit, Mrs. Luke Stone."

Darlina turned to Sally. "Did you hear that? I'm really about to be Mrs. Luke Stone."

Sally squeezed her hand. "This is what you've wanted as long as I've known you. It's almost time. I'm going to go get Lily and Nicole. The photographer is on his way in to take some pictures before the ceremony."

"Okay. I'm ready."

Luke had the ring that would go on her finger in his pocket; another purchase she'd made before leaving Shreveport. It was a simple white gold eternity band. The ring she'd place on Luke's finger was one he'd made out of turquoise and silver while in prison.

The girls had white baskets filled with silk rose petals to carry. Sally had done a beautiful job of decorating the baskets with tiny rose buds and long flowing ribbon streamers.

Darlina had always known of Luke's love for roses, and had lost count of the number of letters that came with a red rose drawn on the letter or the envelope.

So, she would carry a single long stem red rose, the symbol of their love. She inhaled the sweetness of the flower, letting the fragrance burn its memory into her brain. She'd forever associate that sweet smell with Luke and their love that had weathered a tremendous storm.

After the photographer finished, Darlina took a calming breath. It was time. Luke joined her in the foyer and the girls with Sally close behind stood impatiently waiting as Bobby started the music.

Tears caught in Darlina's throat. She dared a glance at Luke only to find his clear blue eyes glued on her.

"I love you," she mouthed.

Luke tightened his grip on her hand and leaned in to whisper in her ear. "Honey, you and these little girls are the most beautiful angels I've ever seen. I'm the luckiest man alive."

They turned their attention to the girls, who tried their best to walk down the aisle dropping rose petals like they'd been instructed, but six-year-old Nicole couldn't help skipping a time or two.

Once the girls reached the front of the church, they turned and waited. Sally joined them next.

On cue, Bobby played *The Wedding March.*

Luke placed his arm through the crook of Darlina's and together they walked toward their future.

The pastor of the Northside Community Baptist Church waited to officially pronounce them man and wife.

The ceremony passed in a blur. All Darlina could focus on was that she would finally and forevermore be Mrs. Luke Stone.

Her voice wavered and her hands shook as Darlina read the poem she'd written for the ceremony. "Today I stand here next to you, to pledge my love faithful and true. At your side, I'll always be, from now throughout eternity. And so, in sight of God and man, I promise as I take your hand, to love you deep and strong and true and with you be, though storms may brew. Never may our love grow cold even though we'll both grow old. So, today, they'll say I belong to you, although that fact we already knew."

Luke chose to speak from the heart. "I've loved you for always and promise to love, protect and adore you for always and forever. You have my pledge to be faithful and true, and you can rest assured I'll never ever lie to you. You and these two girls are my family now and I intend to make sure you never regret this union. You are my everything. You're all I need."

Brother Paul, the minister, instructed them to place the rings on each other's fingers and repeat the traditional wedding vow after him.

Darlina and Luke faced each other, hands joined while Bobby cued the Lionel Richie song. *"Girl, tell me only this, that I'll have your heart for always, and you want me by your side whispering the words, I'll always love you. And forever I will be your lover, and I know if you really care. I will always be there..."*

Tears trickled down Darlina's cheeks as she watched Luke's eyes glisten with emotion.

He reached up and brushed away a stray that found its way to the tip of her nose.

Finally, the ceremony ended. Luke and Darlina joined their families for pictures, a tiered cake decorated with pink roses, and punch.

Darlina hugged her sister, Norma. "Thank you so much for providing the cake and paying for a photographer. I could never have afforded all of it. I owe you so much."

"Ah phooey. You don't owe me a thing. Just be happy and enjoy your new life."

Darlina's mother joined in the celebration, but she didn't pretend to be happy. She adored her granddaughters and no matter how much it seemed Luke had changed she still had her reservations. Time would tell.

Darlina met Luke's children for the first time, and gained two instant grandchildren whom Luke had never seen.

In the chaos of everyone talking and laughing, Darlina linked her arm through Luke's. "We did it, baby. We finally did it. Are you happy?"

Luke gave her a positively sinful grin that made her heart lurch. "Darlin', I'll show you how much a bit later. Bet I can get you out of that beautiful dress in nothin' flat."

Darlina laughed. "Promises, promises"

It was a very big day in the lives of Luke and Darlina Stone. One that would never be forgotten.

A union created in heaven and sealed on earth.

Mr. and Mrs. Luke Stone

Darlina, Lily and Nicole

Darlina's Mother, Darlina, Luke, Luke's Mother

Luke and Darlina Stone

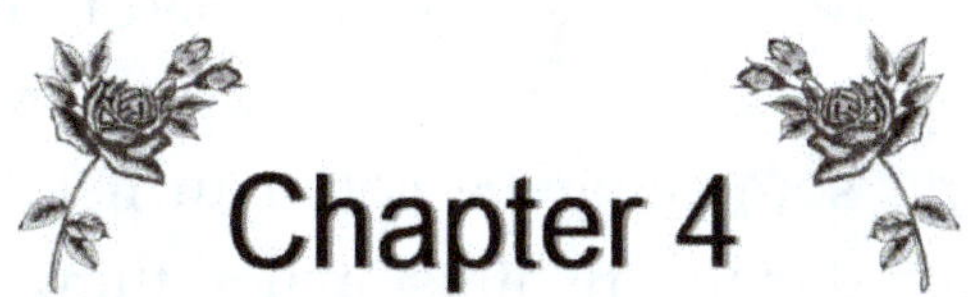

Chapter 4

Bit by bit, Luke became more acclimated to the everyday sounds of life and lost a little of the edginess that plagued him. Nevertheless, he could take a defensive stance in a heartbeat. He'd lived too long behind bars to instantly be comfortable in his new surroundings. In some way, he knew that he'd never be the same self-assured man he was before walking through the doors of prison.

But, prison had taught him one thing and that was to look for opportunities and make the best of what he had where he was.

He and Darlina spent their days at Mom Stone's house undertaking repair and cleaning projects and examining the boxes of Luke's belongings she'd kept stored under the beds for years.

One by one, they unpacked beautiful ceramic pieces, intricately tooled leather handbags as well as oil paintings that had never been unwrapped. One box held nothing but thirty ceramic frogs with wings that Luke had labeled Coon-Ass Canaries. Another held twenty Uni-Frogs, frogs that had a unicorn horn attached.

"Honey, we can sell these. I had forgotten all about them until now, but at the time, that's what I had in mind." Luke set the two boxes aside. He'd seen them as an investment when he'd made them, something he could turn into money later. He'd never suffered from any illusion that things would instantly be perfect and easy as soon as he made it home. There would be hard work and struggles starting over again with nothing at the age of fifty.

"We could have a garage sale here at your mom's house since it's on a main street. I bet we could sell some or we could take them to a flea market somewhere. They're cute." Darlina helped stack them in a separate corner.

In the next two boxes, Luke found belongings that his folks had packed up from his apartment following the arrest fifteen years ago. He couldn't stop the twinge of contrition. His entire previous life came down to a few boxes of worn-out clothes and memories. The signature Rhythm Rebel vest lay in the bottom of a box of clothes, but it was apparent that moths had devoured a good portion of it.

He discovered a pair of brown pointy-toed cowboy boots from the late 60s, with tarnished silver tips still intact. They appeared wearable even though the leather had cracked in places. Luke felt sure that he could bring them back to life with leather balm. He dusted the boots off with his hand and pulled them on. Flashbacks of the many times he'd strode onto the stage wearing them flew through his mind. Oh how he'd swaggered back then. That swagger lingered somewhere deep inside of him, but he'd never revive it. He could not allow himself to be that arrogant egotistical man who had acted as if he ruled the world. Mr. Luke Stone, King of the honky-tonks. His eyes misted over and he hid his face looking down to remove the aging boots.

How could Darlina always know when he needed a soft hand on his shoulder? No words needed to be spoken. He patted the back of her hand, then turned to dig into the next open box.

"Look, sugar." Luke held up a pair of his old jeans from fifteen years ago. "I was a fat man back then."

Darlina giggled. "You sure couldn't fit into them now. They'd fall down around your ankles."

Luke reached under the bed and tugged hard on a box caught on the bed spring. When it came loose, he fell backwards. "Shit." He reached for Darlina's outstretched hand and sat upright. When he pulled the tape off, he found newspapers stuffed inside. "Oh man! Here's my ol' cowboy hat." He pulled a black felt Stetson from inside and blew the dust off. "It's a little worse for wear, but I've got an Indian beaded hatband somewhere in my stuff that I made specifically to go on this hat. That'll spiffy it up." He placed it on his head.

"Looks good on you, baby." Darlina picked up what appeared to be a piece of driftwood that had flown across the floor when the hatbox came unstuck. "What's this?"

Luke took the piece of wood from her and choked on his words. "I'll be damned. I never thought this would have survived all these years. This is a piece of wood I took from a tree that fell on the outlaw Sam Bass's grave in Round Rock, Texas in 1968 or 1969."

Mom Stone leaned against the door frame, cigarette hanging from the corner of her mouth. "Daddy and I wondered what in the world you were doing with all of that firewood in your closet. Daddy said we should keep one piece of it. Son, you ought to enter some of your artwork in the Fiesta de la Paloma coming up in a couple of weeks. There are cash prizes."

Luke raised his head from the box he was deep into. "What the hell is a Fiesta de la Paloma?

Mrs. Stone chuckled. "It's the county fair."

"You think they'd let an ex-con participate?"

"I don't see as that would matter. This town has never seen art like yours. Look at that ceramic bowl with the antelope on top. It's about the prettiest thing I've ever seen."

"Maybe you should, Luke. Lord knows we could use the cash and I have no doubt you'll win with anything you enter." Darlina sat back rubbing her shoulders.

"Where do I sign up, Mom?"

She disappeared only to return with the Coleman newspaper. "It tells all about it in here."

Luke read over the rules for the art show then winked at Darlina. "Want to take me to the Coleman County State Bank to get entry forms, baby?"

"Of course. Let's finish with this one box and we'll go."

Later that afternoon, with the necessary forms completed, Luke asked Darlina's opinion about which pieces he should enter in each category.

The antelope bowl, hand-tooled leather framed picture of a large mouth bass, Indian beaded necklace and a water color painting were the items they settled on. Each entry paid twenty-five dollars for first place.

Early on Saturday morning, September 21st, Luke and Darlina sat across from each other at the kitchen table and drank coffee while Lily and Nicole wolfed down bowls of cereal. The two girls talked non-stop in their excitement about going to the fair.

"Slow down," Luke chuckled and scolded gently. "We're not leaving 'til me and Mama finish our coffee."

Darlina grinned from ear to ear. "I haven't seen them this excited about anything in a long time."

"I don't reckon we've provided them much entertainment. I counted our change and we have a whole fifteen dollars to spend today. I hope they can ride some rides and get cotton candy on that."

"I'm sure they can. Besides that, your mom gave them five dollars yesterday. They'll have fun."

Within an hour, Luke and Darlina packed the art entries into in the trunk of the car while the two girls bounced up and down in the back seat.

The rodeo grounds, on the outskirts of town, was the location of the fair. After several inquiries, Luke found the art exhibit display in a horse barn.

He gave the entries one last backward glance before the four of them walked toward the midway. He whispered a silent prayer to the Great Spirit. Winning this art show would give him instant recognition in the small town for something positive and good. After all, that was what he'd worked so steadfastly toward while he was in prison.

Lily tugged at her mother's hand. "Mama, I wanna ride the tilt-a-whirl."

"Okay, sweetie. Go get in line. Nicole, do you want to ride with her?"

"Yes, but I might get dizzy."

"That's all right, punkin'." Luke smoothed her hair back. "If you get dizzy, I'll hold your hand 'til you're all better."

Nicole smiled up at him. "Okay." With that, she skipped off to join her sister.

Luke and Darlina stood, hand in hand, while the girls went around, waving each time they made the circle. He leaned down and kissed the top of her head. "You know I'm a happy man, don't you?"

She grinned impishly. "I could have guessed it. Thank you."

"For what?"

"For trying so hard to be a daddy to the girls. I know I don't make it easy but I've been used to being everything to them for over seven years. It might take me a while to let go."

"Do you trust me?"

"Of course." Darlina released his hand and put her arm around his waist.

"Then you know I'll never ever hurt them. I want them to grow up strong young women, women that don't have to have a man to be happy in life."

"I want that too."

"Then we're on the same page." Luke circled his arm around her small waist and held her tight against him. His heart swelled with pride. How could a man get so lucky to get a second chance at love, at life?

Once they girls rejoined them, they clamored for another ride. Nicole, proud of herself for not throwing up, held Luke's free hand while Lily took Darlina's, and together the four walked farther down the midway.

Soon, the girls had cotton candy and popcorn and ran ahead to stand in line for more rides.

Luke and Darlina strolled along, making sure they could see the children. A voice bellowed from a booth inviting Luke to play for a prize.

"Come on over. See if you can knock down the bottles. Win a prize for your daughter," the carnie shouted.

Luke chuckled. "Hey man, this is my wife."

"Well ain't you a lucky man. Win a prize for your wife then. Come on, I'll give you two for one."

"No thanks, man." Luke bent down and pressed a kiss to Darlina's lips. "Bet they all wonder what a pretty young thing like you is doing with an old man like me." He loved the way her blue eyes sparkled up at him like shining diamonds.

"Well, they can wonder all they want. You're not an old man to me. I'd dare to say that not one of these young whippersnappers could begin to keep up with you." She leaned in to him discreetly brushing against his arm with her breast.

Luke patted her bottom. "I'd say you're right." This woman continually took his breath away and the bonus prize was the two girls who openly adored him. He looked up at the clear Texas sky that stretched forever and mentally sent up a prayer of thanks to the Great Spirit for the abundant blessing of his freedom and his family.

Later that evening, Luke, Darlina and the children stood at the back of the room as the judges announced each winner in the art show. He dared to hope for at least one prize.

Luke won first place in every category he'd entered. Each time the judge called his name, Darlina squeezed his hand before he strode to the front of the room to accept the award. Then to top it all off, they honored him with the Sweepstakes award for the Fine Arts division of the show.

Several people approached him, shook his hand and welcomed him home. Perhaps it wouldn't be as hard as he'd thought to establish himself in the community.

With pride nearly popping off every button on his shirt, Luke collected a total of one hundred and twenty-five dollars. Once a reporter, from the Coleman newspaper, finished taking pictures Luke joined Darlina and the girls.

"Can you believe this, baby? We've got money. We'll have to go to the bank on Monday and cash them in, but we can catch up on rent and buy some food."

"I'm so proud of you, Luke. I knew you'd win. I can't wait to give you a special award tonight after the lights are out." Her soft mouth teased as she outlined her lips with her tongue.

"This is just the beginning, sweetheart, and I love the award you give me every night. I have to say that I'm surprised at how accepting the community is of an ex-con. I wasn't expecting that."

"It's because everyone knows your family. They're willing to give you a chance to prove yourself, and I know you will."

"Honey, with you by my side, I can do anything. Just like I told the Federal Probation Officer the other day when he came to visit, you are my reason for everything."

Moisture sparkled in Darlina's eyes. "That's all I ever wanted to be."

Together they packed up the precious art pieces, gathered two tired girls, and Darlina drove them back to their apartment.

That night, lying in each other's arms, Luke pulled his angel wife against him, thrilled at the wild beating of her heart against his. He kissed the hollow of her throat, moved up to her eyelids and tantalized her waiting lips with soft touches from his mouth.

His breath stirred her silky hair as he murmured. "You never gave up on me. How can I thank you for having faith in me when I'd lost it in myself?"

"Like this." Darlina positioned herself over him. "Just love me. That's all."

He chuckled. "Oh baby, that I do."

The world was right. It had been tilted off its axis for many years and now, it was back on track. They'd been married almost one whole month and already their lives had changed one hundred and eighty degrees.

Connected as one, they could move forward and build the dream they'd both held on to, like a life raft in a raging sea. Nothing was impossible.

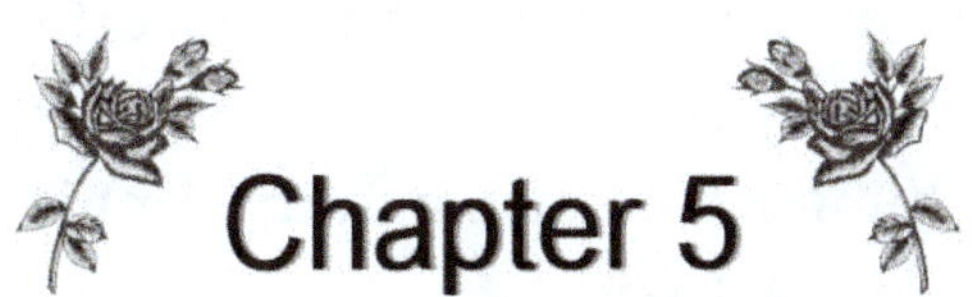

Chapter 5

A little over two months into their marriage, Luke sat at the kitchen table with Darlina, sipping coffee and enjoying the cool October breeze that floated through the open windows.

Her sky blue eyes held worry, worry that brought tightness to his chest. He covered her small hand with his. "Sugar, want to tell me what you're thinking?"

"Luke, I've never lived any place in my adult life where I couldn't find a job of some kind. I've been everywhere in this godforsaken town, looking." She stared out the kitchen window.

Leaning back in his chair, he ran his hands through his hair. "I know, sweetheart. I wish you didn't even have to think about a job. But, the truth is that the sign business Gary's got going is barely more than a back room operation that brings in a few dollars every month."

The tears that welled up in her eyes sent a jabbing pain straight through his heart. He knew he was letting her down, failing his new family.

"We've spent every penny of the money I brought with me from Shreveport, the prize money from the art show is gone and now I've robbed every penny from the girls' piggy banks. There is absolutely nothing left to take and the rent is due again soon. I don't know what else to do."

Luke swallowed hard and lifted her hand to his lips. "Let me do the worrying for us. It helps that you get the few hours a day with the home health working for Mom. Gary says we're gonna make money cuttin' firewood in the next few weeks and Monday I'm hittin' the local businesses and offer to do painting or carpenter work and see what I can rustle up. I don't have any tools or paint brushes, but Mom said she'd kept a lot of Dad's and I can use them."

"This is not the way I imagined it would be for us, Luke," her voice broke.

"Don't give up, princess. Hang with me a little longer. I'm good at pulling rabbits out of the hat. Something will come along. Just don't stop believing in me. But, for now, let's gather the girls and go pick up pecans to sell so we can get enough food for another day." Luke finished his coffee and winked at her.

"I'm not going anywhere or giving up, but something's gotta give." Darlina squeezed his hand. "We can't keep this up."

"I could go back to playing in the honky-tonks in a heartbeat, but that's not the life I want for you and the girls. I'm doing my best and I know you are too."

Luke openly admired her shapely bottom as she stood and placed their cups in the sink. Lord, how she turned him on.

She called to the children. "Girls, get your jackets and come on. We're gonna go pick up pecans."

From the loft where they played, Nicole whined. "Again, Mama? I don't wanna."

Lily intervened. "Stop whining, Nicole. If Mama says we have to, then we have to."

"That's the spirit, Lily," Luke praised. He placed his arms around Darlina and whispered in her ear. "Everything's gonna work out, I promise."

She buried her face in his chest, then stood on tiptoe and kissed his waiting lips. "I sure hope so."

Darlina still did all of the driving for the family. He'd be forever grateful for her understanding. He needed a little more time to settle in. Nevertheless, he felt like he wasn't fulfilling his role as the head of household every time she got behind the wheel.

A vacant house next door to his mother's had two huge pecan trees in the backyard and lately, this had been their choice location for gathering the nuts to sell.

Each of the girls had small red plastic pails while Luke and Darlina filled a battered five gallon bucket together. He found a long limb from one of the trees and used it to dislodge more of the nuts higher in the tree. In two hours, all of the buckets were full. Dammit, his little princesses shouldn't have to do this, and yet they willingly pitched in.

***

Chewing her fingernails, Darlina watched the man at the feed store pour the harvested pecans into a brown bag and put it on the scale. The effort gained them $6.73. With money in their pocket, they headed to the small market just down the street from their apartment.

Luke waited in the car with the girls while Darlina went in to scour for bargains. She gazed longingly at the wheat bread for $2.79 per loaf, then turned to the .59 cent white bread. She hated feeding food to her family that she knew wasn't healthy. What she wouldn't give for a steamed artichoke with garlic butter sauce, a fresh green salad or tofu with stir-fried vegetables.

She pushed those thoughts out of her mind, picked up a box of macaroni and cheese for .39 cents, then walked to the small meat counter. What would be on clearance today?

She left the store with dried pinto beans, bread, milk, hamburger meat that would be out of date in a few hours, a package of wieners, two packages of cornbread mix that were on sale and a carton of eggs. The twenty-one cents left over rattled around in her purse.

They could eat for another couple of days.

The girls had been in school since the end of August and Nicole already had new friends. Lily, on the other hand, hated going to a new school and had thrown up every morning for weeks. She'd told Darlina that she didn't fit in and no one wanted to be her friend, but Darlina simply encouraged her to keep trying. No matter how hard she fought it, Darlina couldn't help thinking back to how settled and happy the children had been in Shreveport.

Her worries kept her gut in a knot. She loved being with Luke, but was realizing that the picture she'd painted in her mind wasn't the way things were turning out. She'd imagined them selling Luke's songs and riding around in a Cadillac. How wrong she'd been. This dirty depressed little town they'd chosen to begin their life in certainly didn't offer much.

She thought about how she'd watched Luke put his guitar in the closet a few days after he'd arrived. She hoped it had only been temporary, but he wasn't showing any signs of going back to it. She missed her handsome rebel musician winking at her from the stage as he belted out one ballad after another. Maybe he simply needed more time to get settled.

These thoughts weighed heavy on her mind along with the financial woes. The nights were the only salvation. When she lay in Luke's arms, the troubles of the day melted into nothingness and gave her renewed hope. She doubled her efforts to find a job, filling out more applications.

By the end of another week, Darlina finally found work at the local mental health office. They offered four hours per day for a receptionist. Now she had two part-time jobs and it had taken her almost four months to get them. It wasn't the kind of work she was accustomed to doing, but at least it was steady income. It would take a full thirty days to get the first paycheck from MHMR, and she would have to go to Brownwood to pick it up every month.

Luke had managed to land a job painting a house. It wasn't much, but better than what they'd had.

With no phone of their own, Luke and Darlina used Mom Stone's telephone to make and receive calls. It was the number Darlina listed on every job application, all of the parole and probation papers and the contact number for the sign business.

Since Darlina worked a few hours a day for her, they could always get messages.

On a Tuesday afternoon during the first week of November, the phone rang as Darlina cleaned the bathroom.

She heard Mom Stone pick up. "Hello."

"No, he isn't here, but his wife is. Would you like to speak with her?"

Darlina put down her sponge and walked to the living room.

"Here she is." She handed the phone to Darlina.

"Hello." Darlina heard a man's deep voice on the other end.

"Mrs. Stone?"

"Yes."

"This is Jim Considine with the Coleman Democrat-Voice. I'm interested in doing an interview with you and your husband for the newspaper. Do you think your husband would speak with me?"

Darlina didn't hesitate. "I'm quite sure he would love talking with you, Mr. Considine. What do you have in mind?"

"Well, I saw the write-up in the newspaper last month when he won all of the awards for the art show at the Fiesta and it piqued my interest. I'd like to interview him about how he developed the varied art skills he has."

"If you want to give me your phone number, I'll have Luke call you tomorrow." She reached for a pad and pencil lying beside the phone.

"He can reach me at 625-4128 during the day."

"All right, sir. I'll give this to him."

"Thank you, Mrs. Stone."

"You're welcome."

"What was that about?" Mom Stone inquired.

"A man from the Coleman newspaper wants to do an interview with Luke. He said the art show winnings impressed him and he wants to know how Luke developed such artistic skills."

"Oh that's wonderful." Mom Stone clapped her hands. "I knew Bubba wouldn't have any trouble fitting in here. This will give him a chance to tell people his story."

"Yes, it will. I'm going to finish up in the bathroom, then I'll go find Luke." Darlina hurried back to her chore. She couldn't wait to tell Luke about this opportunity. Once she stored the cleaning supplies away, she drove two blocks down the street to the makeshift sign shop set up in a garage next to Bobby and Cindy's house.

Luke looked up from a sign he and Gary were painting when she came in the door. He put his brush down, hugged and kissed her. "What are you doing here, honey?"

"Looking for you. Hi, Gary."

"Hi." Gary kept painting.

She still thrilled to Luke's touch and even though it had only been a few hours since she'd seen him, it was new all over again. "There's a man at the newspaper office who wants to do an interview with you. He said he wanted to know how you developed your artistic talents.

Luke chuckled. "I don't mind tellin' him. Wonder just how much he wants to know."

"He didn't say. He just gave me his number and I told him you'd call him tomorrow."

"This could be good for us."

"That's what I thought. When will you be ready to go home?"

"What do you think, Gary? Maybe a couple more hours?"

"Yeah, I think we can wrap this one up." Gary put down his paintbrush and reached for a beer. "Hey, maybe you can give the sign business a free plug, Uncle Bubba."

"You know I will if I get a chance. I'll just have to see what the man wants to know. Honey, can you come back around six and pick me up?"

"Of course." She kissed him lightly and left through the open doors.

***

Luke set the interview up with Mr. Considine for the following Saturday at two. Darlina made a pot of coffee and placed fresh-baked cookies on a tray. She made a separate tray for the girls to take upstairs so they wouldn't interrupt the interview.

Once Mr. Considine arrived at the apartment and the introductions were out of the way, Darlina ushered the girls up to the loft and made sure they had activities to keep them busy for the next hour or so.

Mr. Considine stood close to Luke's height, had a ring of white hair around an otherwise bald head and wore a priest's collar. He held a tape recorder in one hand and once settled in a chair, he turned it on.

The questions flowed and soon the hour turned into two with Mr. Considine going outside to his car for another blank tape. Luke openly shared his story, the years of playing music, fighting, drinking, taking drugs, chasing women, the bank robberies and his part in them, meeting Darlina, then on to prison where he had to decide if he was going to turn all bad or try to do something worthwhile and positive.

Luke shared details of a dream he had while in solitary confinement, or, the hole, as he called it...The dream where a being or angel walked beside him and reflected his own battered and broken soul...The dream that inspired Luke to write the poem, *Discovery*.

Mr. Considine asked to see the poetry and was more than impressed with the large collection of poems along with pen and ink drawings bound in a notebook. "May I print the poem, *Discovery*, in my article?"

"Of course. Maybe someone will read it and be as inspired as I was when I wrote it."

Luke shared his current goals with the man, "I hope to teach ceramics, get back to doing leather tooling work, do more pen and ink drawings and portraits, publish some songs and poetry as well as perfect and patent a couple of inventions I came up with while I was in prison."

Mr. Considine drew Darlina into the interview, asking her questions as well.

Luke did not hesitate to proclaim that Darlina was the reason he decided to try and be a worthwhile human being. "Darlina was totally different from those I had been runnin' with. She is the influence pullin' me out of myself."

When the interview came to an end, Mr. Considine turned off his recorder and sat back in his chair. "Luke Stone, you've got quite a story here. I can't tell it all in one little newspaper article. You should think about writing a book."

Luke chuckled. "In my spare time, I just might do that, sir. Thank you for taking time to listen to me and I'll look forward to reading the article."

Before Mr. Considine bid his farewells, he promised to bring the article by for Darlina and Luke's approval before he printed it in the newspaper.

Once Mr. Considine left and the girls came downstairs, Nicole sat on Luke's lap and asked, "Daddy, are you gonna be famous?"

He ruffled the little girl's hair. "Honey, I don't know, but there is going to be a newspaper article. Do you girls want to learn how to do some artwork?"

Both of the children clamored. "Yes."

While Luke and the girls bounded upstairs to gather art supplies, Darlina headed to the kitchen to cook for her family.

By Luke's side, she was filled with contentment and a love that no words could explain. Just the nearness of him sent her heart racing. She knew she'd never tire of this man who made her world go around.

Luke and Darlina and one of the Prizewinning Art Pieces

Chapter 6

Thanksgiving brought an opportunity for Darlina, Luke and the girls to visit Darlina's mother in East Texas for the holiday. At least there would be a bounty of food and they would all get their fill. As much as she wanted to run to her mother and spill all of their troubles, she knew she had to maintain a front that everything was wonderful. She didn't want a lecture from her mother about Luke.

But, mothers know things. When they arrived, Granny (the name everyone called Darlina's mother) had boxes of clothes for the girls that she'd picked up at garage sales, along with shampoo, toothpaste and an assortment of other necessities. Darlina fought back tears when she opened the box.

As much as Darlina loved being there, knowing how Granny felt about Luke made it stressful. But, he kept a cheerful spirit, and other than Granny's dog biting him once on the ankle, the visit passed without incident.

Darlina bragged to her mother that Luke had been interviewed for the local newspaper and proudly displayed the article from the *Coleman-Democrat Voice* titled, *From Drugs, Crime; Prison to Rehabilitation* with a picture of her and Luke along with one of the ceramic pieces he'd entered in the art show.

The reprieve from their meager existence resembled a warm fire glowing in the Arctic. The girls stayed beside their granny for the entire three days, even insisting on sleeping with her. When it was time to leave, once again, Darlina fought back tears that threatened to break lose. Nicole openly cried and Lily let silent tears run down her cheeks. Granny hugged the girls, with tears of her own and even managed a brief hug for Luke, inviting them to come back soon.

On the road back home, Luke decided he was ready to practice driving. Under Darlina's watchful eye, he managed to maneuver through Waco with only one close call. He shared memories about holidays with his family and the marathon domino games he grew up watching. He wasn't a player himself and thought games were a waste of time, but they were a big deal in his family. To Luke Stone, entertainment was creating something with his hands. Darlina discovered that he had little tolerance for waste of any kind. This was an aspect of Luke she didn't know.

A few days later, as Darlina cleaned house for Mom Stone, Luke repaired the back door. Baby, the sheep, had butted it so many times the screen was loose.

Mom Stone called to both of them. "Kids come in here. There's something I want to talk to you about."

With hands joined, Darlina and Luke strolled in.

"What is it, Mom?" Luke sat on the couch, pulling Darlina down beside him.

"I know things are hard for you kids and I just hate the thought of you having to pay rent on that tiny apartment. I want to deed this extra lot here beside me to you, Son, and then you use it as collateral to get a trailer house."

"Are you sure you want to do that?" Luke tightened his grip on Darlina's hand.

"I'm positive. I'm leaving this house to Bobby when I die and it's only fair that I give you the other lot. Bobby can't do anything to make a living all crippled up and at least they'll always have a place to live. But, you're still strong, Luke, and you can build a place for your family."

"That'd sure be a big help, Mom. And we'd be right here to see about you and help you."

"Then tomorrow, I want you to go with me to talk to mine and Daddy's lawyer, Don Johnson, and get it transferred over into your name."

Darlina stood and hugged Mom Stone. "Thank you so much, Mom. This will mean the world to us."

"Yes, it will. I've been trying to figure a way to get us a place of our own and with the land, I'm sure I can do it." Luke leaned forward on the couch.

"You know me and Daddy always did business with the First National Bank and I'll bet if you talk to them, they'll help you get a trailer house," Mom Stone continued.

Luke chuckled. "I don't know if a bank would loan me money since I'm a convicted bank robber."

She waved him aside. "Horse hockey. Everybody knows you didn't do that and if you go in and talk to Rob McCollum, you'll get a loan. You just need to find a trailer you want first."

Luke turned to Darlina. "Sugar, how about we go to Abilene this weekend and start looking?"

"Sounds good to me. Maybe your mom's right. Maybe the bank would give us a loan. I have good credit and I've been a homeowner. The only problem I see is that our income is small, but at least it's steady."

Luke slapped his leg. "Well, by God, I think we can do this. Thank you, Mom."

"You're welcome. I want to see you kids doing good and not having to scrounge around to put food on the table and pay the bills."

"You and me both." Luke hugged his mother.

Over the next weeks, Luke, Darlina and the girls went shopping for a trailer house every weekend. Finally, they found just the right one in Granbury.

A week later, to Luke's surprise, the First National Bank didn't hesitate to make the loan, with the trailer title and land as collateral. Arrangements were made to move the home onto the vacant lot in January.

Things moved at warp speed, each day racing to meet the next. With so much to be done, Darlina watched Luke tackle the job of clearing the land to make ready for the delivery. It didn't matter that the weather turned bitter cold or that snowflakes fell. Luke had renewed drive that refused to let the icy cold or frozen rain stop him.

On a particularly windy December day, Darlina headed out the back door of Mom Stone's house with a cup of steaming coffee for Luke. She lowered her head against the wind and hugged the warm cup. "Got time for a break, sweetheart?"

"Baby, I always have time for a break if it means spending a minute with you." Luke reached for the cup and hugged her close. "I am grateful to Mom for giving us this chance."

"Me too. It is the hand-up we needed. I'm wondering though, how we're gonna come up with money to get a utility pole set and a gas meter?"

"I've been thinking about that. Let's go in the house for a minute. I wanna run something by Mom."

Darlina appreciated that Luke took care to clean his feet on the back porch so he wouldn't track dirt into the house that she worked so hard to keep clean.

Mrs. Stone looked up. "How's it going out there, Bubba?"

"I'm making progress. I've got an idea I wanna throw at you."

"What is it?"

"There is no damned way we're gonna have money to get a gas meter set plus an electric pole and box. How would you feel about us running the gas and water lines off of yours over here and we'll pay you every month for the bill?"

"I have no problem with that at all. I know exactly where you can tie into the water line but the gas you'll have to get a plumber to do or they'll cut me off."

"Okay. Do you know a plumber that won't rip us off?"

"I sure do. Marvin Stafford used to work with your daddy and he drops in every once in a while to check on me. I'll get him to do it. You'll have to dig the ditches and lay the pipe, then he can hook it up."

Luke rubbed his hands on the cup warming them. "We sure do appreciate all of this, Mom."

"Son, I'm just so glad to have you out of that awful prison and home I don't know what to do. I don't have any money, but you know I'll help any other way I possibly can."

Luke kissed her cheek. "I'll pay you back."

"You already have. I've got some leftover chicken and dumplings if you want some."

"Nah, I'm gonna get back to work. Thanks again, Mom."

Darlina walked with Luke back to the door. She pulled his face down to hers and kissed him with parted lips slipping her tongue into his mouth. "I love you, honey."

"Sugar, you keep that up and I'll forget all about workin'." He patted her on the bottom, slipped on his gloves and ducked out through the door.

Occasionally, Gary would come down and help with heavy tasks. But for the most part, Luke did the work single-handedly.

Since they'd be moving in a few days, Christmas came and went without much fanfare. Darlina set up the beautiful lighted ceramic Christmas tree Luke had made while in prison. Then she wound lights and garland around the stair rail. They purchased a few presents for the girls and on Christmas morning, Darlina had been amused to find that in her distracted state of mind, she'd labeled the presents wrong. Lily giggled when she held up a small nightgown that didn't fit and Nicole opened one that was much too big for her.

Even though Luke and Darlina had agreed on no presents for themselves, early Christmas morning, he handed her a beautifully penned poem with red roses drawn around the border of the paper.

THE MISSING LINK

All my life, I've been fitting you into my heart
Like jigsaw puzzle pieces of delicate art
I find in you qualities I admire and adore
Every wish, every dream I've carefully asked for

You are my destiny my reason and end of my strife
The reason for being and to fulfill my life
As you take me soaring in blissful flight
To peaceful plateaus of wondrous height
My darling Princess, my woman, my wife
I no longer wonder – nor even think
I know I've found the missing link

Tears misted her eyes as she read the words and marveled at the intricate roses drawn with the girls' markers. Her heart full of love for her rebel, she resolved to make any sacrifice necessary to carry on and help him build a life, their life.

To make food go further, Darlina resorted to cooking beans and cornbread frequently. More than anything, she wanted to cook food Luke wanted. After all, he'd been the one deprived from these small pleasures for fifteen years. He loved for her to fix ground hamburger meat with gravy and serve it over toasted bread. She struggled to put a bite of it in her mouth, but when her stomach growled loud enough, she forced it in and swallowed. Everyone had adjustments to make and they were giving it their all. Fresh vegetables and whole food would have to come later when they could grow a garden.

January arrived, along with new excitement as the trailer house was delivered. Even though Luke had done a lot of preparation, it was obvious that it would be another solid month before they could vacate the apartment and move into it.

Anticipation of having their own home kept the momentum going. Luke worked tirelessly from sunup 'til past sundown.

Darlina respected Luke's determination and adored him more for trying so hard.

Every night, they found escape from their struggles in each other's arms. After all, it was love that had brought them together and love that would sustain them through good times and bad.

In those moments, nothing else mattered and in the sweetness of passion, the outside world melted away. They were each other's destiny.

Luke and Darlina and their new home

Chapter 7

The days, weeks and months flew by and when Texas Springtime raised her lovely head, Luke Stone had the solid beginnings of a decent home for his family.

Each day, he made sure he had some small accomplishment to report, a task completed to show for the hours of the day he'd invested and yet progress seemed to move like cold molasses.

Darlina often came home from work to find him still outside pounding away with a hammer and nails.

On this particular April day, she found him under the trailer, nailing up pieces of used insulation Gary's neighbor had given him. She knelt down and watched for a while in silence.

"Luke."

He jumped and bumped his head on a metal beam. "Shit!" He rubbed the knot that was already starting to form.

"I'm sorry, honey. I didn't mean to startle you."

"That's okay. I'll live. This damn insulation is all over me and itching me to death, but I'm almost done. What do you need?"

"I just wanted to say hi."

Luke crawled from under the trailer. "Hi, yourself. I'd kiss you, but I don't want to get this shit all over you." Luke couldn't deny that above everything, she lit a fire inside of him, with her nearness.

"That's alright. You can give me plenty later. Are you okay?"

"Yeah." Luke growled. "Damned frustrated today. I hit my thumb with the hammer earlier and now my fuckin' head."

"I'm sorry. I'll leave you alone so you can finish what you're doin'. Supper will be ready in an hour."

"Okay." He crawled back under the trailer and picked up his hammer.

Even though he'd made huge strides since he'd arrived home in August, Luke couldn't shake the dissatisfaction with his accomplishments.

Dammit! He should be able to do more. Once Darlina went inside the house and he could hear her footsteps on the floor, he stopped hammering and pounded his fists into the dirt. Fuck it all! He had to man up and get more done for her, for his family. This was no time to let negativity overtake him. He thought about the ancient Indian medicine rituals. It'd been a while since he'd offered up smoke along with gratitude to the Great Spirit. He mustn't lose sight of the things he'd learned in prison.

When he crawled out from under the house, he felt sure his face had streaks from the frustrated tears running through the caked on dirt. Unwilling to let Darlina or anyone else see evidence of a moment of weakness, he hurried to the outside faucet. After he rinsed off the best he could, he put on a smile and went inside to his family.

Freshly showered, he joined Darlina, Lily and Nicole at the supper table. The banter between the girls was good medicine for him and he gazed with admiration and appreciation at his sexy wife, while they ate fresh blackeye peas, okra and chicken. No, Luke wouldn't let himself get sucked into anything negative. He hadn't survived prison to be the kind of man that gave in or gave up. Luke Stone wouldn't be beaten.

Trips to the local dump ground had proven beneficial. He'd scavenged pallets and other building materials that he put to good use. The pallets worked great as a makeshift sidewalk to keep their feet out of the mud when the spring rains came. His nephew, Gary, who was fast becoming his right-hand man, freely offered the use of his pickup truck on these hunting expeditions.

Gary stood a little over six feet tall, lanky and lean, had freckles and a shock of red hair. He cursed like a sailor with every breath. Luke was taken aback by the language used in front of his mom or Darlina. It seemed that it was no longer abnormal to curse openly. He often thought about what his father would've said about that. Al Stone never had any tolerance for what he considered disrespect and the foul language would be at the top of his list.

Nevertheless, Gary was the one who stepped up to help Luke with whatever he needed.

Luke watched Darlina move through the days with him. He knew she wasn't afraid of hard work, but hated that he couldn't pamper her in the ways he'd always dreamed of. He wracked his brain to think of any avenue that might make things easier.

"Darlina, sweetheart, I know you're tired and worried, so let's figure out something that might make things better. Sometimes I think I should have stayed in Kansas City and run night clubs for the mafia, but I didn't want that life for you and the girls. Eventually, they would have asked me to do a job for them and you cannot say no. So, I walked away from it and I'm not sorry. Got any ideas you wanna share?" Luke stroked her hair as she lay nestled on his shoulder after their nightly love-making.

"I might have one. You remember a few years back when I filed on Will for not paying child support?"

"Yes, I remember. You had a lawyer friend do that for you."

"Uh huh. Well, the problem back then was that I lived out of state. Now that I'm living in Texas, it might be easier to get something done. He owes a pretty good chunk of money at this point."

"Then I say we pursue that. I don't feel like he owes me any-thing, but he does owe the girls."

"I'll look into it tomorrow," Darlina mumbled, drifting off to sleep.

The following day, Luke and Gary sat at the kitchen table inside the trailer, eating bologna sandwiches for lunch, while rain pattered on the tin roof.

"Gary, I want to talk seriously to you about the sign busi-ness. I really believe that if we start working our asses off and use our heads, we can turn it into something that will support both of our families."

"What are you thinking, Uncle Bubba?"

"We need to get cleaned up nice and go hit the businesses downtown. Have you noticed the faded signs on the old build-ings? We need to convince them that it's time to spiffy up downtown Coleman. If we get one business on board we can use that to leverage the next one. See how it could work?"

"I sure as fuck could use some steady income. All of my damn kids are outgrowing their goddamn clothes and shoes. When do you want to go?"

"Well, since it's raining, how about this afternoon? You can pick me up in an hour. Another thing, we need a sign shop up here on the main road instead of down at your house."

"It damn sure couldn't hurt."

"We could easily turn that abandoned chicken house sitting over next to Mom's into a small sign shop. Hell, we'd already have the framing and a concrete floor."

"Whatever you think. I'd like to see us all making some fuckin' money."

"I believe we can. We just have to get out and work it. Bobby can still draw with his one good arm so he can make patterns for us. I'm just damned ready to make a living for my family. Darlina works her ass off and so do I. Now it's time to make some money."

Luke couldn't wait for Darlina to finish work that evening. He'd dropped in on her at his mom's house before he and Gary took off to drum up some sign business. It hurt like hell to see the circles under her eyes and furrowed brow.

When she walked through the door of the trailer house, he looked up from the kitchen sink. "Hi, Mama."

The girls, standing on either side of him at the sink, chimed in. "Hi, Mama."

"Hi yourselves. What are you doing?"

"We're cleaning up for you, Mama." Nicole puffed her chest out.

Darlina walked up to Luke and the children, hugged each of the girls, then wrapped her arms around Luke's waist. He dried his hands on a towel and turned toward her.

"You girls finish up here. I need to help Mama get comfortable." He winked and grinned.

They walked arm in arm to their bedroom in the back.

"You're in a good mood. What's going on?" She slipped off her shoes.

"I just need to show you how much I love you and we picked up some sign work today that might turn out to be pretty good."

"Oh Luke, that's great."

He slipped her blouse over her head and pulled her toward him.

"You know we can't make love on the bed. The girls will hear the squeaking." Darlina giggled.

"It won't be the first time I've had carpet burns on my knees."

Luke moved slow taking off each piece of clothing until they lay intertwined on the bedroom floor.

A knock on the door startled them both. Darlina called out. "What is it?"

"Mama, are we gonna have supper?" Nicole inquired "What are y'all doing in there?"

"Yes, we're going to have supper and Daddy is just helping me get my clothes changed. Go watch TV with Lily and we'll be out in a minute." She stifled a laugh with the back of her hand.

Luke hoped she could see the love shining in his eyes. "I love it when you're naughty."

"Then I'll be naughty more often. You can tell me about the new work over supper, and I'll tell you what I found out about Will later, but right now, your wife needs you."

Over a simple supper of pork chops, green beans and new potatoes, Luke shared his news about the downtown sign work.

"And, I made another little discovery today," he added.

Darlina raised her eyebrows. "Oh? What's that?"

"I found my old iron bed frame in a storage room down at Bobby's. Remember the one I had in Brownwood?"

Darlina gasped. "Of course I remember. Let's bring it home."

"I fully intend to, but first I want to put on a fresh coat of paint. Then of course, we'll have to break it in." Luke chuckled. He flashed back to the many nights Darlina had lain wrapped in his arms on the antique bed. Just remembering caused his pulse to race.

"Well, of course."

Nicole looked up from her plate. "Mama, why would you and Daddy want to break a bed?"

Darlina laughed. "Honey, we aren't going to break any bed. It's just a manner of speech, like when you break in a new pair of shoes so they'll be comfortable."

Lily poked Nicole. "You're stupid, Nicole."

Nicole puckered her bottom lip. "No, I'm not."

"Girls, we don't call each other stupid ever. Lily, apologize to your sister." Luke insisted.

"Sorry," Lily muttered.

Darlina gently suggested. "When you're done with supper, you need to show me that you're homework's all done, then you can play for a little while before bed."

The girls nodded and finished cleaning their plates.

"So anyway," Luke continued, "I'm gonna get Gary to help me bring the bed frame home tomorrow. Also, I'm ready to start driving again and get my driver's license."

"That's great, baby."

"Then, I want to start looking for an old pickup I can buy cheap just to use for a work truck. It won't matter if it's an old junker. Gary's good at working on engines."

"He's turning out to be a big help to you, isn't he?"

"Yes, he is. My own sons don't have any interest in helping me or even getting to know me, but Gary does and I want to help him learn how to make a living for his family."

Later that evening, after the girls were tucked in bed, Darlina shared what she'd learned from the District Attorney about the back child support issue. Being an old friend of the Stone family, the D.A. willingly took the case with no fee.

"That's great, sugar. Like I said, Will doesn't owe me or you a thing, but he does owe the little girls."

"I'm finally beginning to think we might be able to make a living here in this depressed little town. I've sure had my doubts since I got here."

"It will all work out, I promise. Gary and I are going to make a go of this sign business."

"When are you going to get back to the music that you love and are so good at? Every time I go in the closet and see your guitar case, I remember how you used to sound on stage, and how handsome you were all dressed up in your fancy suits. Surely, we could get someone to record some of your songs. Without a doubt, they're good enough. What about Willie?"

"Sweetheart, I don't exactly know how to explain this to you, but right now, music doesn't fit into our lives. My full focus is on establishing a home for us. Willie doesn't owe me a thing and he has lots of my songs already. If he's ever interested, I'll hear from him. For now, the guitar has to stay in the closet. I have to work with my head and my hands for us. Everything else will come in time."

"I wish they would make my job at MHMR full time, but because it's such a small office, there isn't a chance for that. My boss did inform me today that I'm going to have to start dispensing medicine to some of the clients daily. I don't much like that idea."

"You just make sure you don't get yourself cornered by one of 'em wanting more dope than they've got comin'."

"I'll be careful. Let's go to bed and do what we seem to be best at." Darlina stood and pulled Luke to his feet. Together they turned off the lights and made their way to the one place where everything was right and good...in each other's arms.

***

Full blown summertime found Luke making great strides in establishing Stone Signs as a viable business. A percentage of earnings from each sign job went toward increasing the size of the sign shop, buying paints, brushes and vinyl. Luke's method taught Gary the value of investing back into a business to grow it.

After haggling back and forth, the District Attorney finally contacted Darlina with an offer from Will to settle the back child support he owed.

It seemed that he'd decided to get out of the carpentry line of work and devote himself totally to a new religious cult movement. He offered to trade a long list of tools in lieu of the debt.

Luke and Darlina sat outside, sipping iced tea under a shade tree while watching the girls play with a stray kitten they'd found.

"What do you think about Will's offer?" Darlina placed her tea in her left hand so she could hold Luke's hand.

"I think it's worth doing. With more tools, especially power tools, I could get so much more done. He's making a generous offer and show of support to us."

"Then, I'll contact the DA tomorrow and let him know we accept his offer. But, that doesn't wipe out future child support. He will have to start paying the hundred dollars monthly that he was ordered to pay in the divorce."

"Shit. A hundred dollars is nothing and he shouldn't have any trouble coming up with that for his girls. I'll talk to my old school friend, Red, and see if his sons will go with me to Austin to pick them up. I'll have to get tires on the old band trailer but they have a pickup to pull it with."

"What about Gary? Can't he go?"

"He's got his own shit to deal with. Bobby and Cindy are moving down to South Texas in a few weeks. Cindy's mother lives there and is in pretty bad shape. She needs Cindy to take care of her."

"Will Gary move his family too?"

"He don't know for sure, but I figure he will."

"What about the sign business?"

"If Gary leaves, I'll do it by myself."

Darlina sighed. "Lots of changes, Luke."

Suddenly, Luke let go of Darlina's hand and stood. His brother, Bobby, was slowly hobbling toward the trailer. "We're back here, stud."

Luke would never get used to seeing Bobby all crippled up and unable to speak except through the device that looked like a small black box with a tiny tube attached. It broke his heart and yet he knew there was nothing he could to change any of it. He remembered the wild, crazy, vital man that loved to sing and play piano.

Chapter 8

Bobby paused and waved.

Luke walked toward him. "Let's go inside where it's a little cooler."

With the help of his cane, Bobby hobbled slowly up the steps of the porch with Luke close behind.

Darlina called to the children. "It's time to go inside, girls."

"Can we watch TV, Mama?" Lily asked.

"Can I bring Tiger inside?" Nicole picked up a tabby kitten with one ear smaller than the other.

"No, Nicole. Amanda wouldn't tolerate another cat in the house. Y'all can watch TV for a little while though."

Luke watched her usher the children inside and quickly fill two glasses with ice and tea for him and Bobby. His eyes never left her and every movement she made captivated him. After she set the glasses on the table in front of them, she tossed a bag of popcorn in the microwave for the girls.

When she glanced toward Luke he winked, and watched her blue eyes twinkle. "Honey, when you get the girls situated, come sit here with me and Bobby."

"I will."

Both Luke and Darlina oftentimes had difficulty understanding Bobby's words through the talking device, so Luke had already placed a tablet and pencil in front of him.

"You out gettin' your exercise, brother?" Luke took a sip from his glass.

"I had to get out of the house. Gary's kids were driving me nuts." Bobby lay his talking device on the table and sipped the cold tea Darlina placed in front of him.

"You know you're always welcome down here."

Bobby nodded. "I know. I wanted to tell you that Joseph is coming up in few days." Bobby leaned his cane against the wall.

Darlina pulled up a chair and joined them.

Luke had wondered if and when any of his children would come around. They'd not made an effort to visit with him since his and Darlina's wedding. It would be good to see his oldest son again.

"That's great, Bobby. I haven't forced myself on any of the kids since I got home. It's their choice if they wanna have anything to do with me or not."

"I figured that's what you were thinking."

"I'll never get over the guilt of running out on them." Luke tapped the edge of the table with his finger.

"You didn't run out, brother. You got drug out. They know that. It's just that Joyce had so much anger and bitterness toward you and tried her best to turn them against you and all of us." Bobby stopped, held a handkerchief over the hole in his trachea and coughed.

"I reckon that's my fault too. It didn't help much with the way I carried on while we were married. Dammit, Bobby, I just couldn't get along with her."

"Nobody could get along with her. Joseph lived with us off and on for years. He even came up to Alaska and worked in the oil field some. He has a hard time staying off drugs. We always tried to help him."

"I appreciate that, stud. He's an adult now and if he wants to kick the drug addiction, he'll have to man up and do it. All I can do is tell any of 'em what their old man learned the hard way."

"You and me both. Hey, do you remember Ila Snellgrove?" Bobby got a twinkle in his eyes and laughed which threw him into another coughing spell.

Luke cracked up. "Hell yes, I remember. What we did was pretty sorry."

"It was all in fun. No harm done."

"What are you two talking about?" Darlina asked.

"It was way back when I had the TV show on KPAR in Abilene," Luke explained. "We'd get all kinds of fan mail. One time we got a postcard from this old lady named Ila Snellgrove and we decided to have some fun with her."

Bobby chuckled. "We started sending her fan mail from the Rhythm Rebels, telling her that we'd heard how good she sang and that we wanted her to join the band."

Luke picked up where Bobby left off. "We used to mail her a postcard from wherever we'd be playing and even gave a few to some fellas that went on up North to New York and all over. We could imagine her telling her friends at the beauty shop that she was going to join a honky-tonk band and go on the road. Like Bobby said, we didn't mean any harm. Just havin' a little fun."

"You two should write all of this down." Darlina giggled.

"Nobody would believe it."

"That's for damn sure." Bobby ignored the dribble of tea on his chin. He launched into a long spiel about something neither Luke nor Darlina could understand.

"You're gonna have to write it down, stud." Luke pushed the pad and pencil toward him.

Bobby wrote furiously, scribbling across the page, then pushed it back toward Luke.

"I agree, brother. With a house full of kids, Gary needs to learn how to make money, not just work. I'm trying to teach him what I know."

Bobby nodded. "Half the time, they have to live with us because they can't afford a place."

Luke chuckled. "The nut didn't fall far from the tree. You and Cindy had to live with Mom and Dad lots of times because you couldn't stay sober enough to make a living."

"I know. Wish I had it all to do over again. I'd do it different."

Luke's heart constricted. He'd lived with regrets for fifteen long years, wishing he could go back and change things.

"Me too. But, all we've got is today and I'm damned well gonna do my best and hope that somehow I make up for all the shit I did wrong back down the line."

"Cindy bought me a little keyboard the other day. I can lay it on my lap and play music with one hand."

"I'm sure you can. My guitar's in the closet and I don't have any intention of pullin' it out. I've gotta work with my head and my hands right now. I love music, but I was never what I would call a great musician. You were."

"You were a damned good singer and writer, Luke."

"Yeah, and look where that got me. If I ever go back to music, it'll be after these girls are grown and we're in good financial shape." Luke stood. "Let's move into the living room, stud."

"I need to be going." Bobby struggled to stand.

"Let Darlina take you back home."

"Nah. I'd rather walk. Besides, I need to poke my head in and say hi to Mom."

Luke slapped his brother on the back. "Come see us anytime, man."

Bobby nodded. Luke held the door open and watched until his brother made it down the steps. Darlina stood beside him with her arm around his waist. Once he was on the ground, Bobby turned and waved, then hobbled across to their mother's house.

"That was nice." Darlina said.

"Yeah. You can't imagine what it's like for me to see him in this shape. I've seen Bobby stand in front of the mirror for an hour combing his hair. Everything had to match perfectly and he'd always insist that his shirts were starched and ironed. Life turns some funny ways." Luke leaned down and brushed Darlina's lips with his.

"Come on girls. Tell Daddy goodnight and let's get you two ready for bed."

The children put their popcorn bowls in the sink, hugged Luke and followed their mother toward two small bedrooms.

When they'd first moved into the trailer, they had to share a room, but Luke had turned the room just off the living room into a tiny bedroom for Nicole with twin bunk beds that Darlina had moved from the house in Shreveport. Lily's room was larger and had a full size bed and a small black and white TV on a shelf in the corner that Luke's mom had given them. Between the two rooms was a small bathroom with a toilet and sink. The only full bathroom in the trailer was next to Luke and Darlina's bedroom at the opposite end.

Luke was standing in front of the north facing window staring out at the night, when Darlina returned a few minutes later. He felt her arms slide around him and let her love wrap him in security and peace.

"What's wrong, baby?"

Luke cleared his throat and blinked away tears threatening to form before he turned to face her.

"I wish Joseph, Lexi, Martin and Nathan would let me be their dad again. I understand they don't have much regard for me, but if they'll give me a chance, I can prove to them that I've changed."

"Give them time, honey. You were gone for a very long time and they suffered hardships. Mom was telling me the other day that when Nathan and Martin were teenagers, Joyce up and left one day while they were at school. They didn't know where she'd gone or if she'd be back. Martin tried to take care of them but they eventually got kicked out of the apartment, so they lived in the city park in Midland until she came back months later."

"Mom didn't tell me a lot about shit like that when I was locked up, because she knew there wasn't a damn thing I could do about any of it. I did know about Joyce's good-for-nothing brother molesting Lexi. If I could've torn those bars apart, I'd have killed him. I still would today if the sorry bastard wasn't already dead."

Darlina sucked in her breath. "You know your children are always welcome here and I'll show them nothing but kindness."

Luke reached for her and stroked her hair as she rested her head on his chest. "I love you for so many reasons, sweetheart, but the way you care about other people touches me deep. I'm a rough ol' lump of coal, but you, you're soft and sweet and loving and kind."

She looked up. "I'm just me, baby and I love you."

He lowered his head and filled his nostrils with the sweet smell of her auburn hair. "And I'm just me loving you with all of me. Whatever, whoever I am, you get it all."

"Would you like to have a drink, baby? I still have that bottle of Crown Royal I moved with me from Shreveport."

"I don't need any whiskey. It's been over sixteen years now since I've had a drink and I haven't missed it one bit. I just need you, sweetheart."

"You've got me, for the rest of our lives."

"And then even in death, I'll still be with you." Luke took Darlina's hand and looked deep into her eyes.

"I believe that with all of my heart. Let's go to bed."

Luke chuckled. "Thought you'd never ask. I need you in every way possible." Luke's voice grew husky. "I want to be inside you. I need to feel your heart beat in rhythm with mine. You complete me. You make me believe that I can do anything, even fixing my relationship with my kids. I love you, princess."

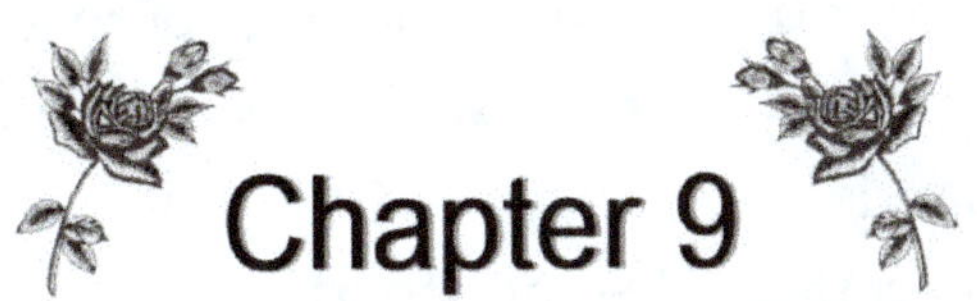

Chapter 9

Two weeks later, Luke sat in the living room with his oldest son, Joseph. As much as he wanted to help his son, all he could do was offer advice, knowing full well the odds of Joseph taking it were slim to none. The anger in his son's flashing brown eyes told him that.

Joseph fidgeted in his chair. "You got anything to drink, Dad?"

"Nothing but coffee, water or tea. Son, I haven't touched a drink in over sixteen years and I can honestly say I haven't missed it."

"Shit, I'd like to go get a six pack. Can you loan me ten bucks?"

"I don't have any money. If you're hungry, we can feed you, but I've got no money to loan."

Joseph snickered. "Why don't you go dig up some of that fuckin' bank money? Don't you think it's about time?"

The words hit Luke with the force of a sledgehammer. He knew he wasn't through paying for his mistakes.

"Don't you realize that if there had ever been any bank money, I wouldn't have spent fifteen years in a goddamn prison? Shit, there was never any money and what little there was, I blew through it like a tornado across the Oklahoma plains." Luke packed his pipe with tobacco trying hard to still his trembling hands.

"Got any cigarettes?" Joseph stood.

"No, and don't go stealing cigarettes from Nanny. She's barely gettin' by herself. I thought you were working steady."

Joseph stood and began to pace. "I've been workin' the rigs around Midland. I make good money."

"Then why don't you have ten dollars for beer and cigarettes? I don't understand."

Joseph stopped and faced his father. "I blow through it just like you did, Dad. Guess the apple didn't fall far from the tree. Mom was right about you. You don't give a shit about none of us. Everything is all about your new family. Well, what about us throwaways?"

Luke winced. "I never ran out on you, Joseph, and up until the day I got drug out, I paid the bills and gave your mom money. She never had to work a day in her life until I got locked up, so don't give me that bullshit."

"You don't know what it's like to grow up without a father," Joseph snarled.

"You're right. I don't, but since you do, you need to make damned sure that your son doesn't grow up without a dad. I don't understand why you can't leave the junk alone. You're an adult and you make the decisions about your life now."

"Well, so far, my life's been pretty fuckin' rotten and I don't give much of a shit."

"Yeah, I thought I didn't give a shit either until they threw me in prison and slammed fifteen doors behind me." Luke grimaced. "Oh, I gave a shit alright. Like you, I just didn't have enough sense to know it."

Joseph sat down and put his head in his hands. "Dad, you don't know what it was like after you left. Mom pretty much fell apart and half the time, Lexi and the two little boys wouldn't have anything to eat if I didn't go steal it. Nanny and PawPaw tried to help, but Mom wouldn't let 'em do much. She said she didn't need handouts, but really we did..." His voice trailed off.

Luke puffed on his pipe. "I know things were tough. My hands were tied and I didn't know half of the crap that went on. Besides, even if I had, there wouldn't have been a damn thing I could've done from where I was."

"The drugs somehow make everything feel better. I'll never forget the first time I put a needle in my arm and pumped it full of heroin. All the struggling stopped in that instant. I could breathe."

Luke put his hand on Joseph's shoulder. "I'd sure like to see you get yourself together and get off that shit."

Joseph looked up. "Yeah me too, but today ain't the day." He stood and pushed the chair in. "Guess I'll go down to Gary's and see if he's got any beer or cigarettes. I'll be around for a few days."

"All right. Come back up anytime you want. I'm always here."

"Yeah." Joseph let himself out the front door.

Luke sat back down and stared at the wall in front of him. He'd failed his first family.

His heart broke for Joseph, Lexi, Martin and Nathan and the hardships they'd had to endure. He knew he couldn't have ever lived with their mother again, even if he hadn't gone to prison, but he would've made damn sure they had what they needed. At least he could have been there to protect them and pick up the pieces when things fell apart.

He cursed fate that he hadn't met Darlina even one year earlier. Things could have been so much different if he'd found her kind of real love before he got knee-deep in the mess that sent him to prison.

He looked up as she came in the front door with their two blonde daughters.

"Daddy, Daddy," Nicole ran to Luke. "Daddy, we found a new kitty today. Can we keep it? Can we?"

Lily joined Nicole. "It's so cute, Daddy. It's white with a little bit of brown around one eye. Wanna see?" She tugged on Luke's hand.

"Sure. Take me to this kitty." He smiled through troubled eyes at Darlina as he let the children lead him outside. "Have you seen this wonderful kitten, Mama?"

"Not yet. I'll go with you and then I'm going to start supper. You okay, sweetheart?" It was uncanny how she seemed to know without a word being spoken when his heart was troubled.

Luke nodded. "I'll tell you later. Right now, we've got a kitty to inspect."

Nicole and Lily darted out the door to catch their new pet. Luke reached for Darlina's hand and squeezed it as they followed.

"Here it is, Daddy." Lily held the white kitten in her arms. "Isn't he cute?"

"He sure is, but he might belong to someone already. Let's see if he stays around before we name him. Would that be alright?"

"Mama, can we bring him in the house?" Nicole begged

"No. I've already told you. One cat in the house is enough and besides that, Amanda would claw its eyes out. He has to stay outside."

"Me and Nicole know how to tell if this is a boy or girl cat." Lily announced proudly.

Luke chuckled. "Oh really? How can you tell?"

"Just turn him over and look at his belly," Nicole chimed in.

Lily continued, "I've already looked and this is a boy cat. I wanna name him Snowball."

"That sounds like a fine name for a white kitty."

Darlina moved toward the porch. "Supper will be ready in half an hour."

"I'll come help you." Luke volunteered.

"Girls, y'all can play with your new kitty 'til suppertime."

"Okay, Mama."

Luke put his arm around Darlina's waist and they walked up the steps together and through the front door. As soon as the door was closed, he pulled her so tight against him that he could feel her heart beating.

"Baby, I love you so much. I never want to live another day of this life without you and these little girls."

"Where is that coming from, Luke? You won't have to because we're right here." She turned her face up toward his. "I want to hear all about what's troubling you. Talk to me while I cook."

Luke leaned against the kitchen counter and while Darlina fried potatoes, opened a can of English peas and popped a sausage link in the oven, he recounted Joseph's visit.

"I want to help Joseph, honey, but I know that even if I had money, giving it to him isn't the answer. It'll go straight into his arm. I wish he'd listen to me. I've learned things the hard way and know what I'm talkin' about."

Darlina stirred the potatoes and tossed a couple of wieners into a pan of boiling water then turned around. "Your mom told me he's going to stay with her for a few days. Maybe somehow, you can get through to him while he's here. All you can do is try. You're right though…he's an adult now and has to make his own choices."

"Joseph has always been tough. I've said many times that of all of my kids, he's the smartest and could survive anywhere. He's built a lot like my dad. He's not a big man, but he's not one that will back down from anyone or anything. If he ever makes up his mind to leave the dope alone, he can. I have no doubt of that."

Darlina gently lay her hand on Luke's cheek. "My heart goes out to all of your kids. I know they were disappointed that you didn't go back with their mother when you came home, and I also know they blame me, but they'll come around. I don't worry about it."

Luke narrowed his eyes. "None of 'em better not ever disrespect you. I won't tolerate that from anyone."

"Don't worry, baby. Nobody's gonna mistreat me or the girls. Do you want to call them in for supper?"

Luke rested his hands on Darlina's bottom and kissed her with all the passion inside him. "Damn, you're sexy, woman."

Darlina laughed. "You better go get the kids before we wind up distracted and have cold food."

Luke wiggled his eyebrows and released a sigh. Then he stepped to the door and called to the girls to come in and wash up.

***

Joseph Stone stayed around for three days, then borrowed money from Gary and disappeared again. This weighed heavy on Luke's heart, but he knew that all he could do was continue to work on building a home for Darlina and the girls and hope that Joseph, Lexi, Martin and Nathan would find it in their hearts to forgive him and let him be their dad again someday.

The one consolation he had was in knowing that he hadn't deliberately run out on them. He'd made bad decisions that resulted in him being taken away, but he'd never intended for things to go that way.

With new resolve, he worked on their home, saving pennies to buy one more piece of tin, or a can of paint to make it better. This was where he belonged and he put all of his energy and efforts into making it the best it could be with what they had.

***

With September came another Fiesta de la Paloma and another chance to enter the art show.

Luke sat with Lily and Nicole at the table, one day after school, with paper, colored pencils, markers and crayons.

"Would either one of you girls like to enter the children's art division at the fair in a couple of weeks?"

"I don't think I'm good enough." Lily glanced down at her drawing.

"Of course you're good enough. Your ol' dad can help you with it, if you want to enter." Luke hated for either of the girls to ever feel inadequate.

"I want to, Daddy," Nicole piped up.

"Okay. Are you sure, Lily?"

"Yeah, I'm sure." She never looked up.

"What would you like to draw, Nicole?"

"I want to draw a Unicorn and a rainbow."

"That's what I'm drawing, Nicole. You do something different." Lily crumpled her drawing and tossed it across the table.

"But, you're not putting yours in the contest, so I want to."

Lily pouted. "You always copy me, Nicole."

Luke broke in. "She wants to copy you because she looks up to you, Lily."

Lily put her marker down and got up from the table bumping into Nicole's chair when she went past into the living room.

Luke spoke sternly. "Lily, come back in here. You can't act like that. What's wrong?"

Tears welled up in Lily's eyes. "She gets to do all the fun stuff. I never get to do anything."

"What do you want to do, Lily?"

"I want to learn to paint like you do."

"Then, sweetheart, let me teach you. But, you have to drop the attitude and stop acting mean toward your sister."

She looked at Nicole. "Sorry."

"Do you mean it?" Luke prodded.

"Yeah. I mean it. Sorry, Nicole." She wiped her eyes with the back of her hand.

Just then, Darlina opened the front door and came in from work. She saw Lily's flushed face and looked from one to the other.

"What's going on?"

"Nothing. Lily and Nicole just had a little spat. They're okay now though," Luke assured.

"Lily?"

"What, Mama?"

"Are you okay?"

"Yes. I got mad at Nicole because she was copying me. But, I'm not mad anymore. Daddy's gonna to teach me how to paint."

"And I'm gonna enter a drawing in the art contest at the fair, Mama." Nicole happily announced.

"Okay, girls. But don't you be giving your daddy a hard time."

"That's the last thing you have to worry about, darlin'." Luke pushed his chair away from the table and pulled Darlina down on his lap, inhaling the perfumed scent of her hair.

"Me and these girls are gettin' along just fine. I'm gonna teach them how to do lots of things. I want them to grow up and be smart and beautiful young ladies."

Both children grinned at that thought.

"Okay, smart, beautiful young ladies. Let's get this table cleared off so I can have the kitchen." Darlina unwrapped herself from Luke's arms and stood.

The girls scrambled to round up the escaping pencils and markers and put them away in a plastic box.

Luke watched all three of his girls with pride. No luckier man had ever walked the face of the earth.

From the stark cold darkness of prison to a home filled with warmth and love still sometimes seemed too good to be true, much like an oasis in the middle of a hot dry desert.

They would always get his very best. That much he knew.

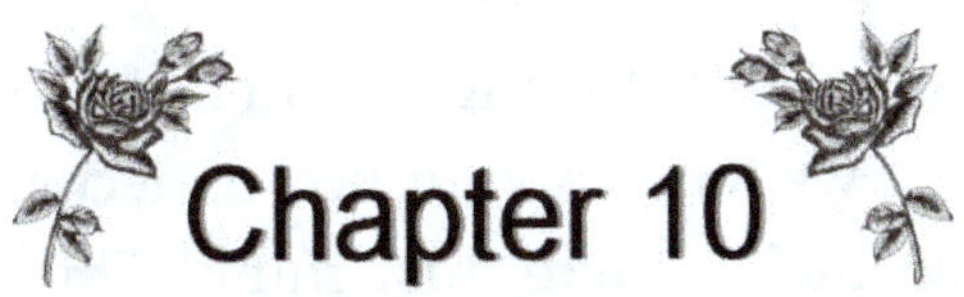

Chapter 10

The summer months rolled into autumn and headed on into winter. Once again, Darlina burst with pride that Luke had won first place with every entry he submitted in the arts and crafts competition in the Fiesta de la Paloma. Nicole had drawn a third place prize in the children's art division with the Unicorn drawing she entered. Luke had helped her, but insisted she do the work.

Darlina loved the way the girls watched and learned from Luke. He patiently showed them lines to draw and how to blend colors together.

The first weekend of December found Luke, Darlina and the girls driving the back roads around the Santa Anna Mountain looking for cedar branches to cut.

"I want like hell to feel the spirit of Christmas again," Luke said as he expertly cut an aromatic cedar branch. "Prison pretty much took it all out of me, but you girls can help me get it back."

"I think decorating our home is a good start." Darlina laid the branch on top of a growing pile in the trunk of the car. "We can put these along the top of the divider between the living room and kitchen and along the west wall too."

"I wanna weave lights through them and put up ribbons and bows or whatever we have in your box of decorations."

"It will be beautiful, Luke. Just think. This is the start of a Christmas tradition for us in our very own home."

Luke chuckled, "Yeah, ours and the bank's. But, it's damn sure better than the little apartment, and something to build from."

Lily rolled down the car window and stuck her head out. "Look, Daddy, it's starting to snow." Within seconds, Nicole's head popped out alongside her sister's.

Luke looked up at the sky. "Would you look at that. It is starting to spit snow." He reached for Darlina who was standing beside the car. "It's snowing, Mama. The Great Spirit heard us talking and is offering up a gift to add to the feeling of Christmas."

Darlina never tired of the easy way she could move into Luke's arms and the instant warmth they provided. "I do believe you're right. I think we have enough cedar branches. How about we go back home and make hot chocolate with marshmallows on top?"

The children clamored. "Yay! Hot chocolate."

She waited for Luke to open her car door then close it. He shut the trunk lid and slid behind the wheel. She was more than happy to turn the driving over to him after he got his driver's license. The only times he had any trouble was when they went into Abilene, which was a rare occasion.

She'd backed off as he moved with more confidence into his role as the head of their household. He told her repeatedly that he wanted nothing more in life than to be exactly where he was. Of course, they both wished for an easier flow of money to make things less difficult, but the love they shared made up for everything else they lacked.

Luke turned the volume up on the radio when *Here Comes Santa Claus* began to play. In unison, all four of them sang along with Gene Autry.

Luke grinned at Darlina and mouthed the words, "You are beautiful."

She blew him a kiss and kept singing.

Darlina peered through the window at the tiny bits of snow that grew larger. She and Luke had been married a year and a half and they'd gone through many adjustments in a short time. The early struggles just to have enough to eat seemed impossible to get past and yet they did. Steady income, even though small, and lots of determination along with hard work had paid off and their life together was slowly taking shape.

She listened to Luke and the girls singing *We wish you a Merry Christmas* and blinked away tears. Never before had she felt so complete.

It astounded her to realize that she and Luke had only had two disagreements since he'd come home.

They had differences in opinion about what Luke expected of the children. Although she knew he would never hurt either of them, he insisted that they work alongside them.

Back in the summer, he'd given them the chore of painting the outside of the trailer and Darlina thought this was a little more than ten and seven year old girls ought to have to do. But, in the end, Luke won out.

Lily had become a great help by the end of summer. Darlina was overjoyed to see her confidence grow. Nicole learned fast how to avoid work and how to manipulate Luke, whereas Lily approached everything head on and open.

Now, wrapped in a blanket of love, Darlina glanced in the back seat at the two sweet faces. More than anything, she wanted them to have a happy childhood. In that moment, with the radio playing Christmas carols and Luke singing along with them, everything was perfect. She sighed. Any differences they encountered, she felt confident they could work through. She reached for Luke's hand and squeezed it. She would never tire of the instant warm response she got or the love that shone in his eyes when he gazed at her.

***

Just one week before Christmas, as Darlina helped Mom Stone bake pies, they heard the front door open. Mom stepped out of the kitchen.

"Well my lord, Sissy. You didn't tell us you were coming down." She embraced Luke's daughter, Lexi.

"I didn't know until this morning, Nanny. We caught a ride with Joseph. Do you have any milk? Sage needs milk in her sippee cup." She carried a red-haired two-year-old baby girl on her hip.

"Of course, I have milk."

Darlina drew in a deep breath and walked into the room. Lexi was so beautiful with her perfectly styled dark hair, manicured fingernails and dark purple lace top over jeans. In an instant, Darlina felt as though she was looking at a little girl playing dress-up.

"Lexi, you remember Darlina, don't you?"

"Of course, Nanny. Hello, Darlina."

"Hi, Lexi." Darlina wished she could hug her. "What a nice surprise. Your daddy will be so happy to see you." She hurried forward. "Here, let me have Sage's cup. I'll rinse it and fill it with milk."

"Thanks." Lexi put the child on the sofa. "Can you watch her for a minute, Nanny? I need to use the bathroom."

"Come here, little girl," Nanny reached her arms out. The baby instantly started crying.

"She's not used to seeing anyone but me. I'll be right out." Lexi darted from the room and closed the bathroom door.

Darlina returned with the cup and reached for Sage. "Here, now. Don't cry. How about some milk?"

The baby hid her face and wailed.

"Let me try." Mom Stone sat in a rocking chair and Darlina placed the screaming child in her arms along with the cup.

By the time Lexi came back into the room, Sage was drinking her milk.

"Oh good, she stopped crying. Nanny, do you have any cigarettes? Joseph took mine."

"Look in the top dresser drawer in my room and get a pack. Why didn't he come in?"

"I dunno. Said he had to see a man about something."

"Oh lord. I hope he isn't in any trouble, or messin' with that ol' dope."

It amazed Darlina how this family could talk so openly about Joseph's drug use.

"He said he'd be back in a few hours." Lexi obviously avoided the remark about drugs and headed to the bedroom for cigarettes.

"Bring me a new pack while you're in there, Sis," Mom Stone said.

In less than a minute, Lexi was back with two packs of cigarettes. She opened one and laid the other beside the rocking chair.

Once she had a cigarette lit, she met Darlina's gaze directly. "How's Dad doing?"

"We're doing really good, Lexi." Darlina refused to differentiate Luke from her and the girls. "You remember my two girls, don't you?"

"Sure."

"They're going to be so excited to play with Sage. How long can you stay?"

"I'll be here 'til Joseph gets back. When will Dad be home?"

"He usually gets in around six or so. He's trying to make Christmas money. He and Gary are painting the courthouse."

"So Gary works with him?" She sounded surprised.

"Yes. When they aren't painting signs, they find something to do."

Mom Stone interrupted. "Sis, do you want something to eat?"

"No, I'm not hungry. Do you have any Dr. Pepper?"

"Lord no. I've got a pitcher of sweet tea, though."

"Since Sage is okay for now, I'm gonna to walk down to Buddy's and get a Dr. Pepper. It will only take a few minutes."

"Sage is fine. Why don't you take my car?"

"It's only a block away, Nanny. I need to walk." Lexi pulled on a denim jacket and left, closing the door behind her.

Darlina returned to the kitchen full of thoughts. Luke would be excited to see his daughter. She wished Lexi wouldn't be so angry at her.

But, that was something only time could remedy. She'd treat her with nothing but kindness. She could see the scared little girl underneath the careful layer of makeup. Her life hadn't been easy with losing her father when she was nine years old, molested by her mother's brother, then married at the age of fifteen, and a baby by the time she was sixteen. Darlina's heart went out to her.

Darlina glanced at the clock. School would be over soon. She wiped her hands on a dish towel and walked back to the living room. "Mom, I've gotta go get the girls. Is there anything you need while I'm gone?"

"No, I can't think of a thing. I have some fish in the freezer. Would you mind taking it out? We can fix it for supper."

"Of course." Darlina quickly located the package of frozen fish and put it in the sink to thaw, then grabbed her keys. "I'll be back in a few minutes."

When Darlina told Lily and Nicole that their step-sister was visiting with her baby, they jumped up and down.

"Hurry home, Mama. I want to play with a baby." Nicole urged.

"Settle down. We'll be there in a minute."

When they rushed in the front door, Sage was sitting in the living room floor playing with bowls and spoons that Mom Stone had gotten out of the cabinet for her.

Lexi sat on the couch sipping on a large Dr. Pepper, but when the girls came in, she stood. "Hello, Lily and Nicole. Remember me?"

Nicole immediately hugged Lexi's leg. "You're my sister.

"That's right, and Sage is your niece." Lexi bent down to hug Nicole.

Lily put her school books on the coffee table and sat on the floor with Sage. "Can I play with you, Sage?"

"How about a hug, Lily?" Lexi prodded.

Lily walked shyly to Lexi. "Thank you for the hug. I always wanted to have a sister and now I have two. We're gonna have a bunch of fun."

Lily nodded and sat back on the floor with Sage and Nicole joined them.

Darlina gave Lexi a warm smile. "Thank you."

"For what?"

"Being sweet to my girls." Darlina went back to the kitchen to finish her chores.

She could hear Lexi talking with Lily and Nicole and Sage while they played. She thought about how wonderful it would have been to have had a role in Lexi's life as she grew up. She sighed. Some things just aren't meant to be. But, maybe in time, Lexi could learn to accept or even like her.

Anything she could do to bring Luke's children back into his life would be worthwhile.

So, she would welcome them with open arms and an open heart and hope Luke could regain a small part of what he'd lost. Not only had he lost his children over the long years he was gone, but he'd lost his home, his livelihood, his dignity and confidence.

Darlina knew that even though it was a slow journey, he'd regained some of his dignity and confidence. And, he worked tirelessly on building a home and livelihood.

The determination he had, inspired hope in her. Hope for better days ahead, hope for a lifetime of love and hope for healing.

Chapter 11

Once Darlina finished cleaning the kitchen, she went back into the living room. "Girls, let's go home and get changed out of your school clothes. Mom, I can fix some potatoes and green beans to go with the fish and we have pie for dessert. Do you think that's enough?"

Mom Stone put out her cigarette. "That sounds fine to me, honey. We can all eat over here tonight. Maybe Joseph will be back in time for supper."

"Luke would like that. Okay, we'll see you in an hour or so. Lexi, do you and Sage want to go over to the trailer with us?"

"I guess we could do that. Lily, you and Nicole wanna show Sage your toys?" Lexi got to her feet and picked Sage up.

"Yes." Nicole pulled on her coat and took Lexi's hand. "I wanna show you my room, Lexi."

Darlina couldn't help but feel a warmth toward Lexi for the attention she showed Lily and Nicole. Maybe she really did want to be a sister to them. It was obvious that the girls thought she was something special.

With her dark hair, flashing brown eyes and flawless skin, Lexi could've been a cover model. Only the Love-Hate tattoos on her hands marred the image. Darlina knew Luke had worshipped the ground she'd walked on when she was a little girl and Lexi had returned the adoration. Now, if only they could get it back after such hard times for both, and many years apart.

Once they got inside the trailer, Darlina saw Lexi's eyes light up. "Oh it smells so good in here. I love cedar."

"It was your dad's idea. We went out and cut branches, then he wove the lights through them. He said he'd missed out on too many Christmases."

A faraway look crossed Lexi's face. "Yeah, he wasn't the only one."

"Lexi, come in here." Nicole stuck her head around the corner. "Look at my room."

"I'm coming, Nicole." She walked toward the child.

Darlina busied herself peeling potatoes while Lexi and Sage went into the girls' bedrooms.

After a while, Lexi came back into the living room. Darlina watched from the corner of her eye as the young girl stared at the pictures on the walls and the beautiful ceramics sitting on the shelves. She reverently touched the Indian peace pipe her father had made and picked up a picture of Luke, Darlina, Lily and Nicole from the wedding.

When she looked up, tears filled her eyes. "I've missed my daddy so much." Her voice broke.

Darlina put down her knife and went to Lexi. She put her arm around her shoulders and Darlina felt her stiffen, then relax against her. "Sweetie, your daddy misses you too. He worries and wants things to be good for you, but he won't interfere. He knows how rough you guys had it. Guilt eats at him every day. He'd love nothing more than a chance to make it right."

Lexi turned to Darlina. "I can't help wishing that he would have come home to Mom. Were you the one that broke up their marriage?"

"No," Darlina said softly. Your daddy hadn't lived with your mom for several years before I came along. I understand you wanting your parents to be together, but you wouldn't want them to be miserable."

Lexi sniffed. "No, I guess not. I really want to hate you, but you're making it hard."

Darlina squeezed her. "Good. Can you check on our girls while I finish cooking? Then we'll head back over to Nanny's. Your daddy will be home soon."

***

Luke knew it was Lexi standing on the front porch of his mom's house before Gary pulled into the driveway to drop him off. She looked like a forlorn little girl and his heart broke all over again for everything she'd been through. The minute he opened the door to the pickup, she ran toward him. Gary turned the motor off and also got out.

"Well, this is a surprise, sweetheart. I didn't know you were coming." Luke wrapped his arms around his dark-haired daughter.

"I didn't either until this morning. I caught a ride with Joseph."

"Hi, Sissy." Gary strode toward her with his long legs covering the space in seconds. "Haven't seen you since the wedding. Where's your worthless brother?"

"Hell if I know, Gary. He dropped me off here and said he'd be back in a few hours."

Luke put his arm around Lexi's shoulders. "Let's go inside, sugar. I'm hungry as a bear."

"Everyone's eating here tonight. Darlina helped Nanny fry catfish. Wanna come in and eat with us, Gary?"

"I'll come in for a minute, but I've got to get on to the house."

Inside the house, everyone seemed to talk at once. All Luke wanted was a chance to visit with his daughter quietly.

Something was wrong. She didn't have to tell him. He simply knew.

But, he waited patiently and enjoyed watching Darlina move with ease among his family. He hoped that Lexi would let her be a friend.

When his mom dished up the last piece of pie and dinner came to an end, Luke lit his pipe and took his daughter's hand. "Come outside with me, Sis."

"Okay. Let me grab my cigarettes and a jacket."

Once they were out on the front porch, Luke took a deep breath of the cool December air. "What's wrong, honey? You don't have to pretend with me. I'm your ol' daddy, remember?"

"I've missed you so much, Daddy. I want to go back to being a little girl again without all the bullshit adults have to deal with."

Luke chuckled. "Well, sweetheart, that's pretty much impossible once you get all grown up. You've got a daughter to think about and what about your son? Have you seen him since you got to town?"

"No. I thought Joseph would be back by now and I was gonna ask him to take me by to see him. He's living at his grandparents' house now."

"Where's David? Why didn't he come with you?"

She avoided looking at Luke but he saw the tremble of her chin. "I'm pretty miserable with David and I don't think I can stay with him much longer. But, me and Sage have nowhere to go and I don't have a job."

"Did he hit you again?"

"Only once," her voice trailed off.

"Dammit!" Luke clenched his fists. "I oughta go kill the sonofabitch, then that'd solve the problem."

"That would only get you sent back to prison, Daddy. Don't worry. I've got my own ways of gettin' even. His toothbrush makes a great scrubber for the toilet."

Lexi's attempt at humor didn't remove the scowl from Luke's face. "If he ever lays another hand on you, I swear I'll kill him. It's a poor excuse of a man that'll hit a woman."

"I know, Daddy, but I promise I can take care of myself."

"How are Nathan and Martin?"

"They're good. Martin has a new girlfriend that I think he's gettin' serious about. Wouldn't surprise me if they don't get married. She's older than him and has a couple of kids."

"I wish we all lived closer. Four hours is too far away for just running over anytime."

"Especially when you're as poor as I am." Lexi lit a new cigarette.

"The main thing with me, Sissy, is that I don't ever want to interfere in any of you kids' lives and I sure don't want a confrontation with your mother."

They both looked up at the sound of a pickup pulling into the driveway.

Joseph left the headlights on and motor running and rolled down the window. "Come on, Lexi. It's time to go back to Midland."

"But, I'm not done visiting, Joe."

"I don't give a shit. If you want a ride back home, you better get Sage and come on."

Luke walked to the pickup. "Why don't you get out and stay a little while, son? Nanny's been worried sick about you."

Joseph growled, "I'm all right. Just need to get back to Midland."

"You're high, aren't you?"

"So what if I am?"

"Then you don't need to drive and especially with your sister and the baby in the truck."

"Who in the hell do you think you are to tell me what I should or shouldn't do?"

Luke jerked the pickup door open. "I'm your father, that's who. So, I suggest you turn the motor off and get the fuck out of this truck before I drag you out."

"Shit!" Joseph killed the motor and headlights. "I'll get out, but I'm going back to Midland tonight with or without Lexi and Sage."

"Son, you need to get the chip off of your shoulder and get over the poor-me-I've-had-a-horrible-life syndrome. Don't you think it's time to man up and take control of your life?"

"Sure thing, Dad. I'll get right on that tomorrow." He slid out of the pickup and stalked toward the house. Luke followed while Lexi stood on the porch and waited.

"Just give me a few minutes, Joe, and I'll get our things together. Will you take me to see Douglas before we leave town?"

"I guess so, but I've gotta be back in Midland tonight."

"Okay. I won't stay long. I just need to see him before I leave."

Luke watched his two children with an aching heart, guilt-ridden at the things they'd had to endure in life because of his selfishness and ignorance. He knew how difficult it must be for Lexi to be apart from her son, but that was not his business. When she'd divorced Douglas's father, he'd won custody of him and she only had visitation rights. Then there was Joseph. What would it take to motivate him to get off the junk and straighten up? Luke didn't know the answer as he followed them into his mother's house.

His eyes met Darlina's the minute he came through the door. He winked at her and forced a smile.

"Joseph, where have you been?" Nanny hugged him.

"I had to go see a man, Nanny. Got any coffee?"

"Of course."

"I'll make it, Mom." Darlina offered. "Hello, Joseph. How do you like your coffee?"

Joseph grinned a crooked smile much like his father's. "Hot."

Darlina laughed. "Okay, I can manage that."

Luke followed her into the kitchen and before she could get the coffee out of the cabinet, grabbed her and pulled her hard against him. "I adore you, sweetheart. Don't you ever forget that."

"I could no more forget our love than I could forget to breathe. What brought this on?"

"Thank you for being good to my kids."

"How else would I be? They're a part of you. Go visit with them before they have to leave. We'll talk later."

He embraced her, nibbled her ear and whispered, "We'll do more than talk later and that's a promise."

He loved the way her eyes lit up and the smile that said much more than words.

"Go on," she prodded as she turned to fill the coffee maker.

Back in the living room, Luke caught the tail end of what Joseph and his grandmother were reminiscing about.

"Nanny, I never saw anyone that could drag a ten pound yellow catfish up on the bank in nothing flat like you could."

She chuckled. "I come from a long line of fishermen. I sure do miss going fishing since I messed up my arm."

"Well, if you would've let us take you to the doctor and get it set right, you could still use it. You're damned hard-headed."

Luke flinched inwardly. Just another on the long list of regrets that he wasn't there to help his mother when she fell and broke her arm.

"I come from a long line of hard-headed people too." Nanny broke out into a belly laugh.

He loved the way she pulled Joseph out of his funk and had him smiling and interacting. He could clearly see the strong bond between grandmother and grandson.

"Nanny, remember the time Mom's girlfriend came looking for me because I had cut up her dildo?" Joseph asked.

"My lord, Joe, I didn't have any idea what that woman was all fired up about but she wasn't getting to you without going through me and my four-ten shotgun first."

Luke joined the conversation. "Mom, when you wrote to me in prison and told me about Joseph cutting up Big E's ditto, I knew you didn't have any idea what it was. I laughed until I cried."

Joseph grinned. "Well, she shouldn't have left the nasty thing layin' around."

"Coffee's ready." Darlina held a steaming cup in her hand. "Here, Joseph."

"Thanks. We really do have to go. Lexi, get our shit ready and after I drink this coffee, I'll take you by to see Douglas for a few minutes."

"I'll be ready when you are." Lexi took Luke's hand. "Dad, when are you and Darlina going to come to Midland to see us?"

"Sugar, I don't know. Seems like we never have a spare dime for anything. But you kids are welcome here anytime."

Within thirty minutes, the two said their goodbyes and drove away.

Luke put his arm around Darlina's shoulders. "You girls ready to go home?"

"We're ready. Thanks so much for letting us all have dinner here tonight, Mom."

"Oh honey, I loved having a house full of people again and it was good to see Joe and Lexi. Darlina, thanks for helping cook and for all the cleaning up you did."

"You're welcome. Goodnight, Mom. Come on girls. Let's go." Darlina reached for her daughters' hands.

The two tired girls walked alongside Luke and Darlina toward home, their breath fogging in the frosty night air.

Luke tightened his grip on Lily's hand and around Darlina's waist. Would it be too much to hope that his grown children might want to be some part of his and Darlina's lives? Time would tell.

He'd already made great strides with Lexi and perhaps Joseph was gaining a bit of respect for him. He longed to see the other two boys and hoped Lexi would relay that message.

While in prison, he'd learned patience, so he'd keep the door open and let his children come to him in their own time.

For now, he felt content to know he'd not make the same selfish and stupid mistakes that had cost them all so much. He would do his best to make amends.

Never would he be such a fool again.

Luke, Lexi and Joseph

Chapter 12

Luke and Darlina greeted the new year of 1987 wrapped in each other's arms, laughing at the girls who'd valiantly tried to stay awake until midnight, but fell asleep on the floor in front of the TV.

"Honey, every year I spend with you and the girls gets sweeter." Luke put a finger under Darlina's chin and tilted her face upward. "So many new years in prison came and went with nothing to celebrate, no hope for anything to change and not much to look forward to."

Tears formed behind Darlina's eyelids. "I can't even imagine how horrible it was for you, so I don't try. I only know that we're together now and that's all that matters and we have lots of years to look forward to."

Words choked in Luke's throat. "Yes we do. Let's cover the girls up and let 'em sleep in here tonight. Happy New year, darlin'. It's gonna be a good'un."

Once spring arrived, warmer weather inspired Luke to build a rock patio in the backyard.

Two weeks ago, when he'd painted a man's house in trade for an old pickup, he felt exhilarated to now have wheels of his own. Another step toward independence.

Many weekends found him driving country roads with Darlina and the children, looking for just the right rocks to create the patio.

He thrived in the outdoors and loved creating with his hands. In fact, he loved everything about freedom. The food he indulged in soon expanded his waistline and his blue jeans no longer buttoned. On a shopping trip to Wal-Mart, he bought two pair of blue bib overalls.

He'd never been so far from the music world he'd once thrived in as he was now, but he'd never been more content with who he was and what he was doing.

Luke Stone had purpose, real purpose that drove him daily.

His next to the youngest son, Martin, came to visit in March. He seemed hungry for anything his father had to say and they sat talking for hours on end.

The next time he came to visit, he brought Lexi, her husband David, Sage and his fiancé, Stormi.

With an anxious grin that indicated Martin wasn't fully comfortable around his dad yet, he made introductions. "Dad, this is Stormi, the woman I'm gonna marry." The need for his father to accept her showed in the way he protectively put his arm around her waist as if to ward off any disapproval.

Luke's uncanny sense of "knowing" kicked in and he immediately liked Stormi. He could tell she was a strong woman and just what Martin needed.

After a while, everyone except Martin, Stormi and Luke went next door.

When Martin carried in their luggage, he handed his father a brown paper bag.

"Hey, Dad, I brought you something," he announced as he came through the door.

"Son, you didn't have to bring me anything." Luke pulled out a bottle of Jim Beam from the bag. "My God, I haven't had a drink of whiskey since 1970. I'm not sure I need it."

"Oh, come on, Dad. I brought a six pack of coke too. Want one, Stormi?"

"Sure. Want me to fix them?" Stormi offered, smiling.

"No, I've got it. Sure you don't want one, Dad?"

"Oh hell, mix me one. One drink couldn't hurt anything."

"I know there is no way you could have influenced me since you were gone when I was growing up, but Jim Beam has always been my choice of whiskey. For a long time, I didn't know it was your favorite. I guess I'm a lot like you in some ways."

Luke chuckled. "I don't know if that's necessarily a good thing."

"When Mom would get mad at me, she'd always tell me I was just like my father. It was the worst thing she could think of to say."

"Well, your mom had lots of reasons to hate me."

Martin went into the kitchen and returned with three full glasses. He handed one to Stormi, then his father. "Here's to you, Dad."

Luke took a swig of the cold liquid and felt the whiskey burn down his throat. "Damn that's good. Tastes just like I remember." Luke looked up as Darlina came through the door. "Hey, sugar, look who's here."

Darlina stopped beside his chair, kissed Luke and then turned to her step-son. "Hi, Martin. It's so good to see you again."

He hoped she wouldn't think he was going back to his hard-drinking ways of the past. He never wanted to disappoint her again.

"Darlina, this is Stormi, my fiancé," Martin gave Darlina a brief hug.

"So very nice to meet you, Stormi. Welcome to our humble abode." She turned back to Luke with a wide grin. "You finally broke down and had a drink?"

"Now don't you go worryin' that I'm gonna start drinkin' and raisin' hell and chasin' women again. I'm just havin' a drink with my son."

"I'm not the least bit worried. I'm happy to see you relaxing." She laid her hand on his arm.

He breathed a sigh of relief that Darlina didn't judge him and couldn't care less that he was having a drink. One more reason he adored this woman.

"The girls saw Lexi standing on Nanny's front porch and headed straight over there when we stopped the car. I'm gonna change clothes and start some supper."

"Can I do anything to help?" Stormi asked.

"You can talk to me while I cook. I always love having company."

Luke stood. "Son, come with me outside. I want to show you my latest home improvement."

"I was wondering what you intend to do with that stack of telephone poles out there."

"The co-op was replacing a bunch of their poles out in the country and giving away the old ones, so I had 'em drop a load off over here. I'm gonna build a fence across the back."

"Shit, Dad, that oughta be like building a fort."

"That's what I have in mind. I wanna close off our corner of the world." He opened the door.

With drinks in hand, Martin followed his dad outside. Luke took great pride in showing off the half-finished patio. The fact that Martin wanted to be in their lives made Luke more than happy.

Luke's wish to have his children back seemed to be coming true, at least with Martin and Lexi. He wanted to make up for his failures.

As they walked around the yard talking and finishing their drinks, Luke shared his vision for the property. Martin interjected some of his own ideas. This was the relationship Luke craved with his adult children.

It wasn't long before Lexi, David and the children joined them and they all went inside.

The smallness of the trailer struck him as Luke gathered extra chairs from the kitchen, with Martin's help. One day when he could, he would expand the rooms and make everything bigger. He wanted a place that all of his family could comfortably fit.

He asked Lily and Nicole to take Sage into their room to play until the food was ready. He grinned at Darlina when she shot him a grateful glance.

Over dinner, Martin made an announcement. "Me and Stormi are gonna get hitched the first of August." He reached for Stormi's hand. "I'd really like for you guys to be at the wedding."

"It would mean a lot to us if you'd come," Stormi added.

Luke glanced at Darlina. "We'd love to son, but I don't know how your mom would feel about that?"

"It's not her wedding, Dad. It's mine and I want you there."

"Then we'll damn sure make it. I'm proud of you. I can tell that Stormi is good for you and like I've tried to tell Joseph, a good woman beside you can make all the difference in the world."

Lexi spoke up. "Dad, don't worry about mom. She won't cause a scene."

"That's good to know, sweetheart, because I don't do scenes anymore."

With conversation and laughter, they finished the meal. By the time the women had cleaned up the dishes and gotten everyone situated for the night, Luke could see the exhaustion on Darlina's face, though she tried to pretend otherwise. He took her hand, turned out the lights and led her to the bedroom.

As they lay in the darkness with her head on his shoulder, Luke talked about how happy he was to have Martin and Lexi there. He was still going on when he heard her soft snores. He turned on his side and molded her soft warm body into his and draped his arm across her stomach.

It meant the world to him that she so easily accepted his children and whoever came with them. He kissed her neck and breathed softly into her hair.

The next day, Martin wanted to take Stormi to see downtown Coleman on a bustling Saturday and especially the drug store that still had an old-fashioned soda fountain. Of course, the girls wanted to tag along and Darlina said they could go.

She looked forward to everyone being out of the house for a few hours so she could clean up. Darlina half-listened to the lecture Lexi gave David and found herself wondering at the conversation.

"David, you damn well better not steal anything while we're in town. This is a small place. Everyone knows everybody and everything. Don't you dare embarrass my dad."

"I don't know what you're talking about, Lexi. Let's just go." David pulled her out the door.

Darlina looked at Luke and he shrugged his shoulders. "Hell if I know, honey."

Once they'd gone, Luke headed out back to work on the patio and Darlina faced the task of cleaning up.

She hummed to herself while she swept and mopped the kitchen floor, then folded bedding and put toys away in Nicole's room. After putting on a large roast to bake, she took time to check on Luke's progress and carry out a fresh glass of tea for him.

"The house is back together, baby, and I have a roast in the oven."

"I know it's a lot of work for you, sweetheart, but having the kids here means so much. What do you think about this big rock I put in the middle of the patio?" He stood on a rock that had imprints of leaves and of a snail embedded in it.

"It's cool. It reminds me of dinosaur fossils."

Luke chuckled. "I reckon it does."

They both looked up at the sound of car doors and walked together toward the house.

Lexi stomped up the steps to the porch and jerked the door open.

"What the hell is wrong, Lexi?" Luke and Darlina walked in behind her.

"I told David not to steal anything but he didn't listen and he stole a candy bar from Owl Drug."

Darlina saw Luke's jaw tighten as he faced David with narrowed eyes. She felt her gut tighten. This wasn't going to be pretty. While never with her, she'd seen his fierce wrath with others.

"Don't you ever come where I'm living and do anything like that again, or I'll bust your head open. I'm working hard to earn the respect of this community and you come and do something stupid like that. On second thought, just don't come back here."

He put his arm around Lexi's shoulders. "You and the baby are welcome here anytime, but leave this sonofabitch at home next time."

"Don't worry, Daddy. I will." She glared at David.

Darlina broke the tension. "Girls, did you behave yourselves downtown?"

"They were great," Stormi offered. "We bought them an ice cream cone." She picked up a bag off the chair. "I bought a new purse at Owl Drug. I just love that place."

"Oh it's beautiful." Darlina admired the colorful purse with intricate detail.

Martin came from the kitchen with a fresh drink while David disappeared out the front door.

"I'm truly sorry, Daddy. He's a damn kleptomaniac."

"I don't care what he is, honey, I just don't need his bullshit around me."

"I won't ever bring him back."

"I'm not mad at you honey. You know that, don't you?"

"I know. I should have left him at home to start with." Anger flashed in her dark eyes. "I love you, Daddy."

"I love you, little girl." Luke embraced her.

Lexi then gathered Sage and headed back over to Mom Stone's.

"Tell Nanny I'll be over in a little bit and introduce Stormi to her." Martin held the door open.

By the time the weekend came to an end, Darlina knew that Luke felt closer to Martin and Lexi in a way he'd not known in a very long time. Great strides had been made toward mending broken fences.

She'd seen how much it meant to him for Martin to want them at his wedding. She also knew he dreaded seeing Joyce, but it was bound to eventually happen. She'd be beside him and it would all be okay.

They stood in the driveway waving to the children when they left and when she gazed up into Luke's shining blue eyes, she saw his contentment and love. Maybe he could finally feel that he'd truly come home at last.

***

Three days later, Darlina came in from work to find Luke sitting at the kitchen table with the girls, helping them draw. He looked up when she came through the door and stood.

"Girls, you keep doing what I showed you and I'll be back in a minute to see it." He walked toward Darlina. "Hello, beautiful. I've got something to show you."

"Hello, girls." She leaned down and kissed each of them on the cheek. "Oh wow, I love what you are both doing. I want to see your pictures when you're finished." She linked her arm through Luke's.

When they reached the bedroom door, Luke stopped. "Close your eyes. I have a surprise for you."

Darlina obeyed and did not open them until Luke gave the okay.

She started laughing. "What in the world, Luke?"

"Sugar, I don't ever want us to settle into being an old married couple. Everything about you excites me and I want us to always keep our love fresh and new. So, I rigged this up for us."

"But, a mirror over the bed, Luke? The girls will ask questions."

"No, they won't, because I fixed it where it easily goes up and comes back down. Luke reached up and slipped the small chains off of hooks in the ceiling and then slipped it into the newly installed brackets on the back of the door. "There, completely disguised. You needed a full length mirror anyway, sweetheart, so it serves a dual purpose."

"Put it back up there, honey." Darlina slipped her blouse over her head.

"Nope." Luke pulled her close to him. "I just wanted you to see it and think it about it all evening until we can try it out, but not right now." He kissed her moist lips. "Right now, we've got artwork to praise, but you can bet I can't wait to get you back in here a little later."

"Oh, I'll be thinking about it alright. You never cease to amaze me, Luke Stone."

"Good. That's just the way I like it."

Luke kissed her again, then re-joined the girls back at the table while Darlina slipped out of her work clothes and changed into comfortable jeans and t-shirt.

Soon she was humming to herself in the kitchen while she prepared the evening meal.

Every time she looked at Luke, he grinned and winked. She didn't have to ask what he was thinking. The lust in his eyes was obvious and she couldn't deny the smoldering fire burning deep inside her.

Becoming an old settled married couple just didn't fit with Luke and Darlina Stone. Passion and excitement carried them on a wave from one day to the next.

Darlina and Luke

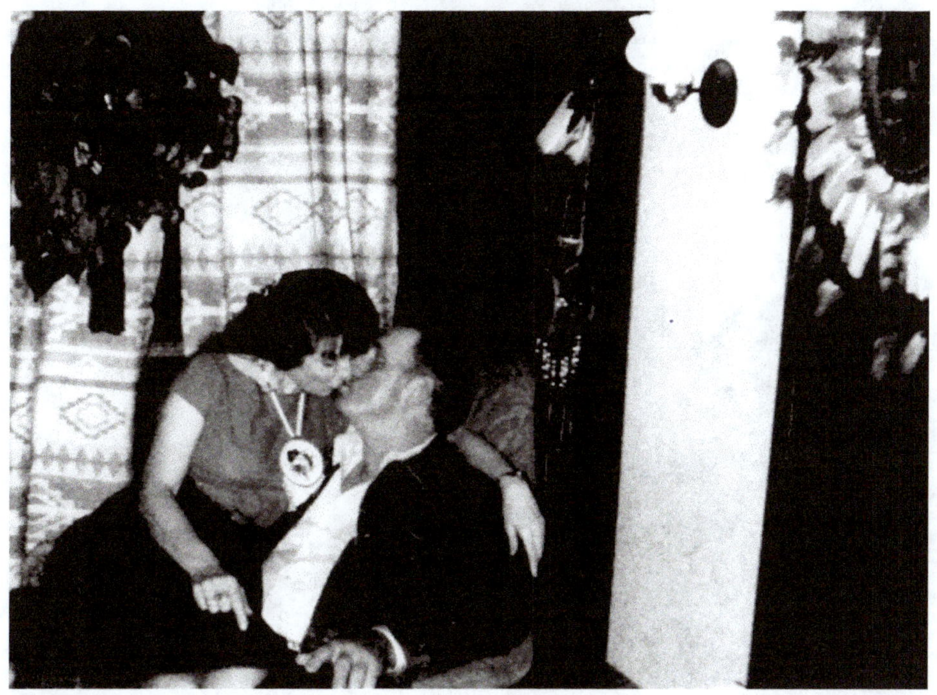

Luke's Daughter, Lexi, and her son, Douglas

Luke and his son, Martin

Chapter 13

Luke Stone wasn't the kind of man given to easily show his emotions. He'd let Darlina see more of his true and deep feelings than anyone. He had a lifetime invested in honing his rough exterior.

But, as he gathered with all of his children for Martin and Stormi's wedding, he constantly fought the lump in his throat and blinked away any sign of weakness. Seventeen years had put a lot of distance between them, and he recognized it was nothing he could remedy in one visit.

Nathan showed indifference toward Luke, yet when they talked, openly admitted that he had no real memory of him. Being the baby, he'd been very young when his father had gone to prison.

Joyce kept her distance and when she finally spoke to Luke, her words were forced and cold. Darlina's warm hand nestled in his own melted the icy gesture. When Luke introduced the two, Joyce kept up her frigid exterior. Darlina returned the greeting warmly just as Luke knew she would. Over and over, he questioned himself as to how and why he deserved this woman who only seemed to know love and giving.

By the time they returned home, Luke felt he'd made even greater strides in establishing relationships with his grown children.

***

The next month, Gary moved down south with Bobby and Cindy. Luke truly hated to see him leave as he was losing not only a business partner, but Gary had become much like a son.

With a small sign shop on a main street to work from, Luke hired a helper. He was determined to make this business a success.

The annual Fiesta de la Paloma was just around the corner. Luke considered entering more artwork, but decided he'd already shown his best pieces. They would take the girls and enjoy the day.

Luke openly shot admiring glances at Darlina as she walked beside him at the Fiesta, dressed in a skirt and blouse and wearing a beautiful Indian beaded necklace and earring set he'd made for her. He kept his arm tightly around her waist, bringing her so close he could feel their thighs brush as they walked.

She paused in front of a picture booth on the midway. "Luke, let's get our picture taken. You look so handsome in your confederate soldier uniform and I could be your Indian princess."

Luke chuckled. "You are that already, but we can take a picture."

They darted inside the booth and emerged with a strip of poorly made pictures that made them both laugh.

A voice interrupted their laughter. "Luke Stone?"

Luke turned. "Well, what a surprise. Hello, cousin." He walked toward a dark-haired woman and embraced her, then turned to include Darlina. "Baby, this is my cousin, Georgia. Georgia, this is my wife, Darlina."

The woman smiled. "Oh my God, you must be a glutton for punishment marrying this one."

Darlina smiled back. "I suppose I am. It's nice to meet you."

Georgia then turned to the man beside her. "This is my friend, Eli."

Luke shook hands with the man and introduced Darlina.

"What are you up to? I had heard you were out of prison," Georgia continued.

"I've been trying to scratch out some kind of a living in this poverty-ridden town. We're living next door to Mom and I'm painting signs. We brought our girls out today to let them have a little fun on the rides. How have you been? Haven't seen you in a hundred years."

"Sure seems like it. I guess the last time I saw you was before Tom and I went overseas. We came out to a club in Midland where you were playing. I'm sure you heard that he died."

"Mom told me and I'm truly sorry. Yes, I remember y'all coming out that night."

"Do you still play music?" Eli questioned.

"Nah. Haven't touched my guitar since I got home. It's stashed in the closet. I have other things to do."

The four found a vacant table and the conversation continued for well over an hour as the two cousins caught up and Luke and Eli got acquainted.

By the time they parted ways, the beginning of a friendship had formed between the two men.

Gathering up two tired girls, they headed for home at the end of the day.

"What a coincidence running into Georgia today and I really liked Eli."

"It was nice, Luke." Darlina slid across the car seat as his arm automatically draped over her shoulders. "I'm glad the girls had a fun day."

"It was fun for me too. We need a break from work every once in a while." Luke glanced in the rearview mirror at the children. They were growing up fast.

"Seems like that is all we do and the girls work hard too."

Luke stiffened. "Shit! They don't have to work nearly as hard as I did when I was their age."

"I'm not complaining, Luke, just stating a fact. Today was good."

"Maybe things won't always be such a struggle. I want you and the girls to have everything good in life, but the truth is that it takes all of us to pull it together." Luke's voice trailed off.

***

In January 1988, Eli came to visit Luke with a proposal.

"I want to open a recording studio and publishing company here in Coleman and I want you to be my partner." Eli took a swig of Crown Royal over ice. Dressed in his usual wrangler jeans, cowboy style shirt, black leather vest, boots and hat, he resembled Waylon Jennings.

"Shit, man, I don't have any money to invest in a recording studio."

"We've got all the cash we need. What we don't have is someone with the knowledge and experience to make it happen, Bubba. I've sat and listened to your stories for months now and also what Georgia has told me and I know you're the right man for the job."

"I don't know, hoss. What in the hell do you need with an old ex-con? Besides that, I haven't picked up my guitar since I've been home."

"I ain't asking you to play your guitar, although I'd damn sure like that. I'm just asking you to come on board as a partner and advisor. I believe it could work."

"A publishing company can succeed anywhere and the way things have changed these days, it's possible to make a hit record anywhere. Hell, I recorded a shitload of songs inside Leavenworth. Not that it means jack other than just making my point."

"All I'm asking is that you think about it. Georgia and I both want you."

Luke lit his pipe and leaned back. "I'll talk it over with Darlina."

"That's all I'm asking, Bubba." Eli stood. "I believe I'll have another drink. Don't you want me to open that bottle of Beam I brought?"

"No, I've gotta get back to work. Come on out to the sign shop and we can talk some more while I paint." Luke reached for his hat and headed to the door.

Eli followed with the blue velvet bag holding his Crown bottle and a full glass.

***

Luke could easily see Darlina's excitement at the prospect of him returning to the music business. When he told her of Eli's proposal, she immediately encouraged him to do it.

"It could mean some late nights working. Would you be okay with that?"

Darlina snuggled against him. "Honey, as long as you always come home to me, I don't care. I'll be here waiting."

Luke rested his cheek on the top of her head. "You know I love the music. I just don't ever want to go back to the lifestyle that goes along with it."

"I know. The girls will be excited about this too. Lily has such a beautiful voice. She could make a great singer."

"Not as long as I have a say. The business is hard as hell for a man, but a woman is shark bait and I won't ever allow Lily to be in that environment."

"I suppose that's true. I'm glad you're going to be doing something with music again." She leaned back and stared up at him. "You know we'll have to get you some new clothes. I don't think your blue overalls will be appropriate for working in the studio."

"I'll check out Goodwill next time we're in Brownwood. I'm not opposed to wearing used clothes. Are you sure this is all right with you?"

"Yes, I'm sure, Luke. I want you to do to it."

The next day, Luke and Eli walked through the large metal building that would serve as the offices and studio for EDP Publishing. With a pad and pen, the men made note of walls that had to come down, where the new ones would go and what area of the building would house the actual recording area.

As they drew plans and talked of the vision, Luke felt an old surge of excitement begin to rise. No matter how much he resolved to stay away from it, he did love music and everything about it.

Every extra hour he could spare, he helped with remodeling the building that had originally been home to an electrical contracting company. He often took Lily with him because she begged to go and loved helping. She'd turned twelve this year and on the rare occasion she was allowed to wear makeup, Luke would swear she was fifteen going on sixteen.

He made baffles for the vocal booth and painted them in brightly colored Indian designs and patterns, soundproofed the drum booth and lay carpeting on the floor to absorb the sound.

It was a far cry from the studio he'd built inside Leavenworth prison with nothing but broken pieces of electronic equipment, egg crates from the kitchen to glue on the walls as a sound buffer, discarded carpeting and drapes from other areas of the prison, but most of all lots of determination and will.

EDP Recording and Publishing would be a state-of-the art studio.

There were many late nights and the more he worked with Eli, the closer the two of them became until they were more like brothers.

He didn't play his guitar or sing, but he took on every aspect of the business from publishing contracts to recording.

The sacrifice of not being home every night to tuck the girls in, then take his big girl to bed, was huge but he knew Darlina supported him.

With the work complete and everything in place, they slated a grand opening for April 23, 1988.

Luke excitedly made a phone call to his old hobo friend and brother, Steam Train Maury Graham, and asked him to come for the grand opening.

Once Steam Train agreed, Luke contacted the local media in Brownwood, San Angelo and Abilene and set up interviews for him.

Steam Train and his wife Miss Wanda arrived in a box-like motor home two days before the festivities.

Luke practically ran toward it, with Darlina, Nicole and Lily not far behind.

When Steam Train opened the door, a small terrier dog shot out and began to sniff the ground. Nicole scooped him up and petted him. Her love for animals never changed. She was always drawn to them.

Steam Train made his way slowly down the steps and embraced Luke. He had flowing white hair he pulled back in a pony tail, long beard and a red bandana tied around his neck.

"My God, Steam, it's been a long time. The last time I saw you, I was still behind bars." Luke's voice cracked.

"Son, I can't tell you how happy I am to see you as a free man, and now you're doing something with the music. I always told you, Luke Stone, you're a music man and that is where your passion lies." Steam Train pulled a bandana from his back pocket and dabbed at his eyes.

"I don't know about that, Steam. My ol' guitar is in the closet and I'm trying my damnedest to build a home for Darlina and these girls." Luke turned and took Darlina's hand. "Steam, this is my angel on earth, Darlina."

Darlina moved forward, ignoring Steam Train's outstretched hand. Instead, she embraced him. "I am so happy to finally get to meet you. Welcome to Texas. These are our two girls." She motioned them forward.

"Well now, ain't these two of the purdiest little gals I've ever seen."

Lily shyly held back, but Nicole came forward still holding the little dog. "Are you Santa Claus?"

Steam Train let out a belly laugh. "As a matter of fact, I am. Every year from Thanksgiving to December, I listen to hundreds of children tell me what they want Santa to bring them for Christmas."

Steam Train then focused on Lily. "And you must be Lily."

She walked toward him. "Yes sir."

At that moment, a white haired lady appeared in the doorway of the motor home and made her way down the steps.

"Everybody, this is my much better half, Miss Wanda."

Miss Wanda hugged both of the girls, then Darlina and finally Luke. "We're so happy to be here and it's such a pleasure to get to meet all of you. I've heard so much about you, Luke, I feel as if I already know you.

The group made their way into the house.

"You're traveling in style these days, Steam." Luke settled into his easy chair and lit his pipe.

The old man chuckled. "These old bones have gotten slower and the trains faster so I had to give it up. Plus this way, I can bring Miz Wanda and her little pooch with me. I spent far too much time away from home and her. We're trying to get reacquainted."

"I suppose in some odd way, that's what Darlina and I are doing. We wrote hundreds of letters back and forth during the many years I was locked away, but you don't really know a person until you live with them. I don't know how she tolerates me, but she is truly a God-given blessing."

Steam laid his hand on his old friend's arm. "We get what we deserve in life."

The two women chatted away in the kitchen while the menfolk did the same and soon, Luke was gathering everyone to the table for a feast. He never ceased to marvel at how Darlina could make everyone feel welcome and feed so many on such little.

The reunion lasted well into the night with so much to catch up on.

***

On the day before the grand opening, under the watchful eye of Steam Train Maury, Georgia and Darlina peeled potatoes and carrots, sliced onions and chopped stew meat to make a large amount of hobo stew.

"If you start peeling a potato and find green under the skin, throw it away because it's no good," Steam Train instructed.

Luke and Eli took Steam Train to the TV stations for interviews, met with newspaper reporters and even visited the hobo jungle outside Abilene.

Early on the morning of the grand opening under Steam Train's supervision, Eli and Luke built a campfire with a tripod over it to hold the large pot of hobo stew. The festivities got under way promptly at 12 noon.

Luke had urged all three of his girls to wear a red bandana around their necks, a gift from Steam Train, and took their pictures with his old friend.

Local musicians and songwriters came from all around the area to check out the new facility. From their interest and enthusiasm, it appeared that this venture would be a success.

Throughout the day, Luke kept a watchful eye on Darlina as he drank a little, ate a little and visited a lot.

He couldn't have been more proud of his family as he watched all three of them serve food to guests, engage in conversation and smile warmly in response.

He realized at that moment, not only were they a family, but a team.

He remembered the many days, weeks and hours he'd spent sitting in his tiny prison cell while the world rushed by without him, wondering if he'd ever be a part of it again. And now his most fervent dreams and wishes had come true. His throat closed with overwhelming emotion and he took a swig of Jim Beam and Coke along with a deep breath.

Maybe this could work. Maybe this would be the avenue to get back into the music business without having to play in the honky-tonks.

More than anything, Luke Stone wanted a means to provide the things for his princesses that they deserved. They needed a break from all of the hard work and scraping by on pennies.

He walked toward Darlina with a huge grin on his face. It didn't matter who saw, he needed to kiss her, touch her and watch smoldering embers that always lay just beneath the surface flame to life. A phrase from a poem echoed in his mind, *"The rose speaks of love silently in a language known only to the heart."*

After all, she was his true rose, his everything.

Front Row - Lexi, Joseph, Nathan Back Row – Martin and Luke

Eli, Luke and "Steam Train" Maury Graham, King of the Hobos

Chapter 14

Darlina dared another glance at the clock on the nightstand beside her empty bed. How could they still be recording after two o'clock in the morning? What if there was another woman and Luke just didn't want to come home? Her stomach turned somersaults and she pushed that thought aside. Wasn't this what she'd wanted; for Luke to be back in the music business? So, she couldn't complain. He'd warned her there would be some late nights.

It's just that they'd become more and more frequent.

She rolled over onto her back and stared at the ceiling above her. Her gaze focused on the tiny hooks almost invisible in the ceiling and she sighed. It had been a long time since they'd even thought about hanging the mirror over the bed.

Not only was Luke still painting signs, but in addition to the evenings in the recording studio, he had been hired to run sound for a couple of local bands.

It had been fun and exciting at first. A break from the daily struggles. But, with summer almost gone and the girls going back to school soon, Darlina needed Luke's arms around her at night. She wanted to fall asleep to the sound of his breathing and the feel of his body curling around hers.

She missed the family dinners and watching him teach the girls art or helping them with projects. They saw each other in passing and more than once, he'd snapped at her or the children over nothing.

He was exhausted. That much she knew. He wanted more for them and banked his hopes on having a breakthrough song come through the doors of EDP studios.

All of that she understood, but it didn't lessen the loneliness of lying in their bed night after night alone until the wee hours of morning.

Just as she was about to doze off, she heard the front door open and Luke's familiar footsteps in the hallway.

She sat up in bed with only the sheet draped over her. "Oh, Luke. You finally made it home."

He plopped down on the edge of the bed with a deep sigh and pulled off his boots. "You should be asleep, baby."

Darlina pressed her warm breasts against his back and nibbled his ear. "I tried, but I couldn't. I miss you."

He pulled off his shirt and turned toward her, the smell of whiskey strong on his breath. He touched her face and she lay her cheek against the palm of his hand. "I told you there would be late nights."

"Yes, you did. Are you drunk?"

Luke slipped off his jeans, slid under the sheet and Darlina draped an arm across his chest. "Darlin', I ain't drunk, but I've had a few. Now do you wanna fight or make love?"

Darlina didn't hesitate. "Make love."

"That's what I thought. You should leave the worryin' to me." He switched off the lamp beside the bed.

Darlina pushed her thoughts aside and kissed Luke. She loved the way he easily pulled her on top of him and the way their bodies fit perfectly together.

Asking Luke to make love when he was so exhausted almost made her feel guilty, but deep inside she knew he needed it as badly as she did.

They moved in unison, Darlina never taking her eyes from Luke's face. She smiled when he groaned with pleasure and didn't relent until they reached the peak together.

Before she could get out a "Goodnight," Luke was fast asleep. She curled up beside him and their breath rose and fell in rhythm.

She looked at him lying peacefully on the pillow. Perhaps she needed to be more patient and stop thinking about her own selfish needs. Luke was trying in every way he knew to make things better. If he believed this venture was going to bring that to them, she'd find a way to be more understanding.

***

Luke hated leaving Darlina and the girls alone so much. He kept telling himself that it was only temporary and once the new company started making money, he wouldn't have to put in so many hours.

Even though he didn't like to admit it, many of the late nights were nothing more than parties with some of the locals joining them from time to time, looking for entertainment.

He sat perched on a stool at the well-stocked bar in the studio on a hot August night. For the first time in months, it was only Luke and Eli.

"What are we doing here, Eli? We've recorded and published a few songs, but nothing that's brought in any money."

"I know, Bubba, but any day the right one will walk in the door. We've still got plenty of money to keep afloat." Eli opened a new bottle of Crown. "You're not losing faith, are you?"

"No, just damned tired of the struggle and always being away from Darlina and the girls."

"Go home. There's nothing going on here."

"It's not just tonight. It's way too many nights. For you, it's different. You don't have a young family waiting at home."

"You're a damned lucky man, Luke Stone. I've never seen anyone love a man more than Darlina loves you."

"I know. That's what's eatin' at me. I want to give her everything but all I'm doin' is makin' things harder."

"You want out?" Eli perched next to Luke.

"No. I want this to succeed. I want us to record a damn song that's so powerful Nashville will be lookin' Coleman up on a map to see where the hell we are."

"You've just got to give it more time." He slapped Luke on the back. "Something will break loose."

"That little gal, Hazel, that we're workin' with has a damned good voice, but she sure ain't much to look at." Luke took a swig from his cup. "What do you reckon we can do with her?"

"I've been thinkin' about somethin'. What if we paired Lily with Hazel as a duet, kinda like the Sweethearts of the Rodeo?"

"Lily does want to sing bad. She begs me all the time. I just hate to get her started in this shitty business." Luke thought about Barbara, a woman who'd sang with the Rhythm Rebels back in the 60s. She'd had a great voice and wasn't bad looking but she had to take a lot of abuse not only from the band, but from the men in the audience. He didn't want that for Lily.

"Luke, she's only twelve years old. Don't you think you'd have control over where she sings and who she's with?"

"Damned straight I would. I'll think about it."

"The deal coming up in Moran in a few weeks would be the perfect place to debut them and Silver Creed can back 'em."

Luke threw back the remains of his drink and stood. "I'll see you tomorrow, stud. I'm goin' home. I've got a young hot wife to take care of."

Eli laughed and motioned toward the door. "Goodnight, Bubba."

Luke found Darlina stretched out on the sofa, wearing shorts and a tank top. An oscillating fan blew across her. He stood in the doorway for a minute taking in the sight of the fan blowing her hair and ruffling the pages of the book she held.

Pitching his keys on the table, he strode to the sofa.

"Hi, baby." She sat up and closed her book.

"Hi, yourself." Luke lowered his large frame to the sofa and patted his lap. "Come over here, little girl."

He loved the way her eyes lit up and the instant smile that graced her lips.

"What do you have in mind, kind sir?" She moved beside him.

Luke easily pulled her onto his lap and lowered his head to catch the scent of her hair. "I love you, angel. You've gotta know that."

"I do and I love you. What's going on?"

"Nothing. Just needed to tell you that."

Luke stroked Darlina's hair as she pressed her cheek against his chest. They sat like this for an hour or more, Luke sharing what he and Eli had talked about and their dreams for the studio.

When he mentioned Lily possibly singing with Hazel, Darlina sat up and looked at him. He saw surprise clearly in her eyes.

"Are you sure you'd be okay with that, Luke? I know she will be thrilled and of course, she'll want to do it. I thought you didn't want her singing."

"I've never said I didn't want her to sing, I just didn't want her to get ideas about making music a career. She's way too smart to settle for that lifestyle." He leaned in, tasting the sweetness of her lips.

He could never tire of her immediate response to him and thrilled to the touch when she put her hand on the back of his neck and deepened the kiss.

"Hmm, I think I've forgotten all about what we were sayin'," Darlina murmured.

Luke stood and pulled her to her feet. "We'll talk with Lily tomorrow, but for now, let's finish what we started."

Sometime later, he lay panting with the damp tangled sheets around them. Darlina seemed to have similar trouble catching her breath as she laid her head on his chest.

Staring up at the ceiling, Luke listened to Darlina's heart beating against his own and sighed. "This is what it really means to be home, sweetheart. I've found the one place on this earth where I finally truly belong."

She traced his lips with her fingertip, then raised herself to place a tender kiss on them. "Of course it's where you belong. I love you with all of me."

He tried to hide the huskiness in his voice. "That's all a man ever has the right to hope for."

He wrapped both arms around her slender frame and held her until he heard her even breathing that told him she was asleep. He gazed at her face. How could he ever do anything good enough to deserve this kind of love?

He didn't know, but was convinced he'd die trying.

***

Over the next few weeks, Luke took Lily with him every evening so that she could practice with Hazel and just as Eli had predicted, their voices blended magically.

Pride didn't even come close to describing what Luke felt for his little girl with a beautiful voice, who was growing up way too fast.

At times Darlina and Nicole came out to listen to them practice and Luke loved the smile Darlina flashed Lily, assuring her she was doing a good job.

By the time the day-long event in Moran rolled around, the girls were polished and ready to go.

Luke sat beside Darlina with Nicole on the other side of him, holding both of their hands as they watched Lily perform.

The girls sang in perfect harmony, "There's one stoplight blinking on and off. Everyone knows when the neighbors cough. They roll up the streets when the sun goes down. I'm a midnight girl in a sunset town."

"Lord, don't leave me in this one-horse town....." Hazel sang.

"Lord, don't leave me in this one-horse town...." Lily repeated.

Darlina, Luke, Nicole, Eli and Georgia all stood and clapped along with others in the audience when the girls finished.

Eli grinned from ear to ear. "Told ya, Bubba."

Luke chuckled. "Yes, you did."

Grabbing Darlina's hand, he made his way up to the stage and enveloped Lily in a warm hug the minute she came off. He looked over her head at Darlina and winked.

He'd never been more proud of his family and it would only continue to grow and get better. It was starting to sink in. He was finally home.

Lily

Chapter 15

An early fall wind whipped bronze colored leaves across the yard. Darlina looked up from the pot she stirred. Outside the kitchen window, she could see the girls pretending to be cheerleaders, as they so often did.

She smiled to herself at their antics. She'd always dreamed that her children would be allowed to do all of the things she'd been deprived of as a child and damned if history wasn't repeating itself anyway.

Every time she'd approached Luke with the idea of the girls participating in extracurricular activities, he vetoed it. There wasn't extra money for such things, he said, and they all did cost money.

She sighed and returned her attention to the stove. She knew that Luke didn't make these decisions to be mean or restrictive, he just didn't see any advantage in spending hard-earned money on frivolous things. He was right, but nevertheless, it left an ache deep inside of her. Children needed room for their dreams to grow as much as they did food and shelter.

In just a few months, Lily would be the big thirteen years old. She already looked older than her years and wanted to wear makeup all of the time.

It took some work to convince Luke that a small amount of makeup wouldn't make her look eighteen and Lily had been thrilled when she could wear a little mascara and eye shadow.

Of course, Nicole wanted to do what her big sister did, but she'd have to wait until she was Lily's age.

Darlina thought about the events of the day and couldn't wait to tell Luke about a job opportunity.

She still worked part-time for MHMR and had become acquainted with some of the women who worked just down the hall at the state welfare office. One of the women had told her of a part-time job opening and encouraged her to apply.

So, she'd picked up her application on her way out of the building and would return it in the morning. The thought of working a full eight hour day excited her. It would make things easier for sure.

Once the table was set, she turned the burners off and headed to the door to call the girls for supper. Just as she reached to turn the knob, Luke opened the door.

"Well, this is some greeting." He bent down and planted a wet kiss on Darlina's lips.

The kiss left an aching hunger inside her. Leaning in to him, she laughed. "I didn't know you were about to come through the door. I was just fixin' to call the girls in for supper. I wasn't expecting you home for a while. What a nice surprise."

"I have to go on out to the studio in a little bit, but I wanted to see my girls."

Standing on her tiptoes, she returned Luke's kiss. "I love surprises. I'll get the girls and I may have some news for you."

Luke slapped her playfully on the bottom as she disappeared through the door.

Over dinner, she shared the news of the pending job possibility and watched his eyes light up.

With a grin, he laid down his fork. "Sweetheart, that'd be wonderful. Maybe it would even turn into full time and you could quit MHMR. I worry about you down there by yourself with all of that dope. Somebody could knock you in the head and steal it."

Dismissing his concern, Darlina wiped her mouth on a napkin. "I'm not always there by myself. The case manager is there sometimes too. But anyway, it would be great if the state job pans out with all of the benefits that would go along with it. I've got my fingers crossed."

"Well, if they have good sense, they'll hire you on the spot." He turned to the girls and ruffled Nicole's hair. "What did you girls do today?"

They took turns telling Luke about their school adventures. Darlina listened as each of the girls chattered on about their friends, their teachers or a test they'd passed.

They tried so hard to please him and lit up when he praised them for any small accomplishment.

It was obvious how much they loved each other.

Anything she could do to make their lives easier, she'd walk on hot coals to do it. She hoped against hope that this job would come through and double her income.

But for now, she brought her attention back to the conversation.

"Lily, remember what I told you about being in the school band?" Luke turned serious.

Lily nodded. Her clear blue eyes lit up and her strawberry blonde hair fell around her shoulders.

"Well, I meant it. You keep your grades up and when you go back from Christmas break, I'll make sure you have an instrument."

"Oh Daddy, I want to play clarinet. That's what my friend Mandy is playing and we could practice together."

"What can I do, Daddy?" Nicole pouted.

"You just stay little and don't grow up like your sister. That's what you can do." He reached for Nicole's hand and pulled toward him. With one arm, he lifted her onto his lap. "When you get bigger, if you want to play in the band and can keep your grades up, you'll get your chance."

The child gazed adoringly at Luke. "I'm smart, Daddy. I can make good grades."

"Of course you can. Just don't grow up too fast on me."

Darlina thought she caught a glint of tears in his eyes, but he quickly changed the subject and told a joke.

"Know what the duck said to the farmer who was eating soup?"

Both girls giggled.

"You wanna quacker?"

They all laughed as Luke stood. "I've gotta run, but you girls be good and do your homework."

Darlina stood and walked with Luke to the door. "Don't be too late coming home, baby."

"Why's that?"

She discreetly brushed her breast against his arm. "Guess you'll just have to come home to find out."

"Sweetheart, you're an expert at keepin' me guessin'." He caressed her cheek and then he was gone.

***

In September, the State of Texas hired Darlina to work four hours per day in the child services office. Finally, after three and a half years, she claimed the status of being a full-time employee.

She made arrangements for someone to take over the home care for her mother-in-law and eagerly went from the MHMR office in the mornings to the Child Protective Services office in the afternoon.

Not only did this job provide more income, but insurance for the family as well.

***

Luke continued juggling three jobs and in every spare minute, he made more improvements to their home.

The latest addition came in sheets of wallboard that resembled red brick. He'd found them discarded at the dump ground. When he nailed them over the paneling on the kitchen wall next to the dining table, it gave the room an old-world look. He happily helped Darlina hang a beautiful ceramic piece that he'd made in prison in the middle of the wall.

"Remember those peppers Felix brought me that I hung out to dry?" He put his arm around Darlina's shoulders.

"Yes. Can we hang them on this wall? They would look great against the brick."

"You read my mind. I'll go get 'em."

He loved making even the tiniest bit of progress. It gave him great satisfaction.

***

Christmas was creeping up on them and with sign work slow, there wouldn't be much money to spare.

Luke had been mulling over a thought for a few days and when it came time to go to the recording studio, he made a decision.

Making sure Darlina wouldn't see him, he took his Martin D-35 guitar out of the closet and put it in the pickup. His girls would have a good Christmas, no matter what.

Eli looked up when he walked into the studio that evening carrying his guitar case. "Well, it's about damned time, Bubba."

"It's not what you think, Eli. I need a favor."

"Anything, Luke. You know that."

"I want to sell this guitar to you for five hundred dollars. I need Christmas money for my family."

"Shit! I don't want to buy your damned guitar, Luke. You oughta be playin' the sonofabitch."

"I'm serious, Eli. It's just sitting in the closet gathering dust, and I need money."

"Just let me give you a loan. You've done a ton of work out here and never drawn any kind of a paycheck." Eli walked behind the bar and twisted the cap off a new bottle of Crown.

"Nope. That wasn't our agreement. If and when the company starts making money, I'll draw some pay, but until then, I won't draw a dime and I damned sure don't need another debt." Luke sat the guitar case down on the floor and perched on a stool.

Eli put ice and coke into a glass, then reached for the Jim Beam bottle. "Have a drink and think about it."

Luke took the fresh drink. "I have thought about it, Eli. If you won't buy it, I'll take it to Brownwood and sell it."

"Damn, man. Don't do that. Hell, the turquoise and silver on the guitar is worth five hundred. I'll tell you what. I'll buy your guitar but I'll build a display case for it. No one will be allowed to play it but you, if you ever decide to." Eli reached into his hip pocket and pulled out a wallet. Opening it, he counted out five one hundred dollar bills and passed them across the bar.

"Do whatever you want with it." Luke pocketed the money. "It's yours now. Let's go to work. Who do we have comin' in tonight?"

"Ol' Escobar. He's written a couple of songs that he wants to record. The biggest challenge will be keeping him sober long enough to sing 'em."

Luke sighed. "Some shit never changes."

Even though he stayed through the recording session, Luke's heart wasn't in it. He couldn't keep his thoughts from wandering to Darlina lying alone in their warm empty bed. He knew she'd been worrying about how they were going to make Christmas happen and he couldn't wait to alleviate those worries.

Eli had no idea what a difference he'd made in their lives for a few days. Luke would be forever grateful. He wanted to buy a heart-shaped ruby and diamond necklace for Darlina. He'd spotted it in the window of the jewelry store downtown when he'd bid on a sign job a few weeks back. Lily would have her clarinet and Nicole would have the new bicycle she wanted.

His girls would have a good Christmas. When he left the studio that evening, he spared a backward glance at the guitar case still sitting on the floor where he'd left it. "Goodbye old friend," he whispered, then quickly closed the door.

On the five-minute drive from the studio back to the trailer, Luke thought about the comfort his guitar had provided in prison. It had seen him through many dark days and nights in the tiny cell behind the forty-foot walls. Yes, they'd been through a lot together and how fitting that it now provided his family with a good Christmas.

He could see their bedroom light burning as he walked up to the front door of the trailer. Cold winter wind whipped around him and he shivered before he opened the door.

The warmth greeted him, soothed his ragged soul and made promises. Promises that he knew would be kept. He would live out the rest of his days on earth here in this home or some home with Darlina. Oh, he never tried to deny the fact that the children would grow up and go their own ways, but he would always be with Darlina.

Even in death, he'd never completely leave her. He walked toward the bedroom door and her waiting arms.

Luke's Guitar

# Chapter 16

Christmas that year was a joyous occasion. When each of the girls opened their present from Luke, they ran and threw their arms around his neck. With the table piled high with food, aromatic cedar branches decorated and hung and Christmas music playing, Luke felt the true spirit of Christmas. What prison drained out of him was slowly being replenished. He only gave a brief thought to the guitar that had helped provide for his girls. Funny that Darlina had never questioned where he'd gotten the money. He was going to tell her they'd sold a big load of firewood, but she never asked. His heart swelled with love for his family. The happiness that the gifts brought to their faces was worth more than ten guitars.

***

Darlina dashed into the house on a blustery February evening, taking off her hat, coat and gloves as she came through the door. "Brrr, it's cold out there. I think 1989 is going to be the coldest year ever. It hasn't gotten above freezing all day."

Luke sat in his easy chair half asleep. "Come here by the fat man, he'll get you warm."

Darlina started to sit in his lap but stopped short, alarmed by his ashen face. "What's wrong, baby?"

"Ah nothin'. I think I might have pulled a muscle in my chest putting up that sign today. Do we have a heating pad?"

"Yes. I'll go get it. I'll get you a couple of aspirin too."

"Thank you, sugar."

Darlina returned within minutes. "Here you go. I was afraid Felix wouldn't be enough help to you."

"He does alright. He's just not as strong as Gary and lifting those eight by ten pieces of plywood over my head and holding them while he screws them down is god-awful hard in this cold wind. Don't worry. I'll be alright."

"Where are the girls?"

"Mom asked if they'd come over and help her make pies after school, so they're still over there. I'm gonna change clothes, then go get them. It's gettin' dark outside early with all of these clouds. You sure you're okay?"

Luke managed a crooked grin. "Yeah, I'm sure."

When Darlina returned from next door with the girls in tow, Luke was sound asleep in his chair. "Shhh," she whispered, "Daddy's asleep."

All three tiptoed in and while the girls went to their rooms to finish homework, Darlina started supper. She cast an occasional glance toward Luke with a worried feeling that wouldn't go away. She wasn't used to him feeling bad. He'd been so vibrant and driven since he returned from prison. But tonight, he was tired and hurting.

Once the meal was cooked, she gently awoke him. "Supper's ready, honey."

"I'm not hungry, but you girls go ahead and eat. I'll get something after awhile if I get hungry."

Darlina didn't push the issue, but again, worry burrowed deep inside her like their cat, Amanda, seeking warmth. This wasn't like Luke. She hoped he wasn't getting the flu or something worse.

She sat quietly at the dinner table, Luke's presence noticeably missed, and half-listened to the girls' chatter. Her attention was on him.

Two days passed with no improvement. Luke didn't have a fever. He only complained of a pulled muscle and continued to work. He had a determination to get the billboard finished so he could get paid. It was the first of the month and bills were due.

Finally after a week, he could no longer lie down on the bed and spent two nights in his chair in the living room. Darlina, stubbornly brought her blanket and pillow to the couch to be close, even though he begged her to go to bed.

Saturday night around 7 o'clock, he sat with the heating pad on the left side of his chest and a blanket over him.

"Darlina, honey, would you run down to the liquor store and get me a pint of whiskey? Maybe a drink would ease this shit. My ol' chest is throbbin' like a sick robin's ass."

"Of course. I'll be right back." She donned her coat and gloves and grabbed the car keys.

She bought a pint of Jim Beam along with a two liter bottle of diet Coke and hurried home. She hoped this would bring Luke the relief he needed.

By 3 am, the pain had worsened and neither Luke nor Darlina had closed their eyes.

"I hate like hell to do this, but I think you're gonna have to take me to the hospital. Something is really wrong. Will you go wake up Mom and see if she'll come and stay here with the girls until we get back?" Luke groaned with pain.

"Yes. I'm glad you're finally doing something. This is more than a pulled muscle, Luke." After throwing on clothes, she woke up Mom Stone. Trying not to cause any alarm, she quickly explained the situation then helped Luke outside and to the car.

"Do you mind, driving?" Luke slid into the passenger side of the car.

"Of course not." Darlina tried not to speed, but urgency pushed her on. She made it to the Brownwood hospital emergency room in record time.

After hours of waiting, a sleepy-eyed doctor arrived to examine Luke.

Darlina listened as the doctor asked what seemed like a million questions; the same questions the nurses had already covered. She could see Luke losing patience.

"Just give it to me straight," Luke snapped.

"This could be a simple case of a cracked rib or even indigestion, Mr. Stone, but we need to do a chest x-ray and EKG to make sure. We'll also draw blood," the doctor finally concluded.

"Shit, doc, if it's indigestion, I've had it for damn near two weeks now." Luke groaned as he pushed himself up from the examining table.

"I'm going to put a couple of Nitro pills under your tongue, Mr. Stone. If you are having a heart attack, they should ease the pain almost instantly."

"Heart attack?" Darlina's breath caught in her throat.

"It's just something we have to rule out, Mrs. Stone." The doctor raised his eyebrows. He then wrote an order and handed it to the nurse. "We'll get to the bottom of it."

Darlina moved to Luke's side and grasped his hand. She couldn't help but think about the shock of losing her father to a heart attack a few years earlier.

The nurse pulled the curtain, closing off the small examining room. "Mr. Stone we need you to get undressed and into a hospital gown and I will get an IV of fluids started."

She handed the gown to Luke and left. Darlina helped him get out of his clothes and put the gown on.

"Lord, honey, I'd rather be butt naked than wear one of these damn backless gowns." He eased back onto the table. "And this table must be made out of stone, it's so damn hard."

Darlina laughed. "You're sure gettin' mighty testy, Mr. Stone."

"You ain't seen nothin' yet. I hate being a sickie. I've got shit to do."

The nurse slipped through the curtain, drew blood and started the IV, then rolled in the cart with the EKG machine on it.

It neared noon on Sunday before Luke and Darlina left the hospital. The tests showed a heart problem, and Luke had a follow-up appointment with a heart doctor back in Brownwood on Monday.

They were silent on the way back to Coleman.

Finally, Luke spoke. "This is probably just showing up because of the rheumatic fever I had as a kid. We'll go see this doctor tomorrow and I'm sure he'll tell us it's nothing. Then we can get on with living."

Darlina squeezed his hand. "I sure hope so, Luke. Thank God I got that job with the state and have insurance."

"Yep, that's a damn good deal."

Lily and Nicole had lots of questions for Luke and Darlina and they did their best to allay their fears. They both assured the children that Luke would be fine.

Darlina wished she could feel as confident as she sounded when she told the girls that Daddy would be okay. She couldn't help thinking about her own father; how he walked into the hospital on his own two feet and came out in a body bag. But, he had other complications that Luke didn't have. She had to keep the hope that this was a simple problem that could be fixed with medication.

Monday morning found Luke and Darlina sitting in the doctor's office listening to words like blockage and damage. She didn't know what it meant except that something was terribly wrong with Luke.

They left with a referral to Abilene for a heart catheter. The doctor explained the procedure. A tiny camera would be inserted through the groin and up into the heart. It would show exactly what was going on.

Anxiety knotted in Darlina's gut. This wasn't in their plans. Luke continually downplayed it and joked that once they looked with the camera they'd see that everything was fine and they could be on their merry way. But, she didn't feel like laughing or joking. Something told her this was serious.

The earliest appointment they could get was for Friday, February 10th at ten o'clock in the morning. Once again, they had to depend on Mom Stone to look after the girls once they got off the school bus.

Darlina and Luke were in the car heading to Abilene by eight-thirty Friday morning. Darlina had taken the girls to school instead of putting them on the school bus. She kissed and assured them she would see them later in the day.

The radio played in the car on the way to Abilene. Darlina had a million thoughts running through her mind but she refrained from voicing them. She didn't want to add anything to Luke on top of what he already had to deal with.

Luke kissed her before going in for the procedure, squeezed her hand and told her not to worry. She wished it was that simple, but the knots in her stomach wouldn't come unwound.

One short hour later, a young doctor sat in a small private conference room next to Darlina.

"We need to keep him, Mrs. Stone. He has five major blocked arteries. It's a miracle he's still alive. He needs immediate bypass surgery."

Darlina only half heard the words. Her heart pounded so loud it drowned out the doctor's voice. Finally, she looked at him. "What did you say your name is?"

"I'm Doctor Robertson."

"We have two children, Doctor Robertson. We need time to prepare for this. Can I see him?"

"Sure, but I can't stress enough how critical this is. When five major arteries are blocked, another heart attack of any kind will most certainly be fatal. I'll take you to Mr. Stone."

She followed the doctor on numb legs. This couldn't be happening. Surely she and Luke hadn't waited and dreamed for so many years of a life together only to have it ripped from them after three and a half short years. She fought against tears that threatened to spill.

The moment she saw Luke's face, she tried to stifle a sob and gripped her hands tightly. He'd been through so much. It didn't seem fair that there had to be more.

She choked out the words, "Luke, Dr. Robertson tells me that you need heart surgery and that you can't go home. Has he told you that?"

"Yes." Luke's gaze met her straight on.

"But, what about the girls? We have to make arrangements. I can call my mom and ask her to come, but it will take her a day to get here." Darlina twisted her purse in her hands.

Luke turned to Dr. Robertson. "Doc, if you'll let me go home over the weekend, I promise I'll be here bright and early Monday morning. But Darlina's right, we have obligations we need to take care of."

"I won't be the one doing your surgery. Dr. Carl is the best heart surgeon in Abilene. He's on his way over now to consult with me. It's against my better judgment to let you go." Dr. Robertson smoothed back his long hair held in a pony tail and looked at Darlina. "Mrs. Stone, if you can promise me that your husband won't move out of his chair or do anything more strenuous than turn on the TV over the weekend, he can leave. But, we have to make sure the artery I just went into isn't going to start bleeding. He'll need to be monitored for several hours. And he'll have to be back here and checked in through admissions by six am on Monday."

"I promise, sir. We just need a little time."

He stood and leaned over Luke. "I'll be back to check on you after you see Dr. Carl." He scribbled something on the chart in his hands.

"Thank you." Darlina's hand went to her throat in relief.

Dr. Robertson left and Darlina pulled a chair up beside Luke's bed. She took his hand in hers and laid her check on it. He stroked her hair. They didn't speak.

Silently, she began to pray.

When she raised her head to meet his gaze, he gently wiped a stray tear that found its way down her cheek.

"Please don't cry, sweetheart. I'm a tough ol' bird and it's gonna take more than a little heart surgery to do me in."

"Oh Luke, this is nothing to take lightly." She choked back a sob. "You just can't leave me. That's all I know."

"Let's not talk about it right now. Once we get out of here, we'll call your mom and I need to talk to Eli."

"We need to think of all the questions we should ask Dr. Carl so we'll know what to expect. Like how long will it take to recover from the surgery? How long will they keep you in the hospital? Things like that so I can tell Mama when I call her. And, I've got to call my boss at both work places."

Luke squeezed her hand. "We'll ask everything we can think of. It's all going to be all right. I just need to make sure you girls will be taken care of while I'm in here."

They both looked up when a tall somber man wearing a white doctor coat, scrubs and surgical hat opened the door. He held a chart in his hands and only glanced up once he'd finished reading. "Mr. Stone?" He extended his hand.

Luke shook his hand. "That's me."

"I'm Dr. Carl and I'm going to be performing the open heart surgery on you." He turned to Darlina. "Are you Mrs. Stone?"

Nodding, she shook his hand.

"I'm sure you have questions and I'll answer everything I can. I know that Dr. Robertson stressed how important it is that you limit your physical activity once you get home and I have the admission papers you'll need to bring back with you on Monday morning." He pulled up an empty chair and stretched his legs out in front of him.

One by one, he answered all of Luke's and Darlina's questions.

Finally, he stood. "Let me take a look at the cath incision." Luke shoved the covers back and the doctor examined the area. "I'd like for you to stay until we're sure this is closed over so there's no danger of bleeding."

Luke nodded.

Once he left the room, Darlina found the phones in the lobby. The first call was to work. She hated to ask for time off after only being on the new job for four months, but there was no choice.

Her boss encouraged her not to worry about a thing and to do what she needed. She assured her that the proper paperwork would be filed for the time off. It would go into time without pay, but none of that mattered to Darlina. All she could think about was Luke.

Open heart surgery. The words stuck fear deep inside her. People died from this. Luke could die and leave her a very young widow. Icy fingers of fear laced themselves through her heart. But, she straightened her spine, lifted her chin and determined not to let Luke see her terror.

Several hours later, they were in the car on the way back to Coleman with lots of explanations to give and plans to make.

Thoughts were jumbled in a mess inside her head as she drove.

Luke stared out the window. When he spoke, he sounded far away. "I loved growing up in this country. I spent many hours huntin' with my little collie dog, and a twenty-two rifle. Those were good days. Funny thing back then, I could smell a squirrel if there was one anywhere around. I won some bets with my buddies over that."

"Maybe sometime you can take me to your old home place. I'd love to see it."

It was almost as if Luke didn't hear her. He seemed lost in reverie. "We were dirt poor, but I had no cares or worries back then other than how I was gonna sneak up on a flock of ducks and pop one to take back to the house for supper." His voice choked and he turned toward Darlina.

Trying to hide the tremor in her voice, she spoke softly, "Luke, I want you to tell me everything you can think of between now and Monday. I want to know all of your thoughts."

He managed a chuckle. "Sweetheart, you don't deserve that kind of punishment. Please try not to worry. Just remember it's not over 'til the fat lady sings and she hasn't even started to hum."

"I hope so, Luke. Truly, I do." But her heart was pounding too loud to hear the words she'd just uttered.

Chapter 17

By the time Luke and Darlina reached home that evening, the sun had slipped behind the horizon, leaving cold darkness. Luke tried to shake off the heavy cloud that settled over him.

The children ran to greet them from Nanny's house the second they pulled into the driveway. He figured they must have been watching out the window and that told him a lot about their anxiety. Damn, he wished he didn't have to tell them the news. Kids weren't supposed to have to worry about things like this. The fact that he would have to tell them soured his stomach. He let go a sigh and pasted on a smile before he opened the car door.

The minute he stepped out of the car, Nicole threw her arms around him. "Daddy, are you okay?"

Lily joined her. "We were so worried."

He ruffled their hair. "I'm gonna be just fine. It's cold out here and you don't even have your coats on. Let's get in the house."

He watched Darlina out of the corner of his eye as she joined them and draped her arm over Nicole's slender shoulders. He also didn't miss the glistening of a tear in her eye or the fact that she said nothing to the children. His gut wrenched. He'd never wanted to put more burdens on her or the children.

The minute Luke opened the door to his mother's house she jumped up from her chair and embraced him. "I'm so glad to see you kids. Tell me what the doctor said."

"Sit down, Mom. I want to tell you and the girls at the same time and Darlina needs to use the phone to call her mother."

"Oh son, it's bad, isn't it? I just knew it." The gray-haired woman who'd brought him into the world and stood by him when everyone else turned away, twisted her hands on her lap.

"Well, it could be better for sure." Lily squeezed in beside him on the couch once he eased himself down and Nicole claimed the other side. He put his arms around them.

Darlina sat beside him and pulled Nicole onto her lap. "Now, girls, don't get upset or start worrying. Just listen to what Daddy has to say."

Luke took a deep breath. In as few words as possible, he explained what had to happen. Mrs. Stone began to sob into her hands.

Silent tears streamed down Lily's face and Nicole buried her face in Darlina's shoulder.

"Now, let's turn off the waterworks. Mom, there's no need in getting so upset and upsetting the girls. It's going to be all right I'll have the best heart surgeon in Abilene."

"Oh son, you know heart disease runs in our family. It's what took your daddy out. We can't lose you so soon after you got home." She removed her glasses and wiped her eyes.

Luke tried to put sternness into his words, but they felt thick and heavy on his tongue. "Don't get all carried away, Mom.

These doctors know what they're doing. They're gonna patch me up and I'll be good as new," he assured them.

Darlina laid a hand on Luke's arm. "Honey, why don't you take the girls on home with you and get that leg up like the doctor said. I'm going to call Mama, then I'll be right on over. Girls, do you have anything over here that you need to take home?"

Nicole sniffled and slid off Darlina's lap. "School books and our coats."

"Well gather them up and go with Daddy. I'll be there in just a few minutes." She helped Nicole into her coat with a quiet calm that she didn't feel, while Lily slipped into hers.

"Come on girls." Luke got to his feet and reached for their hands. "Tell Nanny good night and we'll see her tomorrow. Mom, thank you so much for helping out again."

"Son, you know I'll help anyway I can and these girls are a joy to take care of." She blew her nose loudly and stood. She hugged each of the girls, then turned to Luke and embraced him.

He leaned down and kissed the top of her head. "I love you, Mom. Promise me you won't worry."

She choked on the words, "I can't promise any such thing. I love you, son."

***

Once they were out the door, Darlina took a deep breath, picked up the phone and dialed a familiar number.

After a brief conversation, Darlina sagged against the wall, relieved that her mother would travel from East Texas tomorrow and stay as long as they needed her.

Darlina thanked Mom Stone and hurried home. She didn't want Luke out of her sight any longer than absolutely necessary. The knot that formed in her gut earlier in the day was now a twisted mass of nerves.

She looked up at the twinkling stars against the blackness as she hurried across the yard to the trailer door and prayed a fervent prayer. "God, please don't take Luke from me so soon. Please give us more time. We've just barely gotten started. I'm begging you."

She wiped her tears and pasted on a smile before she opened the door. Her family needed her to be strong and upbeat and she would force that no matter how difficult.

Once the girls were tucked into bed, Luke and Darlina lay on their own bed snuggling close.

"Darlina," Luke began.

Now, regretting her earlier insistence that he tell her everything, she put her fingers on his lips. "Sh. Let's not talk anymore tonight. We need to rest."

"But, I have so much to tell you."

"Then tell me tomorrow. I just want to lie here beside you and pretend everything is like it was a month ago before all of this started."

Luke gathered her closer. "I love you, sweetheart."

A stray tear escaped and she buried her face in the covers. "I love you too, Luke Stone. Never forget that."

Long after Luke's breathing steadied into an easy rhythm, Darlina lay awake with thousands of thoughts racing through her head.

How was she going to hold all of this together and be everything for everyone who needed her? She couldn't allow emotions get the best of her. She had to keep up a happy positive front for Luke and for the children.

But, what if he didn't survive the surgery? A gasp caught in her throat. She must not have these thoughts. Surely, he would be okay and they would have many more years together.

She looked over at him in the darkness and branded to memory the familiar silhouette of his face.

***

Over the next two days, it seemed to Darlina that she was caught in one continuous whirlwind. Eli and Georgia spent several hours visiting with her and Luke. They easily gave their assurances they would look after things for Luke.

She accompanied Luke while he called Lexi and Martin. Both of them drove up from Midland on Sunday to see their dad. Darlina's mother also arrived on Sunday and immediately took over the cooking and tending of the house.

Darlina breathed a sigh of relief. Lily and Nicole were so excited to have their granny with them they didn't focus as much on what was happening. Once Granny had gone to the grocery store and stocked the refrigerator, delicious smells filled the house.

Darlina kept her full attention on Luke and made sure he obeyed the doctor's orders. She listened while he gave Felix instructions on the pending sign work to be completed, then went next door with him to call Gary and ask if he could come help Felix until he got back on his feet.

Finally, by Sunday night, everything was in place as much as it could be.

Georgia and another cousin, Betty, would stay with Darlina at the hospital while Luke underwent surgery.

At last, packed bags sat by the door and lists lay on the kitchen table. This was what family was all about...coming together in hard times and pitching in to help out.

Darlina couldn't have been more grateful for the outpouring of love and support. She began to believe somewhere deep inside that everything just might turn out okay.

Once they were secluded from the world in their bedroom that night, Luke raised himself up on one elbow and looked deep into Darlina's eyes. He lightly ran his fingertips across her lips and smoothed back her hair. "I want to make love to you."

"No, Luke. We promised the doctor."

"The doctor ain't here and if this should be my last night on earth, I'd want to spend it lost in love with you."

She sat up in bed and pulled the covers up around her. "Luke Stone, you stop talking about dying. And I promised the doctor I wouldn't let you do anything to put a strain on your heart. The way we make love most certainly would do that."

"That doesn't stop me from wanting it," Luke grumbled. He pulled her down beside him and she nestled easily into the curve of his side.

"Don't worry. We'll have many more years to make love. Just hold me close and let's rest. Tomorrow is going to be a big day."

"You're my angel," Luke murmured into her hair.

"I'm just me," she whispered, "but I love you."

Just as she'd done the night before, she awoke off and on through the night, watching for Luke's chest rising and falling.

She knew Luke's mother meant well, but the fact that she'd told her three times over the past two days of how Luke's father had died in bed and she'd just thought he'd gone to sleep only heightened her anxiety.

History was not going to repeat itself on her watch. Funny, but she felt a little like a guardian angel. She remembered another time many years ago when Luke lay ravaged with fever and hallucinations that she kept vigil by his bedside for several days and nights until it passed. She'd appointed herself as his guardian angel then. Now the time had come to re-grow her wings.

***

The alarm buzzed at 4:30 on Monday morning and they sprang into action. The first thing Darlina noticed when she got out of bed was that her throat was scratchy. She dismissed it immediately. This was not the time for her to be sick.

"Don't forget the Valentine's cards for the girls," Luke reminded her.

"Mama promised she'd give them the cards at breakfast. How ironic is it that you will have heart surgery on Valentine's Day?"

With a chuckle, Luke replied, "Can't think of a better day to get my ol' heart patched up."

Darlina gave her mother a grateful hug when she handed her a steaming cup of coffee at the door. She promised to call when Luke was out of surgery and then they were off.

About half way to Abilene, Luke broke the silence. "Remember, many years ago, not long after we'd first met, when I went to Oklahoma and asked you to listen to Joan Baez until I got back?"

"Of course I remember. I played that record over and over all night until Sherry was about ready to kill me."

"I'm going to ask you to keep that kind of vigil for me again when I go into surgery. Sort of hold space for me."

"Oh Luke," her voice cracked. "I will hold you in my heart until you are back in my arms again."

He leaned across the seat and placed a warm kiss on her cheek. "That's my girl."

"You've got to promise me that you aren't going anywhere," she choked.

"I can promise you I'm not going anywhere willingly. And you've got to promise me to take care of yourself."

"I will. I'm so glad Georgia and Betty are going to be with me today. I really do appreciate it."

"They're good people and they care. Just remember the things I told you and if for some reason I don't come through this, Eli and Georgia will help you and so will Gary."

"I know, but they're not gonna have to because you'll be fine. We have the best doctors in Abilene." She kept one eye on the road and one on Luke.

He stared out the window into the blackness of early morning. When he spoke, his voice was somber. "I'm just saying that if it does break bad, take the girls and go live close to your mom. You'd have no reason to stay in Coleman."

Darlina dared a glance at Luke's face. She'd never seen him look more grim. She didn't trust herself to speak.

Luke turned the volume of the radio up. *'From a Jack to a King. From loneliness to a wedding ring. I played an ace and I won a queen and walked away with your heart…'*

"I didn't think anybody could ever do that song as good as Ned Miller, but I do believe Ricky Van Shelton has done it. Ned Miller was a nice guy. I enjoyed knowing him."

She nodded. It was good to change the subject and talking about music always came easily to Luke. He talked on as the miles flew past, about days gone by and music artists that had touched his life in one way or another.

It was obvious to Darlina that music would always be a part of Luke Stone, no matter how hard he attempted to squelch it. She swallowed a sob. Dammit! This wasn't fair.

Once they reached the hospital, the admission process went quickly and an orderly escorted them to the third floor where Luke would be prepped for surgery.

Darlina stood quietly by as nurses helped him into a hospital gown, inserted an IV, then shaved his left leg and chest.

Her eyes misted as she watched him joke and make light of the situation. Every time he looked at her, she forced smile, but it was almost more than she could do.

She watched the clock and as each minute ticked away, her heart pounded so loud she wondered if others could hear it. She wanted to yank that clock off the wall and stop the hands that measured her time with Luke.

Finally, the nurses finished and left the two of them alone.

"Come here." Luke patted the bed.

Darlina climbed up and stretched out beside him. He stroked her hair and she struggled to hold back the fountain of tears that clogged her throat.

Words were unnecessary. They'd all been said. They held each other tightly, dreading the sound of squeaky footsteps.

All too soon, the curtain parted and the anesthesiologist strode in. Darlina got off the bed, wiped her eyes and watched while he put medicine into the IV that would put Luke to sleep.

She leaned over, kissed him on the forehead and whispered. "I'll see you soon, my love."

Chapter 18

As Luke sank further and further under the sedation of the drug, Darlina tightly held his hand. When they came to take him to surgery, a young nurse guided her to the waiting room, where she was relieved to see Georgia and Betty already seated.

Her throat had progressed from scratchy to seriously sore. It was getting harder to swallow by the minute and she knew she was getting sick. Just what she didn't need.

Then she panicked. If she was sick, they wouldn't let her back in to see Luke. She had to do something.

She confided in Georgia. Luke's cousin immediately left only to return a short time later, with a bottle of capsules and cough syrup which she handed to Darlina. "I explained everything to my doctor and he called these in for you. Start taking them now and you should be better soon."

"Thank you, Georgia. I simply can't be sick. I just can't." She opened the bottle and downed two of the capsules.

"How about some food?" Betty stood. "I'm going to the cafeteria. Would you like for me to bring you something?"

"Maybe just some coffee for now. I have peanut butter crackers in my purse."

"Honey, you need to keep your strength up. Luke is going to need you," she insisted.

Darlina opened her purse and took out her wallet. "Let me give you some money."

"You will not. Sit tight and I'll be back in a little bit." Betty hurried toward the elevator doors.

Sitting quietly in a waiting room, Darlina searched the faces of people with loved ones in surgery. Lines of worry etched their brows and she knew she wore the same look.

Each time the double wooden door opened and someone got a report from a nurse, her stomach lurched. Four hours dragged by and still nothing.

She tried to focus on conversation with Georgia or Betty, but her heart, soul and mind was with Luke as he lay just beyond those doors, fighting for his life.

Finally, the door opened and a nurse in blue surgical scrubs called her name.

Standing on wooden legs, Darlina hurried toward the nurse with Georgia and Betty on each side. "I'm Mrs. Stone."

"We just wanted to let you know that so far the surgery is going well. Mr. Stone is holding up good and things are progressing. This is a very long surgery, but we'll try to give you an update every hour or so."

Darlina thanked her and then asked. "How much longer do you think it will take?"

"Most likely another three or four hours, but we'll let you know of any change." The nurse's shoes whispered on the shiny floor as she disappeared behind the doors.

The three women walked back to their seats. Betty patted Darlina's leg. "Try not to worry, sweetie. Luke Stone is as strong and stubborn as they come."

Darlina nodded, not trusting her voice. She tried to eat some of the food Betty had brought, but had trouble getting it past the lump in her throat. Through the day, she felt more and more sick, even running a little fever. Dammit! She just couldn't let this happen. Not now.

She loved listening to the stories Georgia and Betty shared about their childhood and the closeness all of their families had when they were small. Their mothers were sisters and sisters to Luke's mother as well. Georgia had dark hair, while Betty was blonde and of slender build. They both carried an intense pride in their family. It gave her a deeper insight into what formed the man she loved.

Twice more a nurse came with a report on the surgery and each time the words were the same. The hours dragged by like thick molasses on cold toast.

When would it be over?

At straight up four o'clock in the afternoon, Dr. Carl strode into the waiting area and sat down beside Darlina.

He still wore surgical scrubs and had slipped the mask down to dangle around his neck. "Mrs. Stone, everything went well. It took longer than I had anticipated, but there was a lot of damage to repair and taking the artery out of the leg gave us a bit of a problem. But, I believe Mr. Stone will fully recover."

"When will I be able to see him?" Her voice quivered. Betty handed a tissue to Darlina and put her arm around her shoulders.

Georgia leaned forward so as not to miss a word.

"He'll remain in recovery for a few hours, then we'll take him to ICU. He'll stay there for at least twenty four hours. Once he is in ICU, you'll be allowed in for a few minutes to see him. I want to warn you, though, that he won't be able to talk. He has a breathing tube in his throat and until that comes out, he can't speak."

"Thank you, Dr. Carl. I appreciate everything you've done for Luke."

"You're welcome. Wait here and after we move him to ICU, someone will come and get you."

Once he left, the three women hugged. "Thank God, Luke is going to be all right." Betty had tears in her eyes. "I'm going to go call Auntie and let her know."

"Thank you, Betty. Will you ask her to go over and tell my mom and maybe she could call Lexi and Martin too?" Darlina asked.

"Okay, sweetie. We'll take care of it."

Georgia stood. "I'm going to go call Eli, then head on back to Coleman. Betty's going to stay here with you tonight. But, you call me if you need anything."

With tears blurring her vision, Darlina stood and hugged her. "Thank you, Georgia. I really do appreciate everything. You girls kept me from thinkin' too much."

By herself for the first time that day, Darlina sank back into the chair she'd occupied for many hours and covered her face with her hands. Luke made it through. Her heart soared and she uttered a prayer of gratitude.

She knew he wasn't out of the woods yet, but he'd made it through the surgery, and that was huge, wasn't it?

When she stood to stretch her legs, Darlina immediately felt dizzy. She tried to think back. Had she eaten? And if so, when? Was it since she'd taken another dose of the medicine? She opened the sandwich that Betty had brought for her and nibbled on it. She had to keep it together.

For Luke, for her family and for herself.

An hour later, Betty returned. "I called everyone, honey. Your mom was over at Auntie's house so she told her the news. Tell you what. I'm going to get a hotel room at a place near the hospital. Then after you see Luke, we can get some rest."

"Oh Betty, I don't have any money for a motel room." The wrinkles on Darlina's brow deepened.

"Don't you worry one bit about that. I'll pay for it."

"I can't let you do that."

"You can't stop me." She put her hands on her hips. "I told you we're stubborn people. You need a good warm bed tonight so you'll feel better tomorrow. If you can't do it for yourself, do it for Luke."

"How can I ever repay you?" Darlina chewed her bottom lip.

"Just take care of my brother. That's how. I'll be back."

Darlina watched as Betty walked away. Her heart overflowed with love for these women who'd stood beside her today. She found it odd that so many of the cousins referred to Luke as their brother. To her, it showed the depth of their feelings for him.

A woman's voice interrupted her thoughts. "Mrs. Stone."

She stood. "I'm Mrs. Stone." Again, she felt dizzy, but took a deep breath and walked toward the nurse.

"I can take you to see Mr. Stone now. You need to prepare yourself for what he looks like. Don't be alarmed by his color. It's completely normal for this type of surgery."

Darlina swallowed the rising panic and followed her down a long hallway to ICU.

Shock rushed through her when she walked into Luke's cubicle. He lay with his eyes closed and a large tube protruding from his mouth. Except for the monitors and sound of oxygen being pumped into his lungs, there was nothing to indicate life.

But the thing that made her suck in her breath and clap her hand over her mouth was the deathly pale gray of his skin. Where was the vital handsome man who'd captured her heart, who completed her world and gave her everything she searched for?

The room began to spin and her spine tingled. Oh God, she was going to faint or throw up. She took a deep breath and steadied herself with the bed railing.

The nurse put a hand on her shoulder. "Are you okay, Mrs. Stone?"

Okay? How could she possibly be okay with any of this?

Darlina nodded, looking desperately around for a chair. Not seeing one, she leaned against the bed. Hands clenched around the bed railing, she took deliberate deep breaths and swallowed hard.

Luke opened his eyes and when he saw Darlina, they lit up for an instant. She leaned over and kissed his cheek. "Hi, baby."

He struggled to move his mouth, which was impossible.

"Don't try to talk." She took his hand in hers.

He turned her hand over and drew a symbol in the palm of her hand.

"I love you too, sweetheart." She patted his hand

Luke shook his head in frustration and drew on her hand again.

"I know," she assured. "Everything's going to be fine."

Three times he tried to communicate. He finally gave up and closed his eyes.

"Your ten minutes are up, Mrs. Stone." The same nurse tapped her on the shoulder.

Tears streamed down her cheeks as she turned back to Luke. His eyes remained closed and he was still. "Is he going to make it?"

The nurse quietly took her arm and led her into the hallway. "I won't lie to you Mrs. Stone. He isn't out of the woods yet."

"When can I see him again?" Darlina swiped her eyes with the back of her hand.

"You can see him when ICU visiting hours open up in the morning and you can visit for a few minutes every four hours. Leave information with the nurse's station as to where you will be tonight in case we need to contact you."

With a lump the size of a grapefruit in her throat she squeaked. "Contact me?"

"We need to know where you will be in case something happens." The nurse spoke calmly and quietly to Darlina. "It's standard procedure."

"Okay." Darlina leaned against the wall.

"I suggest you get some rest. You look like you could use it. He's going to need you to be strong."

Darlina looked with unseeing eyes at the woman. She knew it should make sense, but nothing for the past three weeks had sunk into her brain.

The nurse turned and walked back toward ICU. Darlina stumbled back to the waiting room and collapsed on a chair to wait for Betty.

The image of Luke laying there so gray and helpless replayed in her mind. Silent sobs shook her. She'd never felt so alone and scared. It was all too much.

In less than an hour, Betty returned and took charge. She provided the nurse's station with their hotel phone and room number. Then she held Darlina's arm and guided her to the car.

The short drive to the motel barely registered. She didn't even remember walking into the motel room. She was numb. The door had barely closed behind them when Darlina crumpled in a heap onto one of the beds.

"Honey, I know you're exhausted and half sick, but I'm going to run the bathtub full of hot water and you need to soak for a while. I'm going to go get some chicken noodle soup for you. We've got to get you back on your feet." Betty bustled around the room, turning on lights and closing curtains.

Darlina rolled over. "Thank you. I couldn't have done this without you and Georgia today."

"That's what family is for. Hush, and go get in the bathtub." Betty picked up her purse. "I'll be back in two shakes of a lambs tail."

Forcing herself to shuffle the short distance to the bathroom, Darlina sank down into the tub. She closed her eyes and let her muscles unwind. She tried not to think about Luke just down the street, so hurt, so near death and so all alone. It seemed as if he was a million miles away.

They would get through this. She had to believe that. They hadn't waited all these years to start a life together only to have it ripped away. History wasn't going to repeat itself. She would fight. Suddenly the thought flashed through her mind. In Luke's weakened state, it was up to her to fight hard enough for them both.

She let her memory drift back to when she'd first met Luke that hot summer night in Abilene. Remembering the way he'd flirted and then boldly asked her to go to a motel with him and a lady friend that night made her smile. How naïve she'd been.

A reckless rogue, but oh so charming and handsome he was. She'd loved watching him take the stage and entertain the excited crowds.

Oh how she'd cherished being his woman.

Looking back now, it seemed like another life they'd lived in another place and time. Their love had ignited into an eternal flame and when he'd been taken away to prison, a part of her had gone with him, locked away behind tall forbidding walls.

Luke Stone was everything she'd ever dreamed of and she wasn't about to give up on him now.

She heard Betty return and forced herself to crawl out of the tub. Once she had warm soup in her, she took more medicine and curled up under the covers on one of the beds.

Tomorrow would be a better day.

It had to be. She didn't know if she could get through another day like this one.

She whispered. "Oh Luke, please find the strength to get well. Don't die on me. I need you."

Chapter 19

Even though visiting hours in ICU didn't start until eight the next morning, Darlina was ready to go by seven. "Let's go to the hospital cafeteria and get a bite of breakfast since we've got plenty of time," Betty suggested.

Darlina covered her mouth and gave a deep wracking cough that made her chest rattle. "I could sure use some hot coffee and maybe a bowl of oatmeal. I'm paying though."

"Whatever makes you happy. That cough sounds bad. You know, they may not let you in to see Luke. If they don't, I'll go in and check on him."

Desperation wound through Darlina. She had to see Luke. Dammit! Why did she have to get sick now? She grabbed her purse and coat and followed Betty to the car for the short drive to the hospital.

Sitting in the cafeteria, she pushed the worried thoughts out of her mind and sipped the hot brown liquid. It soothed her throat as it went down. She forced bites of oatmeal down while keeping a close eye on the clock on the wall.

By seven forty-five, they finished their meal and took the elevator to the third floor ICU waiting room.

Darlina ventured to the nurse's station. "Hello. I'm Mrs. Luke Stone. Can you give me an update on his condition?"

The nurse glanced up from her paperwork. "He is about the same as last night. I'm afraid you won't see much change in him today, but by tomorrow, if we can remove the breathing tube, you'll start to see improvement."

"I have to be honest with you. I seem to have a cold, but I must see Luke. Can I wear a mask and go in? Lord knows I don't want to add any problems to what he already has."

The nurse frowned. "Are you running fever?"

"Not today." Darlina fidgeted. She felt like she had to be honest, but couldn't stand the thought of being denied a short visit with her husband.

"Before we take you back, you'll need to thoroughly wash your hands and I'll give you a mask to wear."

"Thank you." Darlina forced a smile.

When she sat back down with Betty, she relayed the information. "After I come out, why don't you go back for a few minutes?"

"I'd love to, but I don't want to cut into any of the short time they give you."

"It'll be okay. I know you have to head home today."

Betty patted Darlina's hand. "Let's go back to the hotel after we get our few minutes with him so you can rest some more before we have to check out."

Darlina nodded. She reached into her bag for the bottle of cough syrup. "I need to be sure I don't cough while I'm in with Luke."

Two minutes later, the nurse came to get her. She handed her a mask and pointed to the restroom.

When she emerged, Darlina had the mask tied securely and her hands were red from scrubbing. Her footsteps echoed as she followed the nurse down the hall to Luke's cubicle.

His blue eyes held questions and he wrinkled his brow when she approached the bed. She quickly reached for his hand.

"It's all right, sweetheart. I have a cold and they want to make sure I don't give it to you. You look a little better today."

Luke squeezed her fingers.

"I can't stay but a few minutes. Betty is going to come in before she goes back to Coleman. She's been wonderful and Georgia got medicine for me so I could get well faster."

Luke began drawing, this time on the back of her hand. She searched his face.

"I don't know what you are trying to tell me, sweetheart. I don't understand."

He shook his head and drew again.

"I love you too, Luke. When you get the breathing tube out, you can tell me what you want me to know."

He struggled to speak.

"Relax, honey. You can't talk until this contraption comes out. Your color is closer to normal today, so that must mean you're improving."

He nodded and drew on her hand again.

She leaned down and kissed his forehead through the mask. "I'm going to let Betty come in and I will see you in a few hours." She stifled a cough. "Just do whatever they tell you and I love you more than life itself."

Luke nodded and closed his eyes.

She walked back toward the waiting room, untying the mask. At least she didn't get dizzy or feel faint this time. And, he did seem to be making progress. Her heart swelled with gratitude. They were going to get through this.

By noon that day, Betty left, and for the first time since the ordeal began, Darlina was alone. The hospital caseworker had signed her up for discounted meals in the cafeteria and another lady in the ICU waiting room had told her about the sleeping arrangements in the hospital.

It seemed that everyone hit the main lobby with pillows and blankets, after the last ICU visiting hours, to stake out a spot on a couch, chair or on the floor.

Darlina was surprised that a hospital allowed this, but at least she'd have a place to pass the nights until they could get Luke into a room.

After a short phone call to Mom Stone to check on the children and her own mother, she settled down in the familiar waiting room. The next chance to visit for the short ten minutes wouldn't come for two more hours.

Upon request, a nurse kindly gave her a pillow and blanket and Darlina curled up in a corner chair to wait.

People came and went. Some spoke to her and some avoided eye contact, seeking solitude. Taking her medicine throughout the day, she began to recuperate somewhat. Thank goodness for the cough syrup as it kept that down to a minimum.

Each time she saw Luke, she thought his color looked less gray. It was obvious he was slowly improving.

That night in the hospital lobby, she managed to get a spot on one of the sofas. She dozed off and on, but even the smallest noise awoke her.

Then a flashing blue light on the wall came on and a voice on the speaker system announced, "Code blue ICU. Code blue ICU."

Everyone in the lobby sat up and wrapped their blankets around them waiting to see who would be called. Darlina held her breath praying that it wasn't Luke.

An older woman openly sobbed when a nurse came to get her.

After a while, everyone settled back down. Darlina discovered over the next few nights, that this was the normal scene. Sometimes they made it through a whole night without a Code Blue but most often they didn't.

The minutes and hours bled together in this strange world where death and the struggle to live bound strangers together into some sort of family.

On the third day, Darlina was relieved to find the breathing tube removed and Luke could have a few ice chips.

His voice sounded hoarse when he tried to talk, but that didn't stop him. "Honey, you scared the hell out of me getting sick."

"Well, mister, you scared the hell out of me too. Now what was it that you've tried so hard to tell me on the back and palm of my hand?"

Luke grinned. "I needed a drink of water terribly bad. I was drawing a W on your hand and I couldn't get you to understand."

"Sweetheart, I couldn't have given you any water. You had a breathing tube shoved down your throat."

"I know that now, but I was so sedated and disoriented I didn't know up from down. It was frustrating that I couldn't make you understand what I needed."

Darlina leaned over and laid her head next to Luke's. "I've missed you so much, baby. I've prayed minute by minute that you'd pull through."

"You look tired," Luke croaked.

"I am, but I'm doin' okay. I'll be glad when they get you moved to a room so I can spend more time with you."

Luke nodded and closed his eyes. Just the small amount of talking had worn him out.

When she was sure he was asleep again, she tiptoed out.

Luke continued to improve and after five days in ICU, the doctor wrote orders to transfer Luke to a room where visiting would be less restrictive.

At the next opportunity, Darlina let Luke know that she needed to make a quick trip home for clean clothes and to see the children.

He agreed and insisted she go and stay the night once they had him situated in a room.

By four o'clock on the fifth day, Luke was placed in a semi-private room with an older man who'd undergone the same heart surgery. Once Darlina was sure he had everything he needed, she left her contact information at the nurse's station and wearily drove the fifty-two miles from Abilene to Coleman.

She was anxious to see the girls and get a real shower. The muscles across her shoulders felt as if they'd been put in a vise and twisted almost to the breaking point. Perhaps Luke was right. She should sleep in her own bed for a night, then head back early in the morning.

Darlina pulled into the driveway, grabbed her bag and ran to the door. She dropped the bag and quickly pulled the door shut to keep out the bitter cold. The girls and their granny were seated at the dinner table. They jumped up and ran to her, both wrapping their arms around her. She hugged them tightly and moved with them still holding on to her, to her mother and embraced her.

Walking into the trailer and smelling good home-cooked food was the comfort Darlina desperately needed. Everything was spic and span. Her mother was, without doubt, an angel.

Tears glistened on her cheeks as all of the tiredness from the many days and nights at the hospital washed over her.

"Honey, you look like death warmed over."

"I've been sick, Mama, and sleeping in the hospital lobby. I'm exhausted. But, they've moved Luke into a room so I'm going to spend the night here tonight and drive back early in the morning. How are things going?"

"We're just fine." Her mother quickly got another plate from the cabinet. "You need to eat."

Darlina took a seat at the table and answered all of the girls' questions while she ate steaming hot homemade enchiladas. They had so much to tell her about school, their friends and games they'd played with their granny. They talked over each other and couldn't get their words out fast enough.

Darlina smiled warmly while they talked. "Sounds like you girls have been busy. Are you being good and helping Granny?" Both nodded. "I'm so proud of both of you, and Mama, I can never ever thank you enough for all of this."

"Oh, phooey. Don't think a thing of it. I've loved being here with my girls. You finish eating. I'm going next door to get

Luke's mother. I know she'll want to hear everything you have to say. That way you'll only have to tell it once."

"Good idea," Darlina said wearily. "I want to shower, wash my hair and go to bed so I can be back in Abilene early in the morning."

After telling both mothers and the children details about Luke, she told them goodnight, excused herself, unpacked her bag and headed to the shower.

Almost before Darlina could turn back the covers and lay her head on the pillow, she fell asleep.

Vaguely, in her subconscious, she could hear the sounds of the washing machine and knew her mother was washing her dirty clothes. She had so much to be thankful for, but most of all, that Luke was on the way to recovery.

The doctor had warned them this would be a slow journey, but it didn't matter as long as each day brought improvements.

If nothing else, this had shown the number of people who cared.

Sometimes wealth wasn't measured in the amount of money you had or the kind of house you lived in. There were times in life when it reached far beyond the physical.

For Luke and Darlina Stone, over and again, their love carried them through tempestuous storms, over insurmountable mountains and across swollen streams. They were blessed and they knew it.

Chapter 20

She was up, dressed and out of the house before six a.m. A good night's sleep had done wonders for Darlina's well-being.

On the drive back to Abilene, she hummed along with the radio. An anxiousness to see Luke filled her.

Arriving at the hospital at such an early hour, she got a good parking place, grabbed her purse and ran to the front door.

The stinging winter wind whipped and tugged at her coat. She gathered it tighter, put her head down and made a dash for it.

Her good mood and light spirit vanished the minute she walked through the door of Luke's hospital room. He thrashed around on the bed, obviously agitated.

"Luke! What's wrong?" She pulled her coat off and tossed it into a nearby chair.

"Call that damn doctor. I want you to get him over here right now."

"Okay, but please tell me what's wrong."

"The goddamn night nurse refused to give me and this man next to me our pain medication and I'm hurtin' like a sonofabitch. The last thing Dr. Carl said to me last night was not to stress and if I hurt, to tell 'em."

"I don't understand, honey. Why wouldn't she give you your medication?"

"Because she was stealing it. She brought me Tylenol and a Colace and told me it was my pain meds. I ain't stupid and I told her so. All I know is that I don't want her in this room again. Now, go call the doctor. Please."

Darlina hurried from the room to the nurse's station. "Can you please page Dr. Carl for me?"

An older lady looked up from the chart she was working on. "What's wrong?"

"My husband is in room 324 and he has been denied pain medication. He is hurting and has been all night. Please page him right away."

The lady stood. "I'll page Dr. Carl, but I will personally be down to see Mr. Stone in just a minute."

"Thank you."

Darlina fairly ran back to the room and told Luke what the nurse said.

His agitation increased. "There's a damn phone right here on the table. Call his office. I don't trust any of these nurses."

Darlina didn't try to argue. She looked the number up in the phone book with shaking hands and placed the call.

Dr. Carl's answering service picked up.

Darlina quickly explained that there was an emergency with one of his patients and would she please contact the doctor.

Just then, the older nurse came into the room with a syringe and pills in hand.

"Mr. Stone, I understand that you are in pain. I've brought you some medicine."

"Lady, I've been in pain all damn night and so has this old gentleman here next to me. The night nurse refused to give us our pain meds."

"I'm so sorry sir. The doctor is on his way, but in the meantime, I'll administer morphine through your IV and that should relieve the discomfort."

"The old man over there needs some too." Luke snapped.

"I'll tend to him."

Darlina chewed her fingernails as she watched. Guilt washed over her. She should have stayed last night and this wouldn't have happened. What if he had a setback?

Once the nurse had dispensed medicine to both men and left the room, Darlina pulled a chair up to the bed and sat, taking Luke's free hand in her own. She could clearly see the agitation subside as the medicine took effect.

"I'm sorry, honey. I should have stayed here last night."

"No, you shouldn't have. That good-for-nothing excuse for a nurse should have picked on someone else to steal their dope. I'm glad you went home. You look like you feel better."

"It was great to see the girls and take a real shower, but even more wonderful to sleep in our own bed. I can't wait to get you back home, sweetheart."

"Yeah, me too." He caressed Darlina's cheek. "I'm gonna do everything I can to get out of here as fast as possible."

"I know you will, honey."

In less than an hour, Dr. Carl strode through the door.

He listened while Luke retold the events of the night. "I can assure you, Mr. Stone, that nurse won't work on this floor again.

I'll see to it. I don't want you in pain. That puts stress on your heart. Those were my written orders."

"Yeah well, Doc, she had another agenda."

"Let me examine you while I'm here."

Darlina moved out of the way and watched as the doctor listened to Luke's heart and lungs, then examined the incisions.

"I want to get you up and moving within the next couple of days, Mr. Stone. That is part of the healing and I know it's going to hurt, but we'll give you medication. The main thing is that we don't want pneumonia to set in."

"Neither do I." Luke shifted in the bed. "Can my wife stay here in the room with me tonight?"

"No sir. As long as you are in a semi-private room, no one is allowed to stay."

"Then, see about moving me to a private room. I don't give a shit what it costs. She doesn't need to sleep in a chair in the lobby."

Dr. Carl glanced at Darlina. "I'll check into it, Mr. Stone. Is there anything else?"

"No sir."

"I'm sorry about your experience last night. Rest assured it won't happen again."

After the doctor had gone, Darlina settled back into the chair next to Luke's bed. With the pain meds in his system, he dozed off. From the snores coming beyond the other side of the curtain, apparently the other patient was asleep too.

When she was sure Luke would be asleep for a while, she picked up her purse and tiptoed from the room.

Making a beeline for the lobby, she dug the insurance card out of her wallet and dialed the eight-hundred-number.

Once she relayed Luke's situation from the night before, the lady on the other end assured her they would approve payment for him to be in a private room.

With a sigh of relief, she grabbed a steaming cup of coffee from the cafeteria and headed upstairs, encouraged that she would soon be able to stay with him.

She hurried back, anxious to make sure he was all right. Relieved to find him still sleeping, she settled into the straight-backed chair next to the bed and sipped her coffee.

She tried to remember when she'd developed such a love for the hot black liquid. Ah yes, it was in her pot-smoking days. Nothing went better with a joint than a cup of coffee. She almost giggled out loud remembering that crazy time in her life. Thank goodness it was short-lived.

She took a book out of her bag and opened it. It was going to be a long day.

***

That evening, Eli and Georgia came to visit Luke. Then, a little later, another cousin who lived in Abilene came in along with Betty.

It was easy to tell that visiting wore him out quickly so Darlina was glad they kept their stay brief.

Once everyone had left and Luke was dozing again, Darlina headed toward the elevator on her way to the cafeteria. A nurse stopped her with good news. Luke would be moved to a private room tomorrow. She quickened her steps to make sure she'd be back when Luke awakened. She couldn't wait to ease his mind with the news. Darlina was determined she would stay in the room with him as long as the nurses would allow it.

When she returned thirty minutes later, he was still asleep.

She sat down in the chair beside his bed and opened her book. After a while, she dozed off, only to wake up with a crick in her neck. She stretched and rolled her shoulders to loosen the muscles.

Luke stirred and opened his eyes. "You're still here, baby."

Darlina reached for his hand. "Of course. Where else would I be?"

"Hell, I figured they'd run you out by now."

"The nurses have been very nice. They're moving you into a private room tomorrow."

Luke gave her a groggy smile. "That's great, sweetheart. I'd give anything if you could crawl up here in the bed beside me."

"Yeah, me too, but we both know that isn't possible. Don't worry. Unless they run me off, I'll be right here with you."

He yawned and shifted in the bed. "They better not mess with my angel."

She laid her hand softly on the side of his face. "Just rest, sweetheart."

"I love you, darlin'." He closed his eyes.

She leaned down, kissed his forehead and whispered, "I love you more."

The nurses came in every four hours like clockwork to monitor vitals and dispense pain medicine, so Luke rested well.

Darlina determined she could do anything for one night and survive it. At least she wasn't out in the cold and she could get up and walk around the hallways when she got too stiff from sitting.

By noon the next day, Luke was in private room. It had a chair that folded out into a bed for Darlina.

***

The hospital stay lasted a total of fourteen days. Twice, Darlina went home for clean clothes and twice, Granny brought the girls and Luke's mother up to see him.

It became obvious this would be a long slow recovery.

With Luke's breastbone split open and an incision that ran down the entire inside length of his left leg, nothing was going to heal quickly.

But, he was alive and getting stronger every day and for that, Darlina gave thanks.

Finally, on March 1, 1989, Luke was released from Humana hospital in Abilene.

Follow-up appointments were set. It seemed there would be many trips back and forth to Abilene for Luke and Darlina Stone over the months ahead.

A male nurse assisted Luke into the car for the ride home. He stretched out on the backseat with a pillow and blanket. Every time the car hit a bump, he groaned.

"I'm sorry, honey," Darlina apologized. "I'm tryin' to miss as many bumps as I can."

"That's all you can do. It just hurts like hell. There is no way to describe what having your chest split open feels like."

She slowed the car and carefully watched the road.

When they reached Coleman, she could tell Luke was in great discomfort and Darlina helped him hobble slowly from the car to the house and drop into his easy chair.

Her mother hovered nearby ready to lend a helping hand. She'd agreed to stay until the weekend to help with getting them settled, then she would go back to East Texas.

Even though Darlina hated to leave Luke, she couldn't wait to go to work the next day. Any routine was welcome after a month of topsy-turvy. At least she knew her mother would keep a watchful eye on him and call if anything went wrong.

Words could not describe how much Luke enjoyed being home and he itched to be back at work. He needed to feel useful again and be doing things with his hands. But that would come in time. For now, he had to be patient and let the healing happen.

He watched his mother-in-law carrying laundry from the girls' rooms and tidying up from breakfast. "Granny, I know you didn't think too much of me when I married Darlina, but I hope I've proven to you how much I love her and these girls."

Granny put down the clothes and sat facing Luke. "I won't lie to you. I had my doubts about Darlina's sanity when she married you. But, surely you understand where I was coming from with you being in prison and all."

"Of course I do. I look at these two little girls and can't imagine what I'd do if they brought a worthless ex-con home to marry."

"I know you're a good man. I think you're too hard on the little girls, but that's your business as long as you don't hurt 'em. That's when it becomes my business."

"I'll never hurt them. I just want to teach them to be responsible adults and to grow up knowing how to do things. I don't want either one of them to be the kind of woman who has to

have a man to do things for them. I want them to be independent and strong."

"I understand. Like I said, I don't agree with your methods,
but I do agree with the theory."

"Thank you for coming and staying through this ordeal. I
can never repay you."

"Yes, you can. You can take care of my daughter and grandchildren. That's all the payment I need or want."

Tears misted Luke's eyes and he choked on his reply. "I give
you my word, Granny."

She set her mouth, stood and picked up the laundry. "Can I
get you anything?"

"No, I'm gonna sit here and rest. I swear I've never hurt like
this in my life."

"Don't push it and let things heal. Eventually, it'll only be a
memory."

"I'm ready for that part." Luke closed his eyes.

He dozed off and on through the morning. Gary came in to
talk about the sign business and his mother came over to keep a
worried eye on him.

When Darlina came through the door on her lunch break, his
eyes lit up. "You're a sight for sore eyes," he murmured when
she leaned down to kiss him.

She grinned. "Too much mothering going on?"

"Maybe just a little. But, I'm glad they're here."

"Me too. It made it easier to go to work." Darlina accepted
the plate her mother handed her. "Have you walked yet
today?"

"No. I was waiting until you got home."

"Then we'll walk a little bit back and forth across the living room before I go back to work. You've got to keep moving."

"I know. I just don't trust myself yet until I get stronger."

"And, you will, baby. We aren't gonna rush anything."

Darlina looked around her. With the two mothers hovering nearby and Luke home, all was right with the world.

Now, they just needed time. Time to heal, time to regroup, time to grow strong again.

Luke recuperating from open-heart surgery

# Chapter 21

The next few weeks brought slow improvement. Luke still couldn't resume working, either at the sign shop or EDP studios.

One morning he sat in his easy chair mindlessly watching TV. He never imagined he'd be sitting in the house watching soap operas until the girls came home from school. How long has it been? A month? More? What was he turning into?

Thankfully, Gary had agreed to stick around and hold the sign business together along with Felix. Luke thought about walking out to the shop to check on things, but the effort of moving ruled that out for now.

He looked longingly at his pipe. Maybe just a couple of puffs on it would soothe his frayed nerves.

The words of Dr. Robertson came flooding back through his mind. *"Mr. Stone, you can keep smoking and we'll see you back in a year or two and do this heart surgery all over again...."*

The hell with him. What did he know anyway? He reached for the pipe, filled it with cherry flavored tobacco and tamped it down. Leaning back, he lit it and took a long draw.

His eyes watered and he started coughing. Oh Lord, how it hurt. He felt as if his chest would explode, even though the breastbone was starting to heal. The pain of each cough took his breath. He quickly laid the pipe back in its holder. That obviously wasn't going to work.

He popped a pain pill in his mouth and leaned back, trying to get his breath.

A knock on the front door startled him. "Come on in," he croaked.

Eli poked his head in. "You up to some company?"

Luke shifted in the chair and blew his nose. "Sure. Have a seat."

Eli sat on the chair next to Luke's. "How are you feeling, Bubba?"

"Like I've been run over by a damned freight train."

Eli chuckled. "I'm sure. Can I do anything for you or get you anything?"

"Nah, I reckon not. I just sit here in this chair like a dawdling old woman day in and day out. Sometimes, I think I'm losing what little mind I have left."

"Why don't you ride with me to the studio? Get out of the house for a few hours."

"I don't really feel like it, Eli." Luke focused on a speck on the ceiling he'd never noticed before.

"I think it'd do you good. We've got some tracks mixed down that I'd like for you to hear."

Luke reluctantly sat forward in the chair. "I guess it wouldn't hurt nothin'. As long as I'm home before the kids get off the school bus."

Eli stood and offered Luke his arm. "Let me help you."

Luke ran his hands through his uncombed hair and jammed a ball cap down on his head. "I can do it. I just have to move slow."

Maybe it would do him good to look at some different walls. It sure got lonely with just himself, his thoughts and the TV. But most of all it was feeling useless that gnawed at his gut.

He was more than anxious to get back to work and help Darlina shoulder the load.

Luke Stone had never been one to roll over and give up. When Dr. Robertson advised him that it would take six months to heal enough to go back to work full-time, he'd scoffed.

But, damned if he could get any strength built up, even though it had been well over a month since the surgery.

"Penny for your thoughts." Eli started the pickup and backed out of the driveway.

Luke refused to pull the seatbelt across his chest and slumped forward to take the pressure of sitting up off his wounded chest.

"Not worth a penny." He snorted. "Tell me what you're taking me to hear."

"That ol' boy from over at Comanche laid down some good tracks last week. I think you're gonna like what we got."

"He has the best song that's come through the door yet." Luke ignored the concerned look Eli shot him.

"Bubba, I know you've been through a lot, but it's time to start trying to live again."

"What the hell do you know about it, man? You ever had your chest split open and your heart laid out on a table?" He didn't attempt to hide the sharpness in his voice.

"You're right. Forget I said anything."

The two men rode in silence and Luke again brushed aside Eli's attempt to help him out of the truck and inside the building.

A man's pride was something he had to hold on to as long as he possibly could and his hung by a thread.

After an hour, he had to admit it felt good to be out of the house and thinking about something other than his damn chest.

Music always lifted him up. He listened intently to the song Eli played. The man had a decent voice and the words told a deep and emotional story about a Vietnam war veteran.

"Well, you're right about one thing, stud. This is the best one yet." Luke sipped ice tea he'd brought with him.

"I'm going to push it everywhere I can and see what happens," Eli said.

By the time Eli brought him back home, he was in better spirits, but very tired.

When the girls got home from school, he was deeply asleep in his chair. The sound of the door opening startled him and for a minute he felt disoriented.

"Who's there?" he called out.

"Daddy, it's just us." Lily sat her school books down on the table with a thud.

"Do you have to be so loud?" he snapped.

"Sorry, Daddy." She picked up the school books and headed to her bedroom with Nicole behind her.

He scolded himself. Why did every little thing bother him so much? He was grouchy and snapping at the girls over nothing, not to mention Darlina.

In that moment, he hated himself. Was he going crazy? He didn't know. Maybe he needed to go back and see the doctor.

Something had to give. He slowly eased his way out of the chair and walked to Lily's bedroom. "Honey, I'm sorry. I didn't mean to yell at you."

Lily looked up with tears wetting her eyes. "I didn't mean to be so loud."

Luke tried to bend down to hug her, but winced with pain. "Come back in the living room and sit with me while you do your homework."

He spied Nicole lingering in the doorway between their rooms. "Come here, Bear." He motioned to her.

Nicole ran forward and hugged Luke. "Are you gonna be alright, Daddy?"

"Of course I am." He ruffled her hair. "I'm just having a bit of a hard time right now. You girls come keep me company."

They both picked up their school work and followed Luke back to the living room.

"Can we have a snack?" Nicole asked.

"Sure. And when you're done with your homework, I want you to pick up after yourselves and wash the dishes in the sink. Mama doesn't need to have to work all day and then do every-thing here."

Darlina had valiantly kept up a good front through this. But, he wasn't blind and could see the stress she carried.

He had to do something to make it better, but what? All he knew to do was recruit the girls to pitch in and help.

By the time Darlina walked in the door, the kitchen sparkled and the living room was neat and tidy.

Luke could see the surprise on her face as she hurried in. "Sorry I'm late, baby. They had to remove some children today and it took a little longer than they anticipated."

Luke turned his face up to her when she stopped beside his chair to bend down and offer a kiss. "I'm glad you're home. I was beginning to worry."

"Oh, before I forget, I made arrangements to have a phone put in tomorrow. I can't stand for you to be here without a way to call me if you need to. Plus, we just need our own phone."

"That's great, honey. We've used Mom's long enough. What do you think about the house?"

Lily and Nicole ran into the living room and hugged their mother.

"Mama, Nicole and I cleaned up for you." Lily stood just under Darlina's chin.

Seeing them side-by-side, Luke wondered again when Lily had gotten so grown up.

"Thank you so much, girls. I thought a couple of fairies broke in and did it. What would you like to have special for supper?"

"Spaghetti."

"Sweetheart, Daddy doesn't like spaghetti, but I'll make some for you girls and make him something different."

Luke scowled. "You shouldn't have to cook two different meals."

Darlina chuckled. "Then maybe you should eat spaghetti." She saw him set his lips in a thin line and go silent. "Honey, I was only joking. Tell me about your day."

"Not much to tell. Went out to the studio with Eli for a bit and came home totally exhausted. I'm just not getting better as fast as I want to." He drummed the arm of the chair with his fingers.

Darlina knelt down and caressed Luke's cheek. "It's going to take time. Don't rush it."

Luke placed his hand over hers. "I thought I learned patience in prison, but damned if I can pull any of it up right now. Will you call Dr. Robertson tomorrow and see if I can get in right away to see him?"

Darlina stood with questions in her eyes. "Of course, Luke. Are you having complications?"

"I don't know what I'm having, but it ain't good. I need to talk to the doc."

He watched her chew her bottom lip and knew he owed her more explanation, but how could he admit to her that he was depressed and fighting suicidal thoughts?

"I'll call first thing in the morning. I'm going to fix supper now and I have a nice piece of deer steak thawed out for you."

"My favorite. Gary bringing the deer meat was a godsend. I need red meat right now. That's the greasy Indian in me."

"And you shall have it, sweetheart." Soon the rattle of pots and pans filled the space.

Luke watched Darlina move around the tiny kitchen. Again, he was plagued with thoughts of failure. She should have a big fancy kitchen to cook in. Hell, she should have a brick home to live in instead of a damned patched-up trailer house.

She'd given up everything to come and be with him and this wasn't what she deserved.

He remembered the books he'd studied in prison about mind control. Perhaps he could will his body to heal quicker. He needed to get back to work.

And he needed to take care of his hot young wife. They hadn't made love in well over two months and that thought stuck in his craw like a bitter pill.

Hell, he was pretty much worthless.

He hated people who pitied themselves. The kind of man he'd always believed he was never ever gave up or had pity parties. So much seemed to be out of his control.

That night, lying in bed, with Darlina's warm body curled up next to him, he stroked her hair and kneaded her back. "Sweetheart, I need to make love to you in a bad way. It's not right that you have to suffer along with me."

Darlina raised her head and looked into his face. "That's what people who love each other do. We'll make love when you're ready."

Luke groaned. "I'm way past ready. My old chest hurts so damn bad, I don't think I can."

Darlina grinned a sinfully wicked grin and ducked her head under the covers. "Just don't you dare have another heart attack and it be my fault."

Luke's breath caught in a gasp as she found his hardness with her mouth. "Oh hell. It'd be worth it."

When she came up, he held her head in both of his hands. "I love you, baby." Tears hung heavy on his lashes. "I want to give you the world. Do you even begin to realize how frustrating all of this is to me?"

"Maybe just a little bit. But, honey, we're going to get through it." She kissed his fingertips and molded her body to his. He knew she took special care not to put her arm over his chest like she'd been accustomed to doing. He owed her so much.

Her words echoed in his mind long after her soft breathing told him she was asleep.

He'd faced illness and even death in prison and he'd survived it alone.

Now he had Darlina and two young girls depending on him to make it through this one.

He sucked in a determined breath. He would get control over this darkness that seemed to take over the minute he was by himself.

If he could just talk to the doctor, maybe he could make some sense of what was going on in his mind during the alone hours.

All he knew was that he had to get a grip, pull his boots on and get back to work.

He watched Darlina sleeping like an angel beside him, her lips slightly parted and her hair spread out on the pillow. She smelled of sweet flowers and for a minute, he almost thought he saw her lips curve into a tender smile.

God, he loved this woman.

Why then did he even think for a second about ending his life? That was no way to repay the woman he loved. He needed answers and he needed them fast.

Chapter 22

Darlina sat with her hands folded on her lap in Dr. Robertson's office, listening to what Luke told the young doctor.

She'd insisted on going in with him, even though he wanted her to stay in the waiting room. Whatever was going on with him, she needed to hear it, and also the doctor's reply.

Worry had plagued her since Luke asked her to get an earlier appointment. She turned her attention to what Luke was telling Dr. Robertson.

"Doc, I don't know what's wrong with me. I feel like I'm going crazy. Every little damn thing gets on my nerves and I've been grouchy with Darlina and the girls over nothing."

Dr. Robertson nodded and Luke continued.

"I can't make love to my young hot wife and that's killing me."

Darlina blushed under Dr. Robertson's gaze.

Luke went on. "But worst of all, I've even had suicidal thoughts."

Darlina gasped out loud. Why hadn't Luke confided in her? Had she locked him out without being aware? She tightened the grip on her hands in her lap.

When Luke finally stopped talking, Dr. Robertson leaned forward in his chair. "Mr. Stone, what you're experiencing is completely normal after open heart surgery. For all intents and purposes, you were dead for a period of time while we worked on your heart. Depression most always goes hand in hand with this surgery."

"Why in the hell didn't you prepare me for this, Doc?" Luke rubbed his forehead.

"Because I didn't want you to think you had to go through it. A few don't. However, the majority do. As far as having sex with your wife, give yourself a little more time." He glanced at Darlina. She blushed again under his gaze. He continued. "And there are more ways to have sex than missionary style."

Luke grinned at the doctor. "Hell, I know lots of different sex positions. I just didn't know if I could do any of them."

"Experiment. Do what works for you. I promise you, Mr. Stone, you'll heal in time."

"That's damned good to hear."

It seemed to Darlina that Luke forced himself to look everywhere in the room except at her. Private man that he was, she knew that he hated for her to hear all of this, but she deserved to know.

"I'd like to prescribe an anti-depressant. It will help level you out." Dr. Robertson scribbled on the chart he held.

"Shit, man. I don't need any dope. I've been down that road before in prison when they gave me Valium until I got so soggy

I couldn't think straight. As long as I know I'm not going crazy, I can deal with it."

Darlina spoke for the first time since they'd sat down with Dr. Robertson. "Are you sure, Luke?"

"Yes, I'm damned sure. Thank you for seeing me, Doc."

"That's what I'm here for. If you have any other complications or concerns, call my office. If you change your mind about the medication, I can call in a script. Otherwise, just keep your next regularly scheduled appointment."

Luke stood and extended his hand. "I appreciate your honesty, Doc."

They walked back to their car in silence. Luke reached for Darlina's hand.

Once inside the car, she turned to him. "Luke, why couldn't you tell me all of that?" Even though she fought it, tears stung her eyelids.

"I didn't want to say the words out loud. Honey, it's pure hell me sittin' there day in and day out, watchin' TV, dozing off and on just waiting…waiting for the girls to get off the school bus…waiting for you to come home from work…waiting to feel like a man again."

She put her hands on each side of Luke's face and looked deep into his eyes. "Don't you ever, I mean ever, let yourself think about suicide again, Luke Stone. I love you and can't imagine life without you. If you want to hurt me to the core, that'd be the quickest way to do it and it would tell me that I mean nothing to you; that all we've faced meant nothing."

Luke placed his hands over hers and closed his eyes. "Sweetheart, you're my whole world. It's not fair that I sit on my ass while you carry the entire load."

Her voice was soft. "It's only temporary. You've got to find some patience."

Opening his eyes and staring past her, he replied, "I'm tryin'."

She turned the key in the engine. "Promise that you'll talk to me when you have crazy thoughts like this. Maybe you need to get into doing some artwork or beadwork to busy your hands. Mama always said that an idle mind is the devil's workshop."

"Yeah, you're right. I've gotta find something to do during the day while you girls are gone. It still hurts like hell to move, but I will have to force myself. You know what else?"

"No, what?"

"As soon as the weather warms up, I want to go fishing. I want to take you girls out to a tank I used to fish in when I was a boy."

"That sounds like fun. See, we have things to look forward to." She caressed Luke's arm. "You can't give up."

She saw a determined set in Luke's mouth. "No, I can't. If you don't give up on me, I damned sure can't give up on myself."

"That's what I need to hear, Luke. And we'll go fishing or camping or whatever you want to do. The girls and I would love that."

"I've been so focused on working and building a home that I haven't allowed myself to think about any kind of pleasure like that, but maybe it's time."

"Yes, maybe it is."

Darlina dared to breathe a sigh of relief. She promised herself she would keep a closer eye on Luke until she was sure he was past this rough time. She would call him during the day and maybe share a funny story or a new song she'd heard on the radio; anything to keep him from feeling completely alone.

***

Springtime brought fresh renewed energy as flowers began to bloom and robins returned to build nests. Nothing more was ever mentioned about Luke's depression or suicidal thoughts, as he found the strength and determination he needed to get past it.

True to his word, the first warm weekend of April, Luke took Darlina, Lily and Nicole fishing in a large stock tank just outside Coleman.

Luke had borrowed fishing rods and reels from his mother, along with his father's tackle box. When he opened the lid to the box, a flood of memories came back. Memories of he and his dad fishing together at Lake Coleman, Hord's Creek, Pecan Bayou or this stock tank where he now stood.

He came from a long line of fishermen. His grandfather had fished most nearly every day of his life until he died. He'd held the title of being the best fisherman in Coleman County for many years.

Now, here Luke was with his girls. He couldn't wait to wet a hook, but first he had to get rigs ready for his princesses.

"Honey, I can't remember the last time I went fishing." Darlina held the rod and reel Luke handed to her and practiced throwing it while Luke rigged cane poles for Lily and Nicole. "And it's such a beautiful day."

Sunlight reflected off her auburn hair and Luke couldn't take his eyes off her. Before he knew it, he stabbed his thumb with a hook. He wiped the drop of blood on his handkerchief and focused on his task. "Here you go, Lily. Can you put a worm on your hook, or do you need help?"

"I can do it." Lily's determination to be independent was not missed by Luke.

"Well, if you need help, let me know." He turned to Nicole. "You ready, Bear?"

"Is it going to hurt the fish, Daddy?" Nicole's soft heart for all animals never changed.

"Nah. They'll never feel it." He finished putting a red and white bobber on the line and handed the pole to Nicole.

"I can't stick a worm with the hook, Daddy. I know that'll hurt the worm."

"Here, let me see your hook." Luke pushed a worm onto the tiny hook. "Now, just drop it in the water and see what happens."

He turned his attention to Darlina. "Do you need any help, baby?"

"Just help me get rigged up and I think I can handle it from there."

Luke took the line and dug around in the tackle box until he found a hook that wasn't rusted, and snapped it onto Darlina's line along with a red and white bobber. He grinned at her. "Sure you can put a worm on?"

"Yes, I'm sure," she replied indignantly.

He couldn't resist patting her pert bottom as she made her way around him, close to where the children were fishing. She flashed him a wide smile.

Luke expertly rigged his rod and reel and cast it out into the tank. He settled down on a rock and watched his girls. Every once in a while, he'd reel his line in and throw it back out.

It didn't matter if they caught a fish or not. Being outdoors in the warm sunshine was good medicine.

More than that, being with his girls topped everything else. He reflected back over the past three months.

How could he have let depression overtake him? What had happened to everything he'd learned in prison? If anything had been depressing, it was finding himself locked behind walls and bars for years on end.

With the infinite expanse of Texas sky overhead, sun shining on his skin and the ones he loved most close by, life was good.

After an hour or so, Nicole screamed and threw down her fishing pole. "Mama, something crawled on me."

Darlina jumped up and ran to the child. "Stop squirming and let me see." She inspected Nicole's arms and legs and found nothing. "Sweetie, I think maybe grass brushed against you. I don't see anything."

"I'm hungry." She folded her arms across her chest.

"Okay. I brought food. Anyone else want anything?" She headed toward the pickup.

Luke started to scold them for making so much noise but stopped himself. What did it matter anyway? He stood and gingerly stretched. "I could use one of those sandwiches you packed, honey."

"I'm hungry too, Mama." Lily leaned her fishing pole against a scrub oak tree.

"Fishing sure does make us hungry, doesn't it?" Luke joined Lily, putting his arm around her shoulders.

She looked up at him and grinned. "Sure does."

His little family spent the entire day at the tank. Lily caught a few small perch. Luke praised her and used them as bait on his own hook.

As soon as Lily caught her first fish, Nicole's interest renewed and with a fresh worm on the line, she sat back down on a rock.

Before long, her pole jiggled and she jerked it out to find a tiny perch. The minute she saw it, she burst into tears.

"What's wrong, Nicole?" Luke went to her.

"I hurt that little fish." She bent over to look at it and through her tears apologized. "I'm sorry little fish." She looked up at Luke. "Can you take it off and put it back, Daddy?"

"Honey, we don't catch 'em to just put 'em back. I can use this one for bait to catch a bigger fish."

Once Luke had the tiny fish off of her hook, she abandoned the pole and the entire idea of fishing. She sat close to Darlina and drew in the dirt with her finger. "Mama, I don't like fishing."

"Well, then just sit here by me or go pick some of those little yellow flowers over there. Or, you can get in the back of the pickup and play with your ponies. That'd be fun."

By the time the sun turned red and began to sink behind the horizon, they had three fair sized catfish and a couple of large yellow perch.

Luke couldn't remember when he'd had a better day. He thought about the many spring seasons he'd spent behind bars, dreaming of sitting in the sunshine with a fishing pole in the water. He'd always wake up to the gray walls and disappointment would wash over him. But no more. That was in the past and with freedom, he had it all.

As they loaded the fishing gear into the back of the pickup, the girls scooted onto the seat, their faces pink from the sun and streaked with dirt.

Once he slammed the tailgate, Luke pulled Darlina close to him. "Baby, I have enjoyed this so much. Did you have fun?"

She pressed herself against him, taking care not to put pressure on his chest. "It was a wonderful day, Luke. It was great to be outside in the sunshine and we actually caught some fish. Thank you for taking mine off the hook for me."

He grinned. "Baby, don't you know by now, I'd do most anything for you."

"I only want one thing. Stay in my life forever."

"Forever's a mighty long time, darlin'." He brushed his fingertips across her lips.

"Not when you're the keeper of someone's heart," she said softly. "Let's go home. I can't wait for bedtime." She walked around to the driver's side of the pickup and slid across the seat next to Nicole.

Luke drove and Lily hummed to herself while Nicole dozed on Darlina's shoulder.

The future offered renewed hope. He glanced over at Darlina and the children. If his chest wasn't already split open, he was sure it would burst with the love he had for them.

How many second chances can one man have? He'd been given a second chance at freedom, having a family and now a second chance at life itself. He would make damn sure he took full advantage of it.

He looked up at the brilliant cinnamon sky and mentally gave thanks to the Great Spirit. *"Just watch me,"* he thought. *"Just watch."*

Chapter 23

Spring of 1992 arrived with all of its West Texas beauty. The cactus flowers bloomed, tiny rosebuds popped out and Luke tilled a large garden plot behind his mother's empty house.

He stretched and pulled his cap down lower on his head. He'd accomplished a hell of a lot since his heart surgery and it made him proud.

Staring at the back of his mother's old house, he thought about the day he and Gary found her unresponsive in her favorite chair. She'd died peacefully and quickly in June of 1990.

He missed stopping in every day to check on her. Sometimes he'd swear he got a whiff of her cigarette smoke.

She'd willed the house to Bobby and Cindy. He was glad he'd been able to purchase it from them for they had no plans to return to Coleman. It only made sense for him and Darlina to take it off their hands.

Then a year and few months later, Bobby gave up his fight and passed away just before Christmas in 1991. He thought about the trip he'd made to see his brother once Bobby had made the decision to *'pull the plug'* as he called it. Even in severe pain with only a few hours of life remaining in his hourglass of time, Bobby managed to play a song on the small keyboard using his one good hand. He admired that spirit.

It saddened him to think that he had no immediate family left. But, he had memories.

He wondered again what they should do with the house. It seemed a waste for it to sit vacant and unused. The answer would come. He just had to be patient.

At the sound of a car door he turned around. That meant it was five o'clock. Darlina walked toward him with her purse slung over her shoulder.

"Hi, sweetheart." He propped the hoe against a bucket and openly admired her slender curves. They'd been married seven years now and his heart still pounded when she came within a mile of him.

He'd always heard men complaining about marriage being humdrum and boring and looked for excitement or sex with other women. And, at one time in life, he'd been that kind of man. But no more. He didn't need or want anyone but his angel and couldn't imagine getting bored with her.

"Hi, yourself. This garden is really taking shape, baby." Darlina stood on tiptoes to kiss him. "I need to change out of my work clothes and then I'll come help you before I start supper."

"I think you might need my help changing clothes. Looks like you have a zipper that'll get stuck." He winked and grinned.

"I'm quite sure I probably do." Darlina flipped her hair back, stepped over the clods of dirt with his arm around her waist as they headed toward the front door. "It's so nice to have an enclosed porch now. And Nicole loves her new big bedroom. You've done so much, Luke."

He tightened his grip. "You girls have helped too. Lily and Nicole have worked as hard as anyone. Lily is gettin' to be a damned good little painter."

"They're growing up fast. You know that, don't you?"

Luke opened the door for her. "I don't even wanna think about it."

The sound of a TV came from Lily's bedroom and Nicole was nowhere in sight. "Shh," He put his finger up to his lips and softly pulled the door shut.

He loved how Darlina slipped her shoes off and quietly tiptoed to the bedroom, glancing back over her shoulder with a mischievous twinkle in her eye.

Once behind the closed door of the bedroom, she turned around for Luke to unzip her dress, then faced him as he slipped it over her shoulders.

The easy way she responded seemed like the most natural thing on earth. No, he'd never tire of her.

Sometime later, they lay tangled in damp sheets and Luke stroked her silky naked back.

Her soft breath ruffled the hairs on his chest and she traced the scar that ran from just beneath his neck to his navel. "I'm so excited to have a garden, Luke. It is going to be wonderful to have fresh vegetables."

He didn't miss the wistfulness in her voice. "You've given up so much for me, honey, and don't think for a minute I don't know."

Pushing herself up on one elbow, she wrinkled her brow. "I gave up nothing and gained everything. Since I was nineteen-years-old, all I wanted was to be your wife. I do have to admit I thought we'd be traveling around in a big tour bus making music and selling hit records. But, it doesn't matter what we're doing as long as we're doing it together."

Luke traced her parted lips with his fingertips. "From the day we first met, you believed in me more than I believed in myself. You were what inspired me to make something out of myself even though I was locked away in prison. I wanted to be good enough to deserve you."

"And I wanted the same. So, here we are. Let's get dressed and I'll go fix supper. We've used up all our gardening time already." She laughed out loud.

"Then let's get moving. Mrs. Stone." Luke sat up and reached for his blue bib overalls.

Darlina's words echoed in his mind. *"I thought we'd be traveling around in a big tour bus selling hit records."* If only he could make that dream come true for her. Under the restriction of double parole, it didn't leave much room for maneuvering around, even if he wanted to.

He thought about his Martin guitar he'd sold to Eli a few Christmases ago, so that he could buy gifts for his girls. Even though he didn't allow himself to dwell on it, he'd always remember the guitar as an old friend that had seen him through many desolate hours and hard times.

But, a deal was a deal and he didn't have the money to buy it back. No matter what, he'd always think of it fondly and knew Eli would take good care of it. He'd not been surprised when EDP studios closed the doors and dissolved the corporation in the spring of 1990. Too much partying and not enough serious work brought it to an end. He honestly enjoyed the time spent working with Eli and Georgia.

***

Two weeks later, early one morning, Darlina stood in their small kitchen filling the coffee pot with aromatic grounds and water, humming a EmmyLou Harris tune. Since she'd been hired full time with the State of Texas, she'd enjoyed having only one job.

That, and Gary moving back to work full time in the sign business with Luke had increased their monthly income. Finally, they were at least making ends meet.

She looked out the kitchen window at the fence Luke had built around the back of the property using discarded telephone poles. It resembled a fort and if he'd had his way, it would have been extended all the way to the front. She'd objected that they'd not be able to see out.

Luke came from the bedroom, walked up behind her and put his arms around her waist. "Sugar, I had a strange dream last night."

"What was it?" She continued pouring water into the tank.

"I dreamed about Mom's house. A sign hung over the front door that said The Saturday Store. I have no idea what that means or what a Saturday Store is, but you know how things come to me in dreams."

"Well, maybe we're supposed to create a Saturday store. Obviously, it would only be open on Saturdays since we have jobs during the week."

"What would we sell?"

She turned to face him. "I don't know. Maybe second-hand stuff of some sort. Coleman could use a place that isn't junked out."

"We'll think on it, but it's time to do something. We discussed the possibility of renting the house out and we decided against it. Maybe this is the answer."

"Maybe so. Let's talk more about it some more when I get home from work today." She touched his cheek and walked toward Lily's and Nicole's bedrooms. "Girls, are you up?"

"Yes, Mama," came two voices.

"Hurry and get ready so I can take you to school on my way to work."

Luke watched Darlina hurrying around the kitchen, making breakfast. She only got prettier with time. He wished he could make her know how truly beautiful she was. "You know, sweetheart, if we could come up with a used car, now that Lily has her driver's license, you wouldn't have to take them to school anymore."

"Very true. If it was possible to build a car with your bare hands, you'd have already done it. The bunkhouse you built out back is beautiful. And the way you put logs around the metal storage building makes it look like they were transported from an old West town."

"It was a lucky break getting to tear down that old barn for Mr. Scott. The wood is what makes it authentic."

"And putting the outdoor kitchen under the awning was another great idea. Luke, do you ever stop and look around at everything you've built?"

"All the time, sweetheart."

"Come on girls. Don't forget your clarinets. Today is a big day for band challenges."

"Okay, Mama." Their voices came in unison.

She grabbed a cup of coffee and headed to the bathroom.

While Luke downed his coffee, an idea formed in his mind. He found Darlina combing her hair and putting on makeup. "Sweetheart, I'm going to take off. I think I'll go visit with Mack Jordan this morning and bounce my Saturday store idea off him. He's been in the hardware business for years and I respect his opinions."

Darlina turned to kiss him. "Okay, honey. See you tonight."

He walked back through the trailer, said goodbye to the girls and went out the door.

Downtown Coleman consisted of one main street with three red lights. Mack Jordan's hardware store covered a large part of one city block. A dark-haired man in his mid-thirties, Mack had inherited the hardware store from his grandfather. Not only had he inherited the store, but also his grandfather's keen sense of business.

Luke and Gary had done sign work for Mack last year. When Luke had taken him the bid, there had been words between them about Luke robbing him. Now, when Luke thought about the incident, he chuckled, but at the time, anger rushed over him and he'd told Mack in no uncertain terms that if he wanted to rob him, he'd stick a pistol to his head and take what he wanted.

From that point forward, they'd become the best of friends with a mutual respect for each other.

Once he parked the pickup in front of Jordan's Hardware, he walked through the doors and straight to the office in the back.

Mack Jordan looked up from his paperwork and reached for a steaming cup of coffee. "What can I do for you, Luke?"

"Got a minute to talk?" Luke pulled up a chair.

Putting the papers aside, Mack replied, "Of course. What's on your mind?"

Luke related the dream about his mom's house and Darlina's suggestion about a second-hand store. "What do you think? I need to do something with the empty house and preferably something that might bring in a little money."

Taking a sip of the hot black coffee, Mack leaned back in his chair. "I think it's a great idea. And, I may have something to help you get started. Do you have time to walk over to the warehouse with me?"

"Of course."

Both men stood and Mack told the store clerk he would be back in a few minutes. They walked the short two blocks to the warehouse.

Mack unlocked the door and turned on the lights. He made his way around piles of lumber, sheetrock and paint to an area in the back. "See all this shit piled in the corner?"

"Yeah."

"I've been wracking my brain trying to decide what I could do with it besides throw it in the garbage. It's all discontinued stuff from the store. What if I inventory it out to you, then you take it out to your place and sell it for pennies on the dollar. You'd only pay me when it sold."

Luke rubbed his forehead and looked closer at the piles Mack pointed to. "This isn't trash, Mack. It's still good stuff. You sure you don't want to put it back in your store?"

"I'm damned sure. You'd be doing me a favor to take it off my hands. I've even got some old shelving I'd give you."

"Let me talk to Darlina about it tonight and I'll get back with you. It would be something to start from. Another idea I've been tossin' around is appliance repair. I worked for Maytag in San Angelo back in the 50s and early 60s when I wasn't playing music. Gary's pretty good at repairing any kind of small engines. Dammit, I want to make a livin' and it's hard as hell in this little town."

The younger man headed toward the front of the building. "Tell me about it, man."

"Shit, Mack, you've got old family money backin' you. You'll never be broke."

"I damned sure don't intend to." Mack chuckled. "Think about my offer and let me know what you decide. As far as appliance repair, I've been using old man Garcia for years, but he's gettin' old. I could give you and Gary some work that way."

Luke couldn't wait to tell Darlina. He hurried to the sign shop to find Gary already there.

After he told Gary about the dream and Mack's offer, the two of them walked next door and Luke turned the key to open the front door. It had been closed for two years and he had to give it a swift kick before it finally gave.

As they walked from room to room, memories flooded back and Luke could almost see his mom sitting in her favorite chair, cigarette hanging out of her mouth. It was past time to do something with this place. It still had life in it and needed to be utilized.

"The first thing will be to paint the ceiling and scrub the nicotine off the paneling." Luke rubbed his hand over the paneling on the living room wall.

"There's been many a shit-kickin' domino game played here and everybody smoked." Gary examined a broken switch plate on the wall.

After Gladys Stone died, Luke, Darlina and the children had worked for weeks emptying the house and selling or giving away everything they couldn't use. Now it badly needed some repairs.

Once they'd finished their inspection of the house, Gary returned to the sign shop and Luke, with list in hand, drove back to Jordan's hardware store. Mack Jordan was nowhere in sight, so he gathered buckets, Murphy's oil soap, sponges, gloves, scrub brushes, a can of Kilz paint for the ceiling and a bottle of Old English oil.

The next stop was the utility office. Luke was thrilled to hear that no deposit would be required since they already had utilities at the trailer. He felt hopeful as he made his way down the streets of the small town.

This idea just might work, and with Mack Jordan's help, would require very little money to get started. He'd recruit the girls to scrub the paneling and just as they'd done everything else, the four of them would work together.

He thought about an argument he'd had with Darlina last summer over how hard the children had to work. But, she said she understood that Luke simply wanted to teach them to be independent. She just didn't always agree with his methods of teaching nor did the kids' granny. Maybe he was too hard on them, but he only knew one way to work; the way he'd learned in the oilfield.

Lily adopted a head-on attitude, and didn't back away from anything, but Nicole still tried to wiggle out of chores whenever she could.

That night before supper, Luke, Darlina and the girls went next door to look it over and make plans.

"I like the idea, Luke, and who knows maybe with doing appliance and lawn mower repairs too, money might actually flow a little better for us and for Gary." Darlina caught her toe on a tear in the linoleum on the kitchen floor and stumbled.

Luke reached out to steady her. "I wanna rip this stuff out and put down some cheap linoleum. This is dangerous and we can't have customers tripping and falling."

"Or us." She leaned on his arm. "What do you think, girls? Can you help us turn Nanny's house into a store?"

"We can work after school." Lily stood in the doorway. "And I can help paint."

"You sure can. You've gotten very good at it." Luke praised. "We can leave the old carpet for now, but eventually, I'd like to tear all of it out too."

"I can help." Nicole bent down to examine a dead bug.

"Of course you can, Bear. There's gonna be plenty of work for everybody." Luke pointed to the ceiling. "It's gonna take more than one coat of Kilz to cover up the nicotine on the ceiling." He turned to Darlina. "All those years I smoked, I had no idea what I was doing to my body. Sure wish I'd not done it."

Darlina looked up at the dingy ceiling. "Honey, we all did things we wish we hadn't. Everyone around you smoked and you didn't know any better. I'm going to head on over and start supper. Y'all come on in a little bit."

"We'll be on over, sweetheart."

"Mama, can I come help you with supper?" Nicole asked.

"Of course. Come on."

After Darlina and Nicole left, Luke moved with Lily from room to room until it was too dark to see. Tomorrow the electricity would be turned on and they could get started. It was obvious that the place would need a lot of elbow grease.

Luke had a saying that he adhered to, *'The harder I work, the luckier I get.'*

Only time would tell. At any rate, the only way he knew to get ahead was by working hard. And he was driven to get ahead for his family.

Luke working in the garden

Chapter 24

Early Saturday morning, July 11th, Darlina and the children stood next to Luke as he turned the key in the lock of The Saturday Store and swung the door wide.

In less than three months, they'd completed renovations and inventoried stock in from Mack Jordan's warehouse. Now they were ready to open for business.

Luke and Gary had cut a wide doorway between what had been the living room and bedroom and braced the ceiling with posts to create a large open space. Shelving installed on the freshly scrubbed walls, bright white ceilings and summer yellow kitchen transformed the house from drab and lifeless to bright and cheerful.

With the sign painted just as Luke had seen in his dream, he and Gary installed it over the doorway the evening before. He hoped a small ad they'd put in the local newspaper would bring in customers.

Luke held the door and his girls walked in ahead of him. "Now to see if the saying, *'build it and they will come'* actually means anything." Hope for success swelled in his heart.

Darlina switched on the lights in each room. "I have no doubt people will come out of curiosity, if nothing else. Look at how many stopped in while we were working to ask what we were doing."

"Everybody at school has been asking me what we're doing over here." Lily held a small cash box.

Luke chuckled. "Small town livin', sweetheart. Everybody knows what you're doin', or at least wants to know." He pulled a small bell out of his pocket and attached it with a screw into the door facing. "There. That'll let us know when somebody comes through the door if we're in another room."

"Good idea." Darlina took the cash box from Lily and sat it on a card table beside the front door. "Nicole, would you please put the cookies you baked on a platter while I start some coffee perking?"

"Okay." Nicole loved everything about baking, from measuring and stirring to pulling it out of the oven and sampling. It appeared that she'd inherited the baking gene from her granny, who was an award-winning pie maker in her own right.

It had been Luke's idea to serve coffee and cookies to customers who came in on the first day. All through the day, he hovered close by as people came and went. He wanted this new venture to work and watched with apprehension as a few purchases were made.

By closing time, twelve or more customers had sauntered through the door. Nicole's cookie platter only had a few crumbs left.

He looked over Darlina's shoulder as she counted the money in the cash box. A grin formed.

She closed the lid, announcing, "We made a total of $29.82. Nothing outstanding, but for a first day, it was a start."

"Since we've spent the entire day here, how about instead of you cooking tonight, I take you girls out for Mexican food?" Luke placed a hand on Darlina's arm.

"Sounds good to me." She stood, flashing a grin. "I think we have something worth celebrating. I'll get my purse."

Luke caught a hint of excitement in the conversation over dinner that evening. He beamed with pride at how his family followed his ideas without question, and how they all had their own input. He gave thanks once more to the Great Spirit for sending him a dream and giving him another second chance at life, love and family.

***

Over the remainder of the year, the business grew slowly but steadily.

Darlina loved the two glass cases Luke bought from a flower shop that folded downtown. They placed them in the front room of the store and Darlina filled them with smaller special items.

Throughout the year, as more and more customers came in looking for antiques and collectibles, Darlina's thoughts returned to a job she'd had in high school, working at an antique store in Hobbs. The elderly lady who owned it taught her a lot about the business. She'd enjoyed learning and wondered now if they could perhaps add some of these kinds of items to their inventory.

While she, Luke and the girls decorated for Christmas, she brought up the idea.

"We could hit garage sales, estate sales and auctions to look for antiques and collectibles. I have a fairly decent knowledge of it."

Luke stopped in the middle of hanging a string of lights. "I think that's a wonderful idea. I say we really start thinking that direction by next spring and see what we can do."

Nicole helped Lily hang ornaments on the garland. "I have an idea."

"What's that, Nicole?"

"How about I bake cookies and brownies to sell?"

Darlina caught Luke's surprised glance. "That's an excellent idea, Nicole. You're a very good baker."

"I learned how to make homemade bread in Home-Ec this year." Lily stretched to reach the corner. "I could bake bread."

Luke finished attaching the lights and looked at both of the girls. "I tell you what. Me and Mama will buy all the ingredients, you girls do the baking and you get to keep the money from your sales. How's that?"

Their faces lit up.

Darlina's heart warmed at Luke's suggestion. She knew he wanted to teach them responsibility, but this was even a step further and she added, "You girls know this means you have to do it every Friday evening, no matter what's going on, so that you are always ready for Saturday morning. And, it would mean not getting to spend two weeks with your granny in the summer."

Lily appeared in deep thought. "On nights we have to play in the band at football games, we can get up early on Saturday morning and do it. Maybe Granny could come here for a couple of weeks this summer."

"Then, I think we should start next Saturday, if you girls are serious." Luke picked up the next strand of Christmas lights. "Lily, can you help me untangle this one?"

"Sure, Dad." She hopped down from the stepstool and took one end of the lights. "Me and Nicole are serious. There isn't a bakery anywhere in Coleman and it's almost Christmas. People could even place special orders if they wanted." She patiently undid one knot at a time.

Darlina grinned. "You're right, Lily, and you know we're starting to get quite a few hunters stopping by here. I'm sure they'd love some fresh baked goods to take to the deer leases."

Even though the small beginning of a store hadn't netted much money in their pockets, with new ideas, Darlina felt hopeful. She'd go to the public library and check out books on antiques to brush up on what she'd learned many years ago.

Luke glanced up at a knock on the door. Darlina rushed to open it only to find Eli.

"Come in out of the cold, Eli." Darlina held the door, accepting a hug as he stepped inside.

"Looking pretty spiffy in here." He turned in a circle taking it all in and hugged the girls as they rushed to meet him.

He ruffled Nicole's hair and turned to Lily. "I sure hope you're still singing, young lady."

She blushed. "I am. I sing in the Methodist church choir and still taking voice lessons."

"That's what I want to hear."

"What are you up to, man?" Luke handed the string of lights to Lily.

"I've got something out here in my truck that I need you to take off my hands." He jammed his hands into his pockets.

"What'cha got, stud?"

Darlina sensed that Luke suspected something, but she had no idea what it could be.

"I just need you to come out here with me and get this shit out of my truck." Eli opened the door.

Luke followed him out and Darlina and the girls watched through the window. She couldn't hear their words, but watched as Eli opened the pickup door and pulled out Luke's guitar case.

Her heart froze. What had Luke done and how had she not even noticed that it was gone?

As she watched, the two men appeared to be arguing, then Luke embraced Eli and they both wiped their eyes. The minute Luke came back inside, she rushed to him. "What was that all about, honey?"

"Back in 1988, the year I bought you the necklace, Lily the clarinet and Nicole the bicycle, I sold this ol' guitar to Eli to make Christmas happen for you girls."

A lump rose in her throat and tears threatened. "Oh, Luke, you didn't."

"And now he's brought it back, wouldn't take any money for it and made me promise to never sell it again." Luke gingerly sat the case down on top of the glass counter and opened it.

"I hope you promised." She stood beside him.

"I did." Luke grazed the strings lightly with his forefinger. "Me and this ol' Martin went through lots of hard times together. Now, she's back home and I'll never get rid of her again."

Darlina swiped at the hot tears that she couldn't keep back, her voice barely more than a whisper. "Maybe someday you'll want to play it again."

Luke sounded distant. "Maybe, but not today." He closed the case and clicked the latches. "I'll never sell it again, though."

***

The girls dove into their baking enthusiastically and word spread quickly that fresh baked goods were available at The Saturday Store.

They asked Luke to paint a sign and put it on the front of the building advertising their goods, and two weeks before Christmas, they both had special orders to fill.

Not only were they busy, but they had Christmas money in their pockets to spend.

Christmas 1992 was a special celebration with Darlina's mother coming to spend a few days with them. The spirit of the season flourished in their household.

Darlina enjoyed showing her mother the store, and talked about their plans to expand. Luke was in the process of installing a kitchen stove so that the girls could bake their cookies and bread in the store to fill the rooms with delicious smells.

Granny loved the whole concept and reminded Darlina of when they'd traveled to flea markets with boxes of carnival glass to sell. And of course, she couldn't have been more proud of Lily and Nicole, as she shared some baking tips with her granddaughters.

***

Many Coleman locals began stopping by when they had things they wanted to sell and most often caught Luke in the sign shop. He explained to Darlina that he hated giving money to people he knew were going to use it to buy drugs, but at the same time, they were going to sell what they had to someone. So, if he thought it was something that they could resell in the store for a profit, he was willing to dish out the cash.

Darlina was never surprised at what she came home to find had been added to their inventory.

***

1993 brought more expansion to the Saturday Store. Along with Gary's help, Luke enclosed what had been his mother's carport and transformed a window into a door leading down to it. Their ever increasing inventory soon filled up that room as well as every other room in the building.

Luke and Darlina frequented garage sales, auctions and estate sales, buying antiques or collectibles they thought they could resell.

Another opportunity for growth came along early that year, when the neighbor on the south side of them offered to sell his house. A trip to the bank soon had Luke and Darlina owning more adjoining property.

Luke and Gary quickly converted that house into the used appliance business they'd talked about off and on for the past two years.

With three businesses now operating on this space of property, there was always a bustle of activity.

Around midday one Saturday in the blazing hot summer that you only find in Texas, the door to the store opened and a curiously dressed woman entered. She wore a cowboy hat, cut-off blue jean shorts, black stockings, bright red lipstick, cowboy boots, dark sunglasses and an array of Indian jewelry.

Darlina sat perched on a stool behind the counter. She watched as the woman walked through the rooms, then back into the front room.

"Is there anything I can help you with?" Darlina offered.

"Do you know Luke Stone?" the woman inquired.

"Yes, he's my husband. Do you need to see him about something?"

"My husband and I are fans of his and we've wanted to meet him for a long time. Is he anywhere around?"

Taken aback, Darlina replied. "I'll get him for you." She walked to the back door and called to Lily. "Honey, can you come sit in the store while I go find Daddy?"

Lily came in and took her post behind the counter. Darlina could see the puzzled look on her face when she saw the strange woman.

"I'll be right back." Darlina opened the door. "By the way, I'm Darlina Stone. What is your name?"

"I'm Judy Gordon. My husband Roxy writes for the Coleman newspaper."

"Oh, I've seen the articles about American Indians. Luke and I always enjoy reading them. How do you know Luke?"

"We don't. We've just always been fans of his and Dean Beard's music."

"Okay. I'll be right back." Darlina hurried next door to the sign shop. She quickly explained and Luke followed her back to the store.

She listened while Luke introduced himself and the woman again explained that she and her husband were fans of his music and wanted to meet him.

"Well, go get your husband and let's get acquainted." Luke leaned against the post separating the two rooms. As soon as Judy had gone out the door, Luke turned to Darlina. "Well, how about that? I still have fans." He grinned his crooked way.

"Besides me, you mean?" She went behind the counter with Lily, but not before sending him a mischievous smile.

When the couple returned, Roxy appeared as oddly dressed as Judy with his long slightly graying hair, black flat-brim hat with a single feather sticking from the band, turquoise jewelry and beads. His pant legs were tucked inside run over boots. Together they looked very out of place in Coleman, Texas. They'd fit right in on an Indian reservation, but not this small conservative West Texas town.

After the introduction, Luke invited the couple to the trailer where he promised to share old band photos from the past and tell stories about the days of playing music. Darlina left Lily in charge of the store and joined them, sending Nicole over to help her sister.

She couldn't help but feel hopeful that somehow these people who knew so much about Luke and his music would inspire him to return to it.

After all, that was his deep passion, even though he kept it disguised and hidden. She knew he still had the clear baritone voice she'd always admired from hearing him sing along with the radio.

Since Eli had brought the guitar back, she checked on it periodically to make sure it stayed where Luke had put it. She'd make damn sure he kept his promise to never let it go again. And, she would never ever lose hope that he would play again.

Maybe, just maybe, this couple, who claimed to be fans, would be the catalyst that sent him back into making music.

Her spine tingled with the thought. She couldn't help but remember the days of being beside him while they drove up and down the roads of Texas playing his unique brand of music.

But more especially, she'd never forget the special flirtatious wink he'd give her from the stage, while he wrapped the audience around his finger. Prison had taken that out of him, or so it seemed.

Something stronger than her belief in him would have to re-kindle that flame. She longed for it and knew that deep down the dream still burned in his chest.

Hope inside her refused to die. That much she knew. She turned her attention back to the couple who sat enthralled with the story he was relating. Even though they'd been repeated over and again, she never got bored with hearing them. And, Luke never seemed to tire of telling them.

Timeless stories of another lifetime, when he was king of the honkytonks and she was his Cinderella princess.

The Saturday Store

Chapter 25

Before the evening was over, Luke and Darlina learned that Roxy and Judy lived in Dallas and that their home on Oram Street was often a landing place for songwriters such as Billy Joe Shaver, Richard Dobson, Ray Wiley Hubbard and Townes Van Zandt, with whom Roxy shared a birthday. Roxy was of Choctaw descent and had been adopted by the Assiniboine Indian Tribe and given the name First Coyote Boy.

Roxy's parents, along with his aging grandmother, resided in a tiny community just south of Coleman. His mother had mailed the article from the Coleman newspaper about Luke returning from prison a few years back, and this had renewed Roxy's desire to meet him.

Judy told a story of how she and Roxy saw Luke and Dean Beard walking down the main street of Coleman back in the 60s but were both too shy to approach them.

They spoke of wanting to move from Dallas with their young son to a slower paced life, but Judy couldn't leave her job.

It became apparent to Darlina they would never get all of their stories exchanged in one short evening. When they left, around midnight, they promised to return the next afternoon for a cookout before they headed back to Dallas.

***

The following day, Luke helped Darlina place chairs around a metal table that sat on the backyard rock patio. He piled mesquite wood into a barbecue pit he and Gary had built. All it needed was a match put to it and soon there would be a perfect mesquite fire to grill over. He'd watched Darlina marinate chicken leg quarters earlier with garlic, lime and cilantro.

He thought about how good it felt to have someone interested in his music again, and knew Roxy and Judy were genuinely sincere. He'd been around enough to know fake from real. He looked forward to more conversation with them.

When the couple arrived around one o'clock, their son, Quanah, was with them. Lily and Nicole graciously offered to play a card game with him while the adults visited.

Roxy handed Luke a package. "Here, Luke, my mom wanted you to have these."

Luke accepted the brown bag. "Hell, you didn't have to bring anything." He opened it to find record albums and 45 rpm records of his and Dean Beard's music. "Shit! I haven't seen these in years."

Roxy waved his hand. "That's nothing, man. You ought to see the house in Dallas. We've got hundreds of record albums plus an attic full."

Luke chuckled. "I used to own a record store here in Coleman back in the fifties. I've recently started buying all the vinyl I can find. Darlina and I go to garage sales and auctions and I'm always pickin' up a box for a dollar or two. I love goin' through 'em and findin' memories. I remember one time back in the 50s when Roy Orbison came through here. He'd just released *Ooby Dooby* and *Go* on a 45. He was broke and needed gas money to get on down the road. I bought a box of his records and got him a gig that afternoon playing intermission at the movie theater downtown."

"Oh hell!" Roxy leaned forward.

Judy spoke up. "Luke, would you please get your guitar and play some music for us?"

"Nah, Judy. I ain't picked it up since I got home from prison. I'm not interested in it anymore. That lifestyle is what landed me behind bars and I won't go back to it."

"Sure we can't change your mind?" Roxy poured Vodka into a glass Darlina offered him and added water.

"I'm sure." Luke quickly changed the subject. "I picked up a Garrard turntable last week and I'm anxious to set it up. I want to play all of these old records. Did you know the most valuable one right now for collectors is Bob Dylan's *Freewheelin'* album?"

"No shit?" Roxy raised his eyebrows.

"No shit. It has to be a specific one though. When it was first released, it had the original version of the *Talkin' John Birch Society Blues* on it. The record company immediately yanked it off the shelves because of the controversy. But a few hundred had already been sold. Then they re-released the album with a different cut on it."

"Hell, Judy. We need to look when we get home," Roxy said. "I know we have that record."

Judy held her cigarette for Roxy to light. "Yes, but I don't know if it's the original version."

Luke watched Darlina flitter around making food, filling drink glasses and stopping to listen, giggle, or interject a word or two into the conversation. She never ceased to amaze him the way she could whip up a delicious feast at the drop of a hat and he loved her special way of making everyone who came to their home feel welcome.

Between the two lengthy visits, Luke and Darlina discovered that Roxy and Judy had done a bit of everything from being the public relations team for David Allen Coe, living with the famous poet Richard Brautigan in California, to spending several years on an Indian reservation in Northern Montana and publishing a music magazine in New Mexico. They were also activists in the American Indian Movement and had been involved in many benefits to free Leonard Peltier from prison. But most of all and above all, Roxy was an artist, writer of songs and poems, a storyteller and an American Indian historian.

And he could drink. Man, could he drink Vodka and lots of it. Judy, coming from a German family, drank beer. She'd grown up in another tiny community just south and west of Coleman and she and Roxy had been together since high school days. Colorful was the only word that truly described these people.

Before they left that day, they'd wrangled a promise from Luke to visit them in Dallas. Roxy was scheduled to be on a show with another artist at Poor David's Pub the next month and he couldn't express enough how much it would mean to have Luke there.

Once they were gone, Luke helped Darlina pick up the leftover food and dishes. "What do you think, sweetheart?"

"About Roxy and Judy?"

"Yep."

"Well, I think they are some of the most interesting people that have crossed our path so far. I love listening to Roxy tell Indian stories. He knows everything about them."

Luke chuckled. "He's a walking encyclopedia. What about going to Dallas next month?"

"I think it'd be fun. I'm curious to see their house and it would be fun to see a Roxy Gordon show."

"Then we'll by god go. I feel a real connection to Roxy, like maybe we've known each other in another lifetime."

Darlina put the last of the dishes into the sink. "And Judy is pretty amazing herself. They've certainly done lots of things, been to lots of interesting places, and know lots of people. I'd like to hear more about the music magazine, *Picking Up The Tempo*, she kept talking about."

***

The next month, Luke and Darlina visited the Gordons in Dallas. Lily and Nicole chose to stay at home. Luke asked Darlina to drive as the thought of maneuvering through the giant of a city overwhelmed him. At least she'd lived in a big city before moving to Coleman and had more confidence in traffic.

When they arrived at the house on Oram Street, it had the appearance of total disarray and yet an artistic orderliness about it. The art pieces painted by Roxy and some by Judy that lined the walls along with various posters of music events were a treat. Most of the art carried the American Indian or American West theme and the posters made Luke feel like they were in a music memorabilia museum.

Luke and Roxy spent hours thumbing through record albums, swapping stories and keeping the turntable spinning, while Judy shared back issues of *Picking up the Tempo* with Darlina.

Before they knew it, it was time to walk the few short blocks to Poor David's Pub for Roxy's show.

Given the amount of alcohol Roxy had consumed throughout the day, Luke was amazed that he was able to stay on his feet, much less remember the words to his poems and songs.

Luke himself had imbibed to the point that he wasn't sure he could walk straight, but knew he could count on Darlina to steady him if need be.

Roxy opened his part of the show with a piece he called Indians. *"Hank Williams was an Indian but John Kennedy was not. And Chuck Berry is an Indian but Michael Jackson ain't..."*

He moved seamlessly from *Indians to Smaller Circles* and *Long Gone Texas Woman.* The raw and unfiltered folk music spoke of real events, real people and real life.

Even though it was a far cry from the kind of music Luke Stone had made back in his heyday, he appreciated the honesty and art of it. And he liked Roxy. He was an old soul like Luke.

***

Over the next few months, as Roxy's parents began to have health issues that came with aging, the trips home came more often. They spoke about Judy taking an early retirement from her job and moving to Coleman County to take care of them.

Roxy's grandmother, well into her nineties, owned a small wood-frame house on a large piece of land, which she gave to Roxy. She could no longer live alone and had moved in with her daughter (Roxy's mother).

On a cool fall Sunday morning, late in October, Roxy and Judy pulled into the driveway at Luke and Darlina's house where they were working on nailing together concrete forms.

Luke laid the hammer down and walked toward the pickup. He leaned against the door. "Good to see you. How is everyone?

"About the same. Hey, man, why don't you and Darlina come out to our place this afternoon?" Roxy leaned out the open window.

Luke glanced at Darlina and she nodded. "Sure. Can we bring anything?"

"You can bring your damn guitar with you and whatever you want to drink. Judy's got a pot of deer chili going."

"I keep tellin' you, stud, I ain't playin' no more, but we'll come out. We've got a few things we need to do here first, so we'll be there around two."

"I'll have Quanah wait at the gate to let you in." Roxy started the pickup.

"See you then." Luke waved and turned back to the project.

At two o'clock, Luke, Darlina, Lily and Nicole pulled onto the caliche road that led to the property. Sure enough, Quanah waited by the gate. Once he'd let Luke through, he wrapped a chain around it, hopped into the back of the pickup and pointed toward the road leading up a steep hill.

The pickup lurched over the pot-holes in the crude road but climbed steadily until they reached a plateau where Roxy's truck sat.

Luke killed the engine. Quanah jumped out of the back and Luke, Darlina and the girls piled from the truck. Roxy and Judy sauntered toward them.

Luke reached into the pickup, pulled a pint of Beam from under the seat and took a long look around. The rugged hill, lined with scrub oak, cedar and prickly pear cacti was one of the highest points for miles around. Directly to the north and east, historic Bead Mountain was clearly visible, then farther east, the Santa Anna Mountain loomed. Bead Mountain stood at 1,978 feet above sea level and Luke figured the hill they now stood on was close to the same.

"Nice view, Roxy."

Roxy laughed. "Yeah, as best as I can figure, this was a prime Indian lookout spot because of the clear view of all of the important peaks. I've found a shit-load of arrowheads, pottery shards and tools around here. I think it was a good spot for Indians to send smoke signals."

"Let me show you around." Judy took Darlina's arm and the group walked toward an encampment.

"This is our house-up." Roxy explained. "I started building it when I was a young boy and my grandfather would come up and help me. I played cowboys and Indians up here. At night, you can see the lights of every little town around here for miles."

The crudely constructed encampment consisted of one room, about an eight by ten with a pot bellied stove against one wall, and another room not as wide but as long, that held two iron frame beds with cotton tick mattresses on top of coil springs.

Luke chuckled. "I'm damn glad I wore my moccasins, Roxy. I feel right at home." He watched Darlina's face as she took in the sight.

Nicole asked the obvious question. "Where is the bathroom?"

Roxy laughed. "Anywhere out there you want it to be. Or at least it is for me."

"Oh, sweetie, don't listen to Roxy. I have a bathroom over here in the back of this shed for us ladies." Judy pointed to a five gallon bucket with a toilet seat perched on top.

"Oh," Nicole said lamely.

"This ain't no Hilton Hotel, girls." Luke walked to the North edge of the hill. "Would you look at this view?" Darlina joined him and he put his arm around her waist. "I dreamed of this when I was in prison. I'd think I was looking out over the countryside and then I'd wake up and see stone walls and iron bars."

"Man, I ain't never been in prison. Spent a night in jail once and that was enough for me." Roxy turned to Judy. "Judy, bring me my Vodka. Luke, I see you brought your own. Darlina, do you want anything?"

"No, I'll be the designated driver so Luke can drink. I hardly ever drink anything. Once in a while, a shot of tequila, but that's about it."

Judy gushed. "Oh, I have a bottle of tequila in here. I'll pour you a shot."

"That's okay, Judy. I'm driving."

They sat on benches and broken down chairs in the middle area between the two haphazardly made structures where rugs lay spread on the ground. Roxy explained the artwork on the sides of the walls. Each year had a theme, depending on what they saw the most of that year. The artwork had everything from flies to scorpions and snakes, crudely drawn and painted. Much like cave drawings or pictographs, they told a story.

As the afternoon flew by, Roxy and Luke discussed every-thing from politics to music and poetry.

"I want to start a militia," Roxy said.

"What kind of militia, Roxy?" Luke stretched his legs out in front of him.

"Nothin' but twenty-year-old girls with big tits and big guns. Think I could start a revolution with that kind of army?"

Luke chuckled. "Hell, Roxy, you could probably start about anything you wanted with an army like that."

Once the sun started to sink behind the horizon, the night air took on a chill. The girls gathered their jackets from the pickup and everyone moved inside the main room with the pot bellied stove. Coal oil lamps provided the only light, and the fire from the stove warmed them.

Luke thought about the contrast between this encampment and their house in Dallas, and yet the two could flow seamlessly together with the same art and vibe that was Roxy and Judy Gordon.

The stories continued around the room, with everyone join-ing in, even the children. Quanah, being bashful, didn't have much to say, but stayed inside with them and sat with the girls.

He and Nicole seemed to be forming a friendship and they got along well.

Roxy brought up Leonard Peltier, knowing Luke had been in Leavenworth where Peltier still was. Luke delicately danced around the subject, saying he'd met the man on a few occasions and that he hadn't been too impressed with him. He couldn't bring himself to tell them that in his opinion, Peltier was a lily-livered coward who'd back down from a fight and whimper like a puppy. He remembered his grandmother teaching him that if he couldn't say anything good about someone not to say anything at all. In this case, the advice seemed to fit. He knew the passion Roxy and Judy had in the fight to free Peltier.

So, he changed the subject as soon as he could and let the matter drop. After a couple of hours, Luke stood and stretched. "It's time to get back to Coleman. Tomorrow's a busy work day and the girls have school."

They said their farewells and with Luke's guidance, Darlina eased the pickup back down the hill, trying to avoid as many holes as she could.

Luke sensed that it was just a matter of time before Roxy and Judy Gordon would leave Dallas and move to grandma's house at the bottom of the hill below the house-up. It fit them to be in a place where life was simpler and moved slower.

***

1994 found Lily in her senior year of high school. College, leaving home, a car and independence were just a few of the adjustments the little family would face with her.

After looking at several college options, she chose to attend Texas Tech in Lubbock, since her best friend was also going there. Darlina knew the idea of leaving the small town and the sheltered life they'd had was exciting, but frightening at the same time. She and Luke had no choice but to give her the wings she needed to fly.

When they went with Lily to help her move into the dorms, they all cried big tears. Luke had sniffled and told her to put her things back in the car and go back home with them, but she chose to stay and face a new exciting life as a college student.

Darlina was proud of her daughter. She had to be scared, but she didn't let that stop her.

Nicole now had the spotlight of attention and quickly took over everything her sister left behind.

As the months went on, nothing stopped Luke's obsession to continue to build and improve the property they owned.

By the end of 1994, he'd built carports, walkways between most of the buildings, fences and gardens. He also planned to build another large room to serve as a den onto the trailer house.

He'd even created a sandblasted sign to hang over their gate that read, 'Hazbin Texas since 1836'.

Luke and Darlina Stone worked tirelessly. Always moving forward, always planning ahead and never looking behind.

No moss would ever grow under their feet if they could help it.

Judy Gordon

Roxy Gordon

Lily graduating

Chapter 26

As the years flew by, what had started out as a very modest beginning, the property Luke and Darlina now owned encompassed the entirety of four city blocks.

Lily brought her boyfriend, Alexander, home to Nicole's high school graduation in May and introduced him to the family. Martin, Stormi, Lexi and her new husband, Walter, came for the big event as well.

Preparations were made for Nicole to leave for college in the fall and she had chosen to attend the University of North Texas at Denton. However, Luke encouraged her to go to Lubbock where her sister already knew the ins and outs at Texas Tech. As the time grew closer for final decisions, Lily transferred from Texas Tech to the University of Texas in Arlington, so Nicole applied to and was accepted by UNT at Denton.

Nicole still helped out in the Saturday Store, but she also had taken on two other jobs for the summer, in order to save up and get ready for college. She worked part time at a local barbeque restaurant and had a private sitting job with an elderly woman.

Both of the girls had won scholarships and taken out student loans. And they worked, just as Luke had taught them.

***

That summer, Luke began to experience another noticeable decline in energy. He still saw Dr. Robertson every six months for routine heart monitoring and the two had moved from a doctor-patient relationship into a true friendship over the years.

Luke hated to think that something new might be wrong. It was most likely just the mid-July heat.

He thought about the doctor in Lubbock that Robertson had sent him to see three years ago to be evaluated for a heart transplant. That doctor had given him a six month death sentence, but here he was, thanks to the countless hours Darlina had spent creating a low fat diet for him. It was her stubborn determination that kept him alive.

Sitting on an overturned bucket under a shade tree, Luke heard Darlina pull the car into the driveway.

She walked toward him. "Hi, Baby," she said, kneeling beside him.

He let his hand drop from his forehead. "Hi, princess."

"Luke, are you okay?"

"Yeah. I'm just tired. This damned heat is zapping me."

Her forehead wrinkled. "You've done enough for today. Come on in and let me fix you some fresh ice tea."

"Go ahead. I've gotta finish planting the last of these rose bushes."

"Let me get changed out of my work clothes and I'll help you."

He stood and wiped his brow. "No, sweetheart, it's too damned hot out here for you. I promise I'll be done soon."

He hated seeing worry on her face and a twinge of guilt rippled through him when he thought about how long it had been since he'd offered to help get her work clothes off and yet she never complained. He owed this woman everything, and each improvement he made, whether it be planting a flower or building a room, was for her. The last thing he wanted was to worry her.

Once inside, he found a frosty glass of iced tea on the end table beside his recliner, along with the TV remote. Darlina with her hair pulled back in a pony tail, dressed in shorts and t-shirt hummed to herself in the kitchen while she prepared their meal.

After a stop at the bathroom to wash up, he walked back into the kitchen. He drew Darlina into the circle of his arms and buried his face in her hair. "You smell delicious, sweetheart."

She turned into him and raised her face for his kiss. "I don't just smell delicious, honey. I'll have to show you after while."

Luke grinned and let his hands slide down to her bottom. "You are a naughty little girl, Darlina Stone. You know that, don't you?"

Just then, Nicole walked into the living room. "Oh Lord, are you two at it again?"

Darlina pushed back from Luke's arms. "Of course we are, sweetie. Even if we are old married folks, we still love each other."

Nicole laughed. "No telling what y'all will do once I'm gone to college."

"Yep, no telling." Luke winked at Darlina and covered the short distance to his chair. "Are you off to work, Bear?"

"Yes. I've got a four hour shift tonight, so I'll be home before midnight." Nicole kissed him on the forehead, waved to her mother and left.

Darlina turned off the burners on the stove, perched on the arm of Luke's chair and wrapped her arms around his neck. "Now, what were you saying before Nicole came in?"

Luke didn't reply, but reached up and easily pulled her down onto his lap. "You know how much I love you, darlin'?"

"I think I've forgotten. You may have to show me."

Without another word, Luke picked her up and carried her to their bed. As always for the two lovers, the world stopped turning and everything faded away except the moment. The moment the two merged into one. That never changed.

***

A few weeks later, Luke and Darlina sat in Dr. Robertson's office waiting for him to arrive. Luke knew he'd have to be honest with the doctor and that meant Darlina would hear what he had to say, but there was no hiding it, something was wrong.

After a short catching-up conversation between the two friends, the doctor got down to business. He examined Luke, listened to his heart and lungs and looked at the blood pressure reading and EKG his nurse, Becky, had already performed.

"What is it, Doc?" Luke asked as the doctor frowned over the readings.

"Have you been feeling all right, Luke?"

"To tell the truth, Doc, I ain't been feelin' worth a damn. I'm tired all the time and get out breath just walking across the yard. I figured it was the heat gettin' to me." He glanced at

Darlina, noticing she sat up straighter in the chair and clasped her hands tightly.

"I don't think it's anything to get alarmed about, but I do think something's going on." Dr. Robertson sat on his stool. "I'd like to schedule a heart cath and take a look."

"Oh hell. I really don't have time for anything like that."

Darlina spoke up. "Luke, you really don't have time for anything *but that*. If Dr. Robertson thinks it's important, then it is." She turned to Dr. Robertson. "Have Becky set it up and I promise you, I'll get him here."

"See what I have to put up with, Doc?" Luke chuckled.

"Yes, I see. Every man should be so lucky. There is a fairly new procedure that I've recently been trained in. It is basically placing a balloon or stent into a blocked area of the heart, opening it up. So far, this has been an extremely effective solution and is replacing many of the bypass surgeries. It is likely that if more blockage has occurred, which is what I suspect, I can insert a stent during the procedure and you can go home the next day." The doctor stood and shook Luke's hand. "Becky will get you scheduled before you leave. Like I said, it may be nothing, but I won't know until I take a look."

Becky set the heart catheterization for the following week.

Damn, here we go again, Luke couldn't stop his thoughts from whirling. What if it couldn't be fixed with a stent? He wasn't sure he could go through another open heart surgery. He glanced across the car. Darlina stared out the window at the passing scenery. How much could he expect her to take? And how did she stay constant even through the worst of times?

Neither of them voiced their fears.

***

Even though the hospital had changed over the years, much of it remained the same and Darlina couldn't help comparing it to the many years before when Luke had spent two weeks there after the open heart surgery.

This time, there would be no sedation, only local anesthesia, and the procedure would take no more than an hour. Also, it was mid-summer instead dead of winter.

There were no words of goodbye or talk of dying and Darlina had no gut wrenching feelings of doom. She brought a book to read while she waited and an overnight bag. They'd learned much from the first hospital stay. Before she left the office where she worked, she had made arrangements for a private room for Luke. They were prepared.

Dr. Robertson, true to his word, was able to put stents in two of the outer blocked arteries. By the time Darlina saw Luke after the procedure, he seemed to feel a hundred percent better already.

"This one was nothing, baby," he joked. "It was just a hundred thousand mile tune-up. I'm good to go now."

She sat close to the bed, her head resting on his hand. He stroked her hair with his other hand. "That's good, Luke, because we've still got lots of stuff to do before either of us checks out."

"You know, the likelihood of me going before you is pretty certain, don't you?"

"Baby, please don't say things like that." She raised her head and gazed into his eyes.

"I'm just stating facts. Being that I am sixteen years older than you, I will most likely die first."

"I suppose so, but not any time soon."

"No, angel, not any time soon." He pushed the button to raise his bed to an incline. "I've always been a dreamer. You know that, but I'm also a realist. I'd like nothing more than to build a brand spanking new home for you, but unless I go to the bank and take out a big loan, that isn't possible. However, I could add on another room to the trailer. What would you think about that?"

"Oh, I'd love to have a big den and dining room, maybe with a fireplace." Her spirits lifted instantly. "And, a carport to park my car under."

"I can do all of that. If you're in agreement with another small bank loan, I can have it built by Christmas."

"I have no objection to another bank loan. Hell, we'll probably both die owing them." She chuckled and sat up straight.

"Is there anything around here I can draw on?"

Darlina rummaged through her purse and came out with a small notepad and pen. She handed it to Luke, then watched as he quickly drew plans for a new addition to the trailer.

She didn't try to hide the excitement in her voice. "We can do this, Luke." She laughed. "Funny, but now that both of the girls will be gone, we're adding rooms on to the trailer. Seems sorta backwards, doesn't it?"

Luke glanced up from his drawing. "Guess I've pretty much done things back-ass-ward my whole life. No point in changin' now."

Darlina and Luke discussed everything that night. It was almost as if they hadn't stopped long enough to really talk since

Luke underwent the bypass surgery. They'd been going ninety-to-nothing and life had a way of slipping by. Darlina vowed to make time to really have a good talk with Luke at least once a week from now on. A lot could happen in a week's time.

***

For the first few weeks in September, after Nicole had left for college, they found themselves spending more time outside the trailer than inside. It wasn't like a death, but there was a definite emptiness.

Roxy and Judy Gordon were regular visitors, as were Luke's daughter, Lexi, and her husband, Walter. Martin and his wife had moved to Las Vegas, Nevada with their jobs and stayed in touch through phone calls.

***

With more cash flow, Luke added another twenty by forty foot room on to the Saturday Store. They now carried lots of antiques and collectibles. The inventory Mack Jordan had started them with several years ago had long since dwindled to nothing, but neither Luke nor Darlina would ever forget the start he gave them.

They filled shelves with antique glassware, old farm implements, tools from days gone by, linens carried out West on wagon trains, quilts, jewelry from a hundred years ago, figurines, a pump organ, an Edison Victrola and everything in between.

Luke had accumulated a vinyl record collection of over two thousand records. Lily helped Darlina create a spreadsheet to catalog the records once she put them in alphabetical order.

He also began pouring concrete and framing the new room on the south side of the trailer. He measured off twenty feet long and twenty feet wide to encompass a carport. Even though he'd made a better drawing than the one on the small notepad in the hospital, he kept the tiny piece of paper.

***

By the time Christmas 1998 arrived, Luke had completed the new den. His oil paintings graced the walls and ceramics sat on shelves. He had bought a large dining room table from a local woman for twenty dollars when she claimed she needed milk for her babies. After he'd thoroughly cleaned and sprayed it for roaches, he placed it in the dining room.

Luke stood back and gave it a critical eye. He might not be able to give his baby diamonds, but he could damn sure give her a den and dining room.

He couldn't wait for everyone to arrive for the holidays. Not only were the girls coming home from college, but Darlina's mother and aunt would also be there. This would be a special celebration.

He loved decorating the house with garlands, lights, tinsel and wreaths with Darlina at his side. The Christmas tree fit perfectly in the new den the lights twinkled like stars.

Luke played records on the stereo system in the corner of the room while they worked. He would put a new one on the turntable as soon as the one playing stopped. Very often, he'd give Darlina a history lesson on the album or the artist.

Once finished, they stood in the middle of the room, arms around each other, and surveyed their work.

"I love this, Luke," Darlina looked up at him. "It's not a new house, but look how spacious it is."

"You deserve so much more, but this is a start. At least we'll have room for everyone this year. Want me to turn on the fireplace?"

"Yes, definitely. The mantle you stained is so beautiful and even though it isn't down here in the den, it is perfect with the rooms all open." She skipped up the two steps to the kitchen. "Want me to fix you anything?"

"Sure. Make me a Beam and Coke and then come sit with me."

She expertly poured a shot of bourbon into the diet Coke and ice and swirled it. As an afterthought, she got down a second glass and made one for herself. "I think I'll join you tonight." She walked back to the den and handed Luke a glass.

He raised his eyebrows. "Oh yeah? Why is that? You got something up your sleeve?"

"Maybe. Would that please you?" She smiled at him over the rim of her glass.

"Honey, everything you do pleases me." He patted the sofa beside him. "We've sure come a long way. We've got both of the girls in college, I'm in good health again and we have a nicer place to live than what we started out with."

"True. But know what matters the most to me?"

"What?" He gazed down at her.

"That we are still in love. It doesn't matter what life throws at us, we'll always come out on top because our love is stronger than anything." She moved closer as he put his arm around her shoulders.

"I've told you a million times but I'll say it again, you are my everything. If I have you, I can conquer the world." He brushed his lips across the top of her hair.

She curled her feet underneath her and sighed. "You'll always have me, Luke Stone. You had my heart even when we couldn't be together in life. Know what?" She looked up expectantly.

"What?"

"You still do."

He leaned down, tilted her chin with his forefinger and kissed the lips that sent tingles down to his toes every single time.

Even though things around them changed, the love they had never wavered. It would beyond any doubt, live on long after they both departed this life.

Nicole graduating

Luke's Handiwork

Hazbin Texas since 1836

Chapter 27

Christmas had been wonderful, with laughter, good food, and plenty of room for everyone with the new addition to the house. Darlina loved the new dishwasher and refrigerator with an icemaker they'd bought. She'd laughed when the girls commented on how it seemed that they were getting all of the modern conveniences since they left home.

Nicole stayed through her entire Christmas break from school. Even though Luke managed to find plenty of chores for her to do, Darlina did notice he'd softened. He let her sleep in and the chores he gave her were nothing more than cleaning up the house or The Saturday Store.

Luke Stone didn't believe in rest and relaxation or playing games. He often said that the years in prison took that away from him. He had to make up for lost time. The only recreation he ever allowed himself was fishing.

This had been the source of most all disagreements Luke and Darlina had over the years. In her opinion, he'd made the girls work too hard. But, he believed this was the way to teach them to be self-sufficient. And now with the girls out on their own, as responsible young adults, the disagreements came no more.

***

Darlina sat on a worn out sofa covered with a horse blanket in the house where Roxy and Judy Gordon now lived. It was a small wood frame house just off the San Angelo highway at the bottom of the hill from the house-up.

The house had no air conditioning and the stifling heat from another Central Texas summer permeated the dwelling. The windows were open and fans blew the hot air across the room.

She listened to the conversation between Roxy and Luke and wondered to herself how she'd not noticed that Luke had gained so much weight.

"Man, I am tellin' you that those Comanches were a mean bunch of damned Indians. Hell, they came down from up north and ran off the Apaches and Jumanos and took over" Roxy shook his finger in emphasis.

"Shit, Roxy, they had to be. Between being tricked by the Spanish and then the white man, they had to be mean. But, at least they weren't cannibals like the Karankawa tribe." Luke took a swig of his Beam and Coke.

Roxy chuckled. "That's true."

The banter went on for a while and eventually, Darlina lost interest.

She joined Judy in the kitchen. "Anything I can do to help?"

"Oh no. I've got it all right here." She pointed to a large boiling pot of water where chunks of German sausage floated.

Darlina cringed at the thought of trying to eat it. She'd never liked sausage of any kind, although she'd forced herself to cook it for Luke over the years. "How are you feeling, Judy?"

"Good. I only had one seizure this week. My doctor is adjusting my medication. They can't figure out why they just suddenly started. I'm fine most of the time. It's just this damn shaking that I can't seem to stop." She held her hands out palms down to demonstrate the tremor.

Darlina flashed to an incident, a few weeks back, when Judy had an epileptic seizure at the trailer and how scared she'd been. She'd ran for Roxy and chewed her nails while he knelt beside her waiting for the seizure to pass. No one seemed to know what caused them, but Darlina suspected that Vodka might have something to do with it. Judy still liked her beer, but leaned more toward Vodka since moving from Dallas a couple of years ago.

By the time they sat at the square wooden table to eat, a slightly cooler evening breeze graced them. Darlina reached for a piece of bread and small chunk of the sausage. She took tiny nibbles until she felt gristle in her mouth. She gagged and discreetly spat it into a paper towel. She ate the bread and left the rest of the sausage lying on the plate.

She and her sister, Leann, had never cared much for meat because of fat and gristle. They couldn't stand it in their mouths.

One thing that struck her as humorous was the fact that they ate on antique blue willow plates and even Cynthia, the dog, ate her food off of one of the beautiful plates.

As always, with Roxy and Judy Gordon, there was irony. Yin and Yang, black and white.

***

Toward the end of 1999, Roxy's abdomen began to swell. He complained to Luke that the Coleman doctors couldn't find anything wrong and only wanted to lecture him about drinking.

Luke watched with growing concern as his friend and spirit brother fell seriously ill.

"Honey, I'm really worried about Roxy," he confided one evening as they sat side by side watching TV.

"I know. He looks like he's nine months pregnant."

"It's that damned ol' Vodka that's eatin' him up, but he refuses to see it." Luke reached for Darlina's hand. "I've been doin' some thinkin' about my own self. I've gotten too fat and am drinking way too much. It's time to pull back on all of it."

He watched the familiar cloud of worry cross Darlina's eyes. "I agree, Luke. You know what Dr. Robertson said the last time you saw him. He wants you to lose weight and slow down on the booze."

"You know me, sweetheart. I can't just eat rabbit food. I need meat."

"I understand, but if you'll let me, I can go back to the way I learned to fix things you like that aren't fattening."

"I guess that means no more fried potatoes," Luke grumbled.

"No, it just means not every meal."

"I'll start next week. But, for now, would you fry me up some of that deer steak and potatoes for supper?"

Darlina laughed. "Of course." She stood, kissed Luke's forehead and sauntered to the kitchen. "I've really enjoyed meeting Roxy and Judy's friends over the past couple of years. Bob and

Sally Ackerman were wonderful and it was a treat hearing them sing and play. Richard Dobson is a great songwriter and how ironic that he and Edith chose to marry here in Coleman County. They all seem to be fascinated by your history and love the stories you share."

"Yeah, Bob and Sally were great. Richard is very talented. He is what I call a wordsmith. I thought it was pretty amazing that he and Edith came from Switzerland to get married here."

"You know, honey, all of these musicians would like nothing better than for you to get your guitar out and play with them."

"Tell you what. Next time they come over, I'll break it out and dust the cobwebs off. Nobody's touched it in a very long time."

"Oh, Luke! Let me go get it. You can serenade me while I fix supper."

"Are you sure? It could be painful." It never ceased to amaze him how she always believed in him.

"I don't think that for a minute. It will be wonderful to hear you play and I even have a request."

"You cook. I'll go get it." Luke walked across the kitchen toward the bedroom closet where his guitar sat. "Hell, honey, you better hear me play before you start making requests."

"I don't have to. I know how good you are," she said loud enough for him to hear in the next room.

He returned with the guitar case in hand, sat down on a kitchen chair and laid the case on the table. The familiar click of the latches caused his heart to beat a little faster.

With the guitar resting on his lap, he searched for a tuner. "Well, I'll be damned. This tuner still works. I figured the batteries were long dead. I'm sure the strings are."

"It'll sound great, sweetheart. Just play."

Luke tuned the strings, slung the guitar strap around his neck and fastened it to the instrument. He strummed a C chord. "No, that ain't right." He reached into the case for a pocket-sized notebook with all the songs he'd performed so many years ago listed and the chords written beside them.

"That's better." He strummed a D chord. "I always did a lot of songs in D."

"That means nothing to me, I just know when it sounds good." Darlina put the sliced potatoes in a cast iron skillet and breaded the steak.

He began to strum and sing. "Don't worry about me. It's all over now. Though I may be blue, I'll manage somehow..."

He looked up to see tears shining in Darlina's clear blue eyes and a smile plastered across her face.

Damn, that felt good. And Darlina was always a supportive audience and never seemed to mind if he missed a chord or forgot a line.

By the time supper was ready, Luke had warmed his fingers and voice up. "I have to admit it feels good to play again."

He caught a twinkle in her eyes when she turned toward him. "See. I told you so. Roxy's been telling you. Everyone's been telling you. You just needed to do it." She wrapped her arms around his neck. "Thank you, Luke."

He wiped down the guitar and put it back in the case. "It'll take a while to get calluses back on my fingers. Hell, maybe I'll leave it out of the closet."

"Those words are music to my ears, sweetheart. Let's eat." Darlina set plates on the small kitchen table for two they used unless they had company.

While he ate, he thought of Dr. Robertson's words of warning about his diet and the drinking. Roxy's condition worried him. He looked across the table at the queen of his heart.

He owed it to her to take better care of himself. Hell, he owed everything to her and she didn't need to watch him abuse his body with food and alcohol. They'd been through too much to let his indulgences get the best of him. No, it was up to him to change things.

Recalling the hard lessons he'd learned in prison and the self-control he'd mastered while behind bars, he knew it was time to bring some of that forward. He simply would not let the freedom he valued be the thing that destroyed it all.

***

Around noon on February 5, 2000, the phone rang. Luke picked up. "Stone Signs."

Between sobs, he heard Judy's voice. "They're care-flighting Roxy to Abilene. He's bleeding internally and they can't help him here in Coleman."

"Calm down, Judy. I'll call Darlina and we'll meet you in Abilene. Is Quanah with you?"

"Yes." She blew her nose loudly. "Luke, he can't die. I can't live without Roxy."

"Don't talk like that, Judy. There are some good doctors in Abilene. What hospital are they taking him to?"

"Hendricks."

"Okay, sugar. Keep it together and we'll meet you there."

When he hung up the phone, he stared at the wall for a long minute. This had been coming. He picked up the phone receiver and called Darlina at work. "Honey, think you can get off a little early this afternoon?"

"I have appointments until three, but I could leave after then. Why?"

Luke explained Judy's phone call, then added. "I have a bad feeling about this."

"I'll be home as soon as I can, honey. I love you."

"I love you too." The words echoed in Luke's brain. How easily they spoke those three little words. But, they were so much more. They were an expression from the heart. He did love her with every fiber of his being.

His clenched gut told him his friend and spirit brother, Roxy Gordon, might not make it. He went into the house and reached for a jar high on a shelf that held the American Indian Sweet-grass Roxy had given him.

He lit it and waved smoke in the four directions. All he could do now was ask the Great Spirit to guide his brother across the great divide if it be his time to make the journey.

Darlina made it home from work and Luke told her that Judy had called again. They'd admitted Roxy into the ICU unit at Hendricks hospital and were trying to find where the internal bleeding was coming from.

As they drove, he caught Darlina up on everything he knew. He adored the way she calmly reached for his hand across the car seat and silently squeezed his fingers.

He blinked away tears that threatened and flipped on the radio.

He watched the fence posts fly by as he drove well over the speed limit. Urgency drew him on.

The DJ's voice announced, "Now we're pullin' up an oldie but goodie with a jewel from the great Hank Williams Senior."

"Hear that lonesome whippoorwill, he sounds too blue to fly. That midnight train is whining low, I'm so lonesome I could cry..."

Luke's breath caught in his throat and he couldn't swallow past the lump. Roxy's favorite song and one he'd insisted on being played at his wake once he was gone. Bits and pieces of conversations drifted through his head. Discussions they'd had over the difference between the Beatles and the Rolling Stones, Waylon and Willie and those damned Comanche Indians.

"Roxy is way too damned young to die," he croaked.

He saw Darlina brush away her own tears. "Maybe he'll be okay. Maybe the doctors can fix him up."

Luke didn't say anything else and the miles flew by. Just past the tiny town of Lawn, Luke spotted a Coyote hanging on a fence. He knew that was a sign, Roxy, First Coyote Boy, was not going to make it. He just knew.

On February 7, 2000, Roxy Gordon passed from this life at the age of fifty-five years.

February 11, 2000, Luke Stone wrote this tribute to Roxy.

To *the family; in memory of my friend, Roxy Gordon, my brother in soul and in spirit, I say, Roxy was a man who dared to be himself at all cost. He was as he said and said as he was. This is indeed a quality found most rarely. I have met many people in this span of life on earth, but none anymore sincere and true to themselves than my brother, Roxy, who shines brightly in the galaxy of stars above; which he and I often discussed as special spirits looking upon us mortals who are yet to join in the array above to shine for those left behind. Look up and see Bob, Sarah and Roxy, for they shine upon us."*

Roxy's death devastated Luke more than he dared let anyone know. Hell, he was a lot older than Roxy, had a heart problem and he was still alive. There was a reason and maybe it was as Roxy so often said, for him to play and write more music.

He needed to make some changes and by God, he could and would. First of all, he would never return his guitar to the closet. Instead, he vowed to play it often. Second, he would slow down on the eating and drinking. He had a beautiful young wife and he couldn't imagine leaving her a young widow as Roxy had done Judy.

They, along with many other friends, rallied around Judy Gordon and helped her through the dark days that lay ahead.

Roxy left behind a legacy of writings, recordings, poems and art. It made Luke stop and think what he would leave behind for Darlina.

He'd built a home from scratch and helped raise the girls. Now perhaps it was the right time to return to his first love and passion, writing and performing music. Only, he'd be smarter about it this time.

He owed it to Darlina to do it right. He owed Roxy and hell, he even owed himself.

Chapter 28

Judy Gordon arranged a service for Roxy at a local funeral home, on February 12th, followed by a wake at the small house where they'd lived. Folks came from New Mexico, California and all over Texas to honor Roxy.

A poet and writer from Dallas, Bob Trammell, spoke with Luke extensively. He expressed his desire to put together a memorial for Roxy in Dallas and he wanted Luke's promise of participation.

"Ah, man, I don't know. I ain't been on a public stage in damned near thirty years." Luke stood in the yard outside Roxy and Judy's house.

"Just think about it. But, I will tell you that Judy insists you be there and she's pretty damned determined about this." Bob hooked his thumbs in his belt loops.

Judy sauntered up hearing the last part of the conversation. She slipped her arm around Luke's waist and leaned shakily against him. "Luke, you know Roxy's going to be watching and he'll expect you to be there. You just have to say yes."

He hugged her. "I said I'd think about it, Judy. Have you seen Darlina?"

"She's in the house, waiting on folks. You know how she likes to make everyone comfortable."

Luke chuckled. "Yes, I know. Y'all excuse me." He headed for the front steps and through the door. He spotted Darlina in the kitchen putting more chips and salsa out. "You doin' okay, sweetheart?" He reached for a chip.

"Of course. You?"

"Have I told you lately how beautiful you are?"

"Just this morning, as a matter of fact."

"Make sure you don't forget." Luke winked and turned back to visit with another guest.

***

Two weeks later, Bob Trammell called Luke. He'd set a date for Roxy's memorial and he wanted to add Luke's name to the music lineup.

That evening over dinner, Luke shared the news with Darlina. "Sugar, what if I'm not good enough to be up on stage anymore? I sure don't want to get up there and make a fool of myself."

Darlina put her fork down. "How on earth could you even think that, Luke? I've been listening to you play here at the house. Yes, you forget a line or two now and then, but you just figure out what songs you want to do and practice them. You know how it's done."

Luke swallowed a bite of broccoli. "I suppose you're right. Will you help me pick out six songs to focus on?"

"I know for sure you should do a couple of the Marty Robbins' songs. Your voice fits them well."

"I can't quite get the high notes like I could when I was thirty, but I can work around that. What else?"

Darlina stood and picked up their empty plates. "Let's go over your list as soon as I get these few dishes washed." She placed the dishes in the sink and cleared the table.

Luke moved to the den and opened his guitar case. He'd already staked out a corner of the room where he placed a picking stool, a guitar stand and end table. Yes, it would appear that Luke Stone was finally going back to the business of making music.

He could visualize Roxy Gordon, Steam Train Maury Graham and maybe even his mom, dad and brother shaking their heads and saying, *"It's about damned time!"*

***

On Mother's Day, Sunday, May 14, 2000, at the famed Son's of Hermann Hall in Dallas, Texas, Luke and Darlina arrived to find a large group of people already gathering to honor the life of Roxy Gordon.

Luke took Darlina's hand as they climbed the steps to the old hall. "Honey, you know I played here one time way back in the very early sixties. Things sure have changed."

"I love this old building. I bet if it could talk, it could sure tell some stories."

Luke nodded. Judy met them at the top of the steps. "Oh, you made it!" She hugged Darlina, then Luke. "Look how handsome you are, cowboy, all dressed up. And you're always beautiful, Darlina. I love the Indian jewelry. Come on. I want to introduce you to some folks."

They followed Judy into a large upstairs room where they were greeted by the Ackermans, Richard and Edith Dobson, poet and writer Charley Moon, and a writer from Austin, Kendall McCook.

Then Judy introduced them to Terry Allen, a Choctaw Indian, Glenn Watson, famed songwriter, Steve Young and so many more it all became a blur. Luke hoped Darlina was taking note of the many faces and names because he was sure he would never remember them all.

The memorial opened with the Indian, Glenn Watson, sprinkling sage, cedar and Sweetgrass incense around the room, then offering a prayer to the Great Spirit with his flute.

When it came close to time for Luke to go on stage, he felt his palms get sweaty and his heart pounded. He turned to Darlina. "I've got to find a quiet place to tune my guitar. Will you come with me?"

Darlina nodded and followed him downstairs and to the car to get his guitar. Then he located a vacant room where he tried to tune.

"Dammit!" He turned the tuner off and back on. "It's picking up the noise from upstairs. I'll never get this damn thing in tune."

"Honey, relax. I know you're nervous, but you're gonna do just fine."

"Easy for you to say. It's not you under the gun. Maybe this was a bad idea."

Darlina placed her hand over his. "I believe in you, Luke Stone. And it's not a bad idea, it's wonderful. Folks want to hear you sing and play. Sweetheart, you're a legend of sorts."

"Maybe in my own mind. I'm just damned twisted up inside."

"Maybe you should have a drink to settle your nerves."

"Hell no. I ain't gonna have a drop until I'm done with my part of this show. I need all of my senses workin'."

After twenty minutes, Luke finally put the tuner down. "Guess that's the best it's gonna get."

Darlina glanced at her watch. "It's almost time."

Luke drew in a shaky breath. "Okay. Let's go." He placed the guitar back in the case and closed the lid. Together they joined the others in the large open room at the top of the stairs.

Luke tapped his fingers on the edge of the table as the Ackermans drew their set to a close.

He saw Bob Trammell motion to him. He stood, opened the case and slung the guitar strap around his neck. He leaned over and gave Darlina a peck on the cheek, then made his way to the edge of the stage.

He adjusted the strap, pulled his cowboy hat down low on his head and took a deep breath, as he listened to Bob.

"Now, folks we have a living legend in Texas music coming up next to play. Many of you have had the pleasure of visiting with Luke Stone and hearing some of his many stories, but now here at the Sons of Hermann Hall for the first time in thirty years, he will grace us with a performance. Please put your hands together and make Luke feel welcome."

Luke tipped his hat to Bob as they passed. Without a word, he stepped up to the microphone and strummed an opening chord, then he opened his mouth and sang. "If we never love again, I know it's my fault. But, I want you back again, that's the reason I called. If you take half of all that we ever owned, you'll leave me half of this and half of that and all alone..."

By the time he started into the second verse, the sweaty palms dried and he no longer felt the jangle of nerves. He guessed it was true that playing music was just like riding a bicycle. Once you got back on, it came naturally.

After he rang out the last notes of the old Wynn Stewart song and the applause died down, he spoke into the mic. "Thank you all so much. Thank you, Judy, for asking me to be here today. Roxy always kept after me to play my guitar and I regret that I didn't get it out and play for him before he died." His words choked. "He just left too damned soon."

He cleared his throat, rang out a G chord and went into *I Walk Alone*, then from that to *Legend In My Time* and on until he'd completed his set.

Again, he waited for the applause to end. "Thank you. Truly, I thank you from the bottom of my heart. God bless Roxy Gordon."

With that, he tipped his hat to the audience, took the guitar from around his neck and strode off the stage back to Darlina. He didn't miss the brightness of her eyes or the width of her smile when she stood and walked into the circle of his arms.

"Honey, that was great. Honestly, you picked right up where you left off thirty years ago. I'm so proud of you. I know it wasn't easy."

Before he could reply, others were slapping him on the back, Judy hugged him as the next act took the stage.

He opened his guitar case, wiped down the strings, then carefully placed his old friend, the Martin D-35, into the case and snapped the lid closed. "Now I'm ready for that drink, honey."

Darlina hurried to the bar area and ordered a diet Coke, then opened the bottle of Jim Beam. "You seriously did a good job, sweetheart." She handed him the drink.

Luke grinned and winked. "Thank you, ma'am."

For a minute it was almost as he if was transported back thirty years when Darlina waited at the band table for him to come off stage. So much time had passed, mistakes made, lessons learned. Lots of water under the bridge and some things could never be the same.

Nevertheless, he couldn't deny the familiar excitement of being on stage and bringing the audience along with him.

He didn't know where it would go from here, but he did know he'd never put his guitar away again even if he only played at home or for friends when they visited.

As he sat with the drink between his hands, he reflected on the exhilaration he always experienced when on stage. He'd spent a large part of his life doing this every night of the week. Getting back up there today was almost like coming home.

Yet different. No longer was he the arrogant egotistical man he'd been when he first met Darlina thirty years ago. He gazed over at her and caught her blue eyes twinkling at him. She'd believed in him when he thought there wasn't a chance in hell at salvaging anything—not a life, not love or even himself.

She still saw the best in him despite everything. And for her, for all the people who depended on him, he would give music one more whirl.

Only this time, he'd be wiser.

This time, he'd have Darlina at his side loving him and cheering him on. Hell, who knows, maybe he could even get her involved in it with him. He smiled at that thought. It'd be like Johnny and June.

Thinking back again to the adrenaline rush of being on stage, he almost voiced the words out loud, *I'm finally home.*

Darlina's soft hand on his arm drew his attention. "Are you all right, baby?"

He placed his other hand over hers. "With you by my side, I'm more than all right, sugar."

Nothing would ever tear him away from her again.

Not even the finality of death would sever their bond of love.

Luke Stone on stage at Son's of Hermann Hall 2000

Darlina, Luke and the infamous songwriter, Steve Young

Darlina, Luke and the infamous songwriter, Steve Young

About the Author

Award winning author, Jan Sikes, began writing around the age of eight.

The stories she writes (so far) are <u>true stories</u> about the journey of two people moving through adversity in order to grow and learn to become better humans. She believes with all her heart, there is something that is worthy of sharing in these stories. Bits and pieces of wisdom, hard-learned lessons and above and beyond all, love…True love that you read about in fiction stories…and yet this is truth. The old saying that *truth is stranger than fiction* fits the stories that she shares.

The Convict and the Rose, her second book, has been awarded the book of the year in the Fiction/Biography category with the Texas Association of Authors.

She is passionate about her writing projects and is driven to tell a story with the hope that it might touch someone's heart or life in a positive way.

She also releases a music CD of original songs along with each book that fits the time period of the story. Why? Because the stories revolve and evolve around a deep-rooted passion for music

Jan resides in North Texas, has five grandchildren and in her spare time, loves to volunteer at Texas music festivals.

New Release coming in late summer!
'Til Death Do Us Part along with the CD, Etchings in Stone.

A wild outlaw Texas musician, a naive young girl, and Texas honky-tonks in 1970 lay the groundwork for this true story of passion and peril.

Available on Amazon.com and www.jansikes.com

Rebel Texas musician, Luke Stone, loses everything he treasures in life to the forty foot walls and iron bars of Leavenworth Penitentiary. Locked in her own prison attempting to live with only half a heart, Darlina Flowers holds to nothing but memories and a dream.

Available on Amazon.com and www.jansikes.com